CHASING SHADOW DEMONS

John Moore

Dedication

For those who dream

CONTENTS

CHAPTER ONE
ON THE ROAD

THIS ISN'T HALF bad for a prison cell, I thought. I'm sure there were worse
jails in Mexico where guards committed unspeakable acts against
helpless prisoners, but this didn't seem to be one of them. Maybe
because we were protesters from the United States, we were receiving
the Mexican police's version of the red-carpet treatment. Fifteen from
our group ROLL, which stood for Rivers, Oceans, and Lakes League,
had traveled to Mexico to protest the pesticides and herbicides US
corporate farmers were spraying on Mexican tomato crops. Our protest
pissed off the local authorities and landed us in jail. It was worth it
because while these international conglomerates were poisoning some
bugs and weeds, they were mostly poisoning the local residents. These
gigantic corporate agribusinesses and chemical companies disguised
themselves as farm operations, but they were really demons destroying
the lives of people all over the world in the name of greed.

The indigenous Mexican population experienced an increase of
cancers, neurological disorders, and an assortment of other health
issues. Was their compromised health just a coincidence? If it was, it
was a coincidence shared by people in many other parts of the world
where industrialized corporate farming practices prevailed. Sure,

industrial farms provided some jobs to the locals: Jobs that trapped them in an endless cycle of mindless, hard labor until their bodies gave out, earning just enough to survive. But quality of life as we think of it did not exist in their world. Their plight reminded me of the days when farmers used mules to pull their plows. They penned the mules in barns and fed them to keep them strong enough to work. Those mules would have preferred to roam vast prairies, free to graze on green grass splashed from coast to coast. Just like the mules, the Mexican farm workers were trapped, with no memory of hope of a better life.

I hated what the corporations were doing to families most of all. Families could no longer support themselves, so children left home to work in sweatshop factories, and their parents were scattered to the winds—often to the US—to look for work as domestic servants or laborers, living in the shadows to avoid deportation. So we came to Mexico to give them some old-fashioned American protesting, and the politicians didn't care too much for it.

Poor little Amanda was the youngest among us. She was a twenty-three-year-old, fresh-faced, naive idealist, new to the group. She came along to express her opposition to the overuse of pesticides, having learned in her Tulane University biology classes that the poisons in the pesticides remained in the intestinal tract of everyone who ate the tomatoes. No one seemed to care, even though researchers had concluded they led to liver and kidney problems. If that weren't bad enough, these toxins circulated through the body to wreak havoc on every cell, causing malaise, loss of memory, and numerous other maladies. No one seemed to care enough to stop gobbling them down as fast as they could in every fast food joint from sea to shining sea.

Like most idealists, Amanda had no idea which pesticides were being sprayed or by which companies, but she knew she was against it. I think our experience in Mexico was more than she bargained for, though. She hadn't expected to be arrested and thrown in a Mexican jail. She thought we would be treated the same as if we were in the US, exercising our right of free speech. Now that she was in jail, she was scared to death. *Not like protesting on Facebook,* I thought. The truth was, I knew how she felt. As an idealistic young school girl, I had to go to the principal's office for spreading the word that the food my school was serving us was out of date when I was not much younger than she. I didn't have to go to jail, but it scared the living crap out of me. The principal had just yelled at me.

Amanda slinked into a corner of the cell, and I slid next to her to calm her. I put my arm around her and reassured her that our stay in the gray bar hotel was temporary. I understood what it was like to be scared. Hell, I'd been scared most of my life. She smiled at me to thank me as Mexican policemen leered at us through the rusty bars—steel, living long past its natural life, and forged during better times. Montezuma's revenge hid in every bite of tamale on our plates. Tamales, prepared with red chili peppers hot enough to bring the entire 1,896 miles of flowing Rio Grande River to a rapid boil; not the kind of accommodations the travel agents promoted.

"We were just protesting, not committing any serious crimes," I said to Amanda. "Look at those cops. They are harmless. They just want to see our boobs." I unbuttoned the top button of my blouse—a little uncharacteristic for me, but what the hell. I was careful not to reveal too much; after all, my mother and the entire church congregation from my hometown in Indiana watched my every move from heaven. At least I hoped they did.

Just enough to show some cleavage, my mind told me. God had graced me with big boobs that sometimes came in handy. I thought the cops were going to crap their pants. "Boobs, the universal language," I whispered to Amanda. We both cracked up, her smile revealing the snowy white teeth years of wearing braces had straightened.

The incident that prompted me to join my boyfriend, Tom's group of protesters, ROLL, was when Bart Rogan, the Armak Chemical Company's thug, tried to kill me. He wanted me dead to hide his criminal pollution, theft, and murder, but it didn't work out as he'd planned. I'd exposed all of his dirty deeds, and now he was in jail in India awaiting trial for a disaster he caused in Bhopal. He was sure to get a long prison sentence. I didn't think even Master-of-Slime Bart Rogan could buy his way out of this one. He'd caused so many deaths, surely he'd rot in a prison worse than this one. At least that's what I told myself.

ROLL protested pollution all over the globe. They were tame compared to the members of the other secret organizations Tom and I belonged to. One was an offshoot of ROLL called ROLF: Rivers, Oceans, and Lakes Fighters, and fight was exactly what our group did. ROLF's crusade against polluters frequently led to violence, and its membership was a strictly guarded secret. Every member used a code name. "Bab" was mine, given to me by Tom as an inside joke. Bab was the acronym for Bad-Ass Bitch, but I wasn't bad at all. I was a small-town girl from an Indiana corn farm. Well, until I was cornered. Then I'd been known to do a few not-so-ladylike things. Amanda would learn just like I did. There is evil in the world, and you had to learn how to fight it.

This episode wasn't much of a lesson for her, though. Our peaceful protest here in Mexico was only going to get us politely escorted out of the country. That's what I hoped would happen. Amanda seemed to be a lost soul searching for meaning. She had led a sheltered life growing up in South Louisiana. The most excitement she'd seen was the Mardi Gras celebration in her small town of Oberlin. Cajun Mardi Gras didn't resemble the New Orleans version. There were no beads, nor floats. Their celebration of Fat Tuesday began in the early morning hours when costumed men on horseback gathered in a pastoral area on the outskirts of town. From there they rode to the farmhouses sprinkled along the way, their mission to gather meat for the community gumbo. The captain of the krewe wielded a length of eight grass sacks tied together to form a gargantuan whip. The captain rode about twenty paces ahead of the pack, beseeching each farmer to contribute to the Mardi Gras gumbo. Most farmers turned a chicken loose in their field to be sacrificed for the festivities and food. The captain gave the go-ahead, and riders barely sober enough to dismount their horses chased the doomed chicken, tripping, falling, and running until the unfortunate bird was caught and dispatched to wherever chickens go in the hereafter. The clumsy chase and apprehension was sometimes captured on video and posted on YouTube for posterity. Good times, to be sure, unless you were the chicken, of course.

Once collected, the bounty was taken to town hall by the staggering riders, their masked costumes rank with sweat and discolored with grime. There, the ladies of Oberlin added the meat to a gumbo large enough to feed the entire parish. When the ride was complete, the krewe promenaded down Main Street proudly displaying their colorful costumes and equestrian skills. Families attended the festivities together to have fun, South Louisiana style. I know this because I went to this celebration three years ago. What an experience, real people having real fun. Now poor, sheltered Amanda was in a completely different world, feeling more like the chicken than the rider.

I noticed Tom in a corner of the cell talking to one of the Mexican members of ROLL. When we made eye contact, my mind took me to the first time we met at Pat O'Brien's in the French Quarter. We had instant chemistry; warmth filled my body and the small hairs on my arms rose when we met. My thoughts flashed to Mardi Gras night when Tom took me from behind on the balcony of Mr. Broussard's condo, right there on Bourbon Street. I could still feel his hands on my hips pulling me to him. Oh my God, what a magical night in an enchanted place. Tom was a good guy, and he was sexy. Not that Tom was an altar boy or anything like that; he was just strong, principled, and all kinds of handsome. Frankly, I didn't understand what women saw in the bad boys. *I've had enough "bad" in my life, thank you very much*, I thought.

"I was just taking to Hector Gonzales," Tom said as he put his arm around me and whispered in my ear. Lost in my thoughts, I hadn't noticed he'd crossed the room to nuzzle next to me. "He told me ACC has teamed with a large industrial farming company, Aggrow, to lobby the Mexican government to change farming practices in South Central Mexico. Aggrow is buying up all the land they can from desperate, poverty-stricken local farmers."

Hearing his voice snapped me back to the present, electricity surging through me when his hand touched my shoulder. "ACC" was what most people called Armak Chemical Company. The company was known to ROLF's members as one of the most notorious polluters on the planet. ACC was ROLF's favorite target.

"When we get back to New Orleans, we should research Hector's story and see if there is something we can do about his problem," Tom said. But I had other thoughts on my mind, thinking we could also catch up on time in bed.

Tom and I were interrupted by the cell door opening. Two policemen, smelling of corn tortillas, grabbed us by the arms and dragged us out of the cell. They dragged us to an office and sat us in front of a wicked-looking Mexican captain, who was finishing a telephone call, no doubt receiving orders about us. Someone else pulled the strings on men like him. He'd sold himself more times than the prostitutes in a US and Mexico border town.

"You two look like the leaders," he said. "We don't like you interfering in our affairs. We may have to charge you as eco-terrorists, and you will both get long prison sentences. Now, if you agree to stay out of Mexico, maybe we can give you a break."

When I saw Tom's face redden, I kicked him under the table, and he snapped his head around to look at me. His cornflower-blue eyes were on fire. I put my finger to his lips to help him contain the onslaught of words he was desperately trying to hold in.

"We don't think we will be back except as tourists to Cancun, Cabo San Lucas, or one of your other beautiful resort cities," I said, batting my eyes, noticing his were helping him mentally unbutton the next button on my blouse. "You wouldn't mind that, would you?"

He didn't answer me. Instead, he looked at us both like we were some type of disease-infested rodents. "Do you two have any kids? You know, *niños*?"

I didn't know where he was going with his odd question, but I knew it couldn't be good. "No, it's just the two of us," I said, wanting to punch him in his mustache-covered mouth. I held back to avoid spending the rest of my life in a Mexican jail.

"Take them back to the cell with the others. You may be with us for a while," he said, laughing as his disgusting belly bounced up and down, rippling like a bowl of brown Jell-O.

We went back in the cell, and Tom thanked me for having a cool head. "No problem. Do you think they would really charge us with terrorism?"

"I hope not," Tom said. "If they do, the US government probably wouldn't do much to help us." He looked around to make sure no one else could hear him and whispered in my ear, the light making his eyes look iridescent. "We might be in serious trouble. If they charge us with terrorism, it could be years before they take us to trial."

My heart raced, and I almost peed myself thinking about being stuck in prison. Amanda was freaking out, too. Taking Tom and I out of the cell like that nearly sent her over the edge. Tears ran down her face, and her eyes darted back and forth, reminding me of a trapped rat. Her mind had convinced her we were going to the gallows. I put my arm around her again and calmed her down. *Wow*, I thought, *I remind myself of Sarah*. Maybe she was reaching down from heaven to guide me, because I was freaking on the inside but maintained a composed exterior. As it turned out, Amanda didn't have long to fret. Our jailers unlocked our cells and escorted her and the rest of the protesters to the outer offices to collect their valuables. Tom and I were ordered to stay in the cell.

Oh shit, what does this mean? Are we getting charged with terrorism? I thought. Tom still wasn't showing any signs of concern. He was much more committed to the cause than I. He'd also had much more experience on the front lines. I, on the other hand, was about to pee my pants even more than before.

Tom, still on task, had that "I'm about to deliver a lecture" look on his face. He turned to me and said, "Alexandra, Hector lives in the south-central state of Tlaxcala, Mexico. The state's name, Tlaxcala, means 'people of corn.' Their way of life is being threatened by international farming corporations who want to bring industrialized methods of farming to Tlaxcala. Hector told me his family plants several varieties indigenous to their region of Mexico. They make many types of tortillas from their harvested corn. They grind the corn and prepare blue corn, yellow corn, and white corn tortillas. Tortillas are a staple; most Mexicans eat tortillas every day just as their ancestors have done for hundreds of years."

He had a tendency to lecture a little bit, but I didn't mind, because smart was sexy in my mind. I'd learned a lot from Tom.

"What do the industrial farmers want to do differently?" I asked.

"Hector said they want to plant genetically modified corn in the fields, or, as it is known in the food business, GM. The Mexican government forbids planting GMs in the southern states but allows it in the North. The industrial farmers are attempting to persuade the Mexican government to allow GMs in the South," Tom said.

"But if the corn has been genetically modified to produce more per acre," I said, "won't that help the Mexican farmers?"

"Not according to Hector. Ever since the passage of the North American Free Trade Agreement, NAFTA, the United States has increased corn exports to Mexico. The effect has been to drive the price of corn down. The American corn is of lower quality, but the poverty-stricken locals are starting to buy it. The pesticide-ridden imported corn is replacing the Tlaxcala farmers' corn," Tom said.

Then I understood, and I shuddered to consider the future consequences for the local farmers. "Tom, I know you know this, but I just have to say it out loud. Corn farming is subsidized by the US government, so really it's the American taxpayers putting money in the pockets of these huge industrial conglomerates. Mexican farmers can't possibly compete. Families will be destroyed. But why is ACC so interested in persuading the Mexican government to change its policies?"

"Alexandra, you know how devious those ACC bastards are. It makes sense. They are teamed with the large industrial farmers. They spray pesticides and herbicides on everything to sell more of their poison. The farm operations know if they poison the insects and weeds and fertilize the shit out of the ground, they'll get more yield per acre. They don't care about the environmental damage," Tom said.

I recognized the flaring nostrils and reddening face as signs of how passionately he felt about Hector's people's problems, and I felt that way, too. Whenever he explained something new to me, I'd get all worked up—but I knew that to fight something takes time and energy, and we had lives in New Orleans that needed attention. I had a public relations business as well as my family farm in Indiana to worry about.

I feared this Mexican jail and its rusty bars, bad food, and smelly guards would be my new home for the next few years.

CHAPTER TWO
SARAH'S HOUSE

~~

FINALLY, AFTER TWO more hours of suspense, two policemen escorted Tom and me to the fat captain's office again, their feet shuffling as they walked. "We have decided to let you go. But we have your names. If you come back to Mexico, it had better be as tourists."

Our plane landed at the Louis Armstrong International Airport and taxied to the terminal. I loved returning to New Orleans, jazz music booming from speakers throughout the terminal and the smell of red beans and rice filling our noses and making our mouths water. There just wasn't another place on earth like it. I almost got on my knees and kissed the ground I was so happy to be back in the good ole USA, and New Orleans to boot.

Our ordeal in Mexico had worn us both out completely. Sleep was next on my agenda, the adrenaline rush from landing safely at home fading. Tom and I were dealing with our Mexican experience differently. He didn't seem perturbed at all, but I, on the other hand, was not sure I'd put myself at risk like that again.

~~

The ringing of my cell phone woke us. *Charlotte*, I thought. *Why is she calling me this early?* My God, what time was it? We'd overslept. Guess it was a form of jet lag.

"Hi, Charlotte. What's up?"

"Did you and Tom make it home from your vacation in Mexico okay?" she asked.

"Yes, yes, we did. What time is it?"

"I didn't wake you, did I? It's eight-thirty a.m.," she said.

"Holy shit. I can't remember the last time I slept this late," I said. "Thanks for waking me. I have so much to do."

"Really? 'Cause I was hoping you could hang with me today," Charlotte said, halfway whining.

"Charlotte, I'd love to, but I have already planned to go to the shelter today. They have moved into Sarah's House, and I want to spend some time with Susan McAllister, the director."

"No problem," she said. "Today is Thursday. How about tomorrow? I'll take the day off. I would love to spend the day in the French Quarter with you. I hardly see you anymore since I introduced you to Tom."

I paused for a minute to collect my thoughts. Tom had to work today and tomorrow. What the hell? Charlotte was a hoot, and we always had fun together.

"Sure, Charlotte, I'd love to spend the day in the Quarter with you tomorrow. What time would you like to meet?"

"Let's say ten o'clock Friday morning at Café Du Monde," she said. "That should give you and Tom plenty of time to get caught up on your backlog of things to do—to each other," she added with a little chuckle.

We both giggled like schoolgirls. Tom rolled over and smiled at me because he'd heard Charlotte's comment. He was ready to make another memory, and so we did, murmuring endearments to each other in Spanish, just for a change. He even tasted a little spicy.

Sated on love for the moment, we sat at my kitchen table drinking coffee, easing back into our lives. He asked about my blog and all of the young women reported missing. He couldn't believe there were so many missing young women in the United States.

"How can people disappear without a trace in this day and age?" he asked. "The police have the technology to track cell phones. There are cameras everywhere. How is it even possible to disappear?"

I shrugged my shoulders. Cameras weren't everywhere. Cell phones could be disabled. It wasn't the how, but the why and the consequences for those left behind that really disturbed me. How many families were torn apart by their children mysteriously disappearing?

Tom headed to work and I jumped in the shower. I was very excited to see the new center for battered women. I had donated the house I inherited from Sarah to them. The center's new name was Sarah's House for Battered Women, and I loved spending time with the residents. These were broken families going through the worst days of their lives. Reassuring them that their lives could get better gave me such energy.

I made it to Sarah's House by ten, and Susan greeted me with her characteristic hug and kiss. She always gave me the biggest smile when I saw her. Susan was the perfect mix of fairy godmother and ringmaster, and she loved taking care of the hodgepodge of residents that came through the center. I knew the house well, having spent many hours with Sarah there. I missed her, but I could feel her spirit as Susan and I poured our coffee and headed to her office.

"How are things working out here, Susan?" I asked.

"Alexandra, this house is amazing. The whole place seems to be filled with Sarah's love. Even the residents who never met Sarah comment on the positive vibe that comes from the walls. This home will change lives and save lives," Susan said.

"How are the finances working out?" I asked.

"So far, so good. We can talk another time about efforts to raise money. Right now I want to know about you. How you've been?" she asked.

I gave her the cleaned-up overview of my blog and PR career. I saw no need to go into my environmental activist activities with ROLL or the fact that I'd spent the night in a Mexican jail. She had too much on her plate already with all the problems the residents carried with them into the center.

"Would you like to meet some of our residents?" she asked.

"You know I would," I said, unable to hide my enthusiasm.

"Let's go outside to the patio. The children are enjoying the playground equipment we purchased."

We walked through the French doors onto the patio. Sarah had furnished the house inside and out with gorgeous yet practical furniture: leather couches and chairs, breakable items beyond the children's reach, and sturdy lamps casting warm light in every room. The ladies sat together on wicker chairs, drinking sweet tea and chatting about their lives and futures. Some were hopeful. Some were not.

Susan introduced me to the group. A young lady spouted, "Oh my God! You are Alexandra from *Alex's Daily Planet* blog."

The entire group of seven women began clapping as if I were a celebrity. Susan just smiled, watching the scene unfold. As my face reddened, I wanted to shrink back into the house, embarrassed by being the center of attention.

"Yes, I am. But how do you know that?" I asked.

"We all read your blog. We loved it when you put Bart Rogan in jail. He was a bad man. My name is Joan Fontenot, and I am a huge fan," she said.

"Well, thank you. I had no idea you read my blog."

Carol Guidry, another resident, spoke up. "Oh, you better believe we do. Alexandra, most of us have nowhere to go. We read about the horrible serial killers roaming the streets. They scare us. We already fear our husbands and boyfriends. If we end up on the streets, we have to watch out for these guys, too. We worry for ourselves and our kids."

Joan added, "I read about all of those missing girls. My sister went missing from a mall in Houma, Louisiana two years ago. We haven't heard a word from her since. She never went more than a few hours without checking in with one of us in the family. She always carried her purse with her makeup and her cell phone. Both were found abandoned in her car parked at the mall. The police said she probably ran away with someone she met. No way!"

Each resident knew of some young girl from their community who'd disappeared without a trace, and they took turns sharing the details of the cases. I was taken aback by the lack of police action, each case going cold.

After they finished their stories, Susan took me to a bedroom where a young girl, no more than seventeen, sat in a rocking chair holding an eight-month-old baby boy.

"Karen, I'd like you to meet Alexandra," Susan said.

"Hi, Karen, I'm so pleased to meet you," I said.

"I'm sorry, I can't get up. My baby has a fever."

"Why don't you take him to a doctor?" I asked.

"I don't have any money. The wait at the free hospital is too long, and I have no way to get there anyway. I am also afraid that my boyfriend will be watching for me there," she said.

I wanted to cry. This poor child, caring for a child, with nowhere to go and no way to get there. She looked as if she hadn't slept in days. Karen's facial expressions betrayed her attempt to conceal her disgust with herself. She was ashamed of the choices she'd made and felt guilty for the circumstances she and her infant were in. She was helpless to provide for the baby she'd brought into this world.

"How long has your baby had a fever?"

"Two days," she answered.

"You're coming with me," I said.

I scooped her up and put her and her child in my car, the city whizzing by as we headed to the Tulane Medical Center emergency room. The doctors working at Tulane were always so kind to the center's residents. They examined the child, diagnosed him with an ear infection, wrote a prescription for eardrops, and quickly discharged Karen and her baby. I took both of them straight to a pharmacy and filled the prescription, the child sleeping peacefully in her arms.

"Thank you, Alexandra," she said. "I didn't know what to do. I don't know how to care for my baby. No one in my family took the time to teach me much of anything. They kicked me out of the house because they hated my boyfriend. When I get a job and get back on my feet, I'll pay you back, I promise."

"You don't owe me anything, Karen. I've been lucky, and I am grateful to have the chance to do something nice for others."

There were so many vulnerable people in the world. Who took care of them? What happened to them? Did they suffer and die? I didn't like the answers to these rhetorical questions I'd asked myself. So many lives fell through the cracks. I remembered the opulence of the Rex Mardi Gras ball I attended where the wealthy krewe members spent tens of thousands of dollars on costumes for one night's frivolity. How could so many, with so much, do so little for those with nothing? I decided to change that situation right then and there.

I took Karen back to Sarah's House. Karen's exhaustion got the better of her, and she fell asleep sitting up with her child in her arms. I took her baby from her and rocked the child to sleep before I put Karen in her bedroom and her child in the crib next to her.

I latched onto Susan and walked her to her office. I closed the door.

"Who provides medical care to the residents and their children?" I asked.

Susan looked down, avoiding eye contact, and said, "Sadly, no one. We have a few doctors who volunteer to stitch girls up from time to time. But we don't have anything set up for regular medical care. Most of our residents are poor. They can't afford doctors or prescriptions. You know our financial situation; we can't afford to pay their medical bills."

"What happens if they really need medical care?" I asked.

"Charity Hospital was closed after Hurricane Katrina. The state has no plans to reopen it. The Interim LSU Hospital takes care of indigent patients now, but they are very busy and the waiting times are long. As you know, I can't stay with the girls and wait for the doctors to see them. I drop them off and return when I can. They are all frightened their boyfriends or husbands might find them and hurt them," Susan said.

"We have to do better," I said. "I have an idea. It'll take some effort, but I think I can make it work."

Susan and I spent the remainder of the day playing with the children. I learned I really sucked at video games, but the kids didn't seem to care. They were happy to have someone show them some attention.

These were destroyed families. The hopes and dreams that fairy tales promised them were gone, their road in life having turned into a never-ending slog of despair. I left Sarah's House thinking how rough life was for those poor women. Tomorrow I pledged to work to help them get some medical help. I'd committed to shopping with Charlotte in the French Quarter, and she was part of my plan.

I walked into my condo and sat at my computer. My blog had become popular with people searching for lost young girls. Many of the posts provided photos of the missing girls. Most were very young. Many were last seen at shopping malls, which I guess made sense in a weird sort of way. Young girls spent a great deal of their time at malls. Food courts were a prime meeting place. Teens gathered to hang out with each other and talk about who was dating whom.

Some of the girls came from distressed backgrounds. Maybe they only claimed they were heading to the mall and just ran away. Even if they did voluntarily leave their homes, how did they survive? Did they live on the streets? It wasn't like they had great street survival skills when they left their homes. They seemed so vulnerable. I blogged back and forth with several of the parents, learning more details of the disappearances and sightings. It must have been frustrating for them to know their children needed their help without having any way to give it to them.

Tom texted me to tell me that he was picking up a Fresh Market baked chicken and some vegetables. *Wow, what a wonderful man*, I thought. The two of us had it made. We both had good jobs, financial security, and each other, making me feel a little guilty since the women in Sarah's House had nothing but troubles.

I met Tom at the door and gave him a huge kiss, like the ones soldiers got from their wives upon returning from war overseas. He didn't fight it. He'd learned to just go with it. When our kiss broke he stepped back a little, out of breath. His mouth curved in a smile.

"I'll have to go to Fresh Market more often. Didn't know you liked it that much," he said.

"Don't be silly. I'm just glad to see you. We are lucky to have each other," I said.

Tom knew I'd gone to Sarah's House that day. He knew me well enough to conclude I felt sorry for the women in the shelter and was thankful for what we had. Tom was good like that. So tuned in to me. Our chemistry was unmatchable.

Tom served the food, sat across from me, and asked, "How was your day at the shelter?"

"It was very emotional," I said. "Did you know the women and children at the shelter have no medical care? They are all too destitute to have medical insurance. When their children are sick they can't help them."

"Doesn't Obamacare provide for them?" Tom asked.

"Not really. They're too poor. Obama's plan for people like them was to expand Medicaid and pay for most of it with federal dollars. But Louisiana refused to accept the money for political reasons. When the Charity Hospital was destroyed by Katrina, the state decided not to reopen it. Instead, they shifted care for the indigent to the LSU Hospital System. Budget cuts in state government have affected care for the poor more than anyone else. As a practical matter, they have no way of getting proper care," I said.

"Alexandra, I know that look. What are you planning to do?"

"I am going to put together financial donors and medical professionals willing to donate their time and money to help them," I said, giving him a determined look.

Tom met my eyes, but his were shadowed. "You're already spread too thin. You have committed to chasing serial killers, both individual and corporate. That work is very important. When you stop a corporation from poisoning people, you save many more lives than helping a handful at the center."

"Maybe that's true, Tom Sanders. But today I held a sick baby in my arms. His mother was a seventeen-year-old with no money, no insurance, and no hope. I cannot turn my back on her or anyone like her. You can either help me or get out of the way 'cause I'm doing this no matter what it takes."

I surprised myself at how passionate I'd become about helping these women. Tom wasn't being insensitive; he was thinking about what was practical. How was I going to do everything I wanted to do? We couldn't save the world. I didn't know how I was going to accomplish any of it at that moment. I just knew I was going to.

"Look, Tom, I know you feel strongly about the damage done by large corporate polluters, and I am with you. But I can't let these families, whom I have already committed to help by housing them at the center, suffer for lack of medical care. Do you understand how I feel?"

He looked at me with faithful eyes, like a dog you'd raised from a pup looks at you when you get home, and said, "If you are committed to this, then so am I."

"I love you," I said.

He hugged me and replied, "Now can we go to bed?"

I kissed him on the cheek and shook my head yes. I needed to sleep because I was emotionally exhausted. Besides, tomorrow I was going shopping in the French Quarter with Charlotte.

Tomorrow was going to be a great day!

CHAPTER THREE
CHARLOTTE'S WEB

~ɔ

CHARLOTTE AND I always had fun together. We both loved watching *The Walking Dead* television show or, really, zombie anything. Spending the day in the French Quarter with Charlotte promised to be a delight.

I met her at the Café Du Monde precisely at ten o'clock, and I was proud of my new habit of being on time. Charlotte was all smiles as she hugged me, and we stood in the line to get our café au lait. We both passed on the beignets, which would have been unthinkable a few months ago, but summer was upon us and bikinis were displayed in the stores. I was actually looking forward to wearing a bikini for the first time in my life, having lost twenty-five pounds by cutting way down on sugar and starch, discovering I wasn't big-boned after all. I was just a corn-fed, plus-sized, Midwestern girl making better food choices, and I loved the results. Passing on the beignets was a small price to pay for a healthy body.

It was a sunny day, and we were both dressed comfortably wearing our serious walking and shopping Nikes. Today she wanted to shop the antique and art stores in the Quarter, and I loved browsing them as well. The Café Du Monde was always crowded because it was that rare place tourists and locals both loved. We grabbed a table outside under the green and white canopy, positioned to see the cafe's usual odd mixture of people. One man stood out because he was so strikingly handsome, and he checked me out as he walked by our table. What the hell? He was checking *me* out, not Charlotte? That never happened. She was the train-stopping beautiful one. He had broad shoulders and piercing green eyes. His dark gray sports coat had a green handkerchief placed in the pocket, accenting his emerald green eyes. *I don't think I've ever seen a man this handsome*, I thought. *Maybe they were making another movie in town? He must be gay if he's looking at me instead of Charlotte.* Gay men loved my big boobs. I guess they looked like fun.

Charlotte laughed at me. "He's hot, but I'll bet he's a heartbreaker. Remember Tom?" she said, breaking me from my trance. "So what did you and Tom do in Mexico?"

"You know me. I always look at the desserts, but I never order one," I said, glancing back at the handsome man. "At least, not anymore." She giggled, taking in both meanings. "Tom and I did the usual touristy things. We saw sights neither of us had ever seen, and we mingled with the locals." And every word of that was true. She didn't need to know we'd done most of our mingling with the locals in a Mexican jail.

"Have you been watching *The Walking Dead*?" Charlotte asked.

"Not really. I feel like I have been living it," I said.

"Oh, Alexandra, I am so sorry," she said. "That was insensitive of me."

Misspeaking was uncharacteristic for Charlotte. She was your typical "always knows the right thing to say" person. She felt bad since I'd witnessed a man get shot and killed and a woman get her head cut off, and I was nearly killed myself. Not your average series of events. I assured her I was not offended. She was my friend, and I needed to be normal again.

"Don't worry, Charlotte. Let's just finish our coffee and get to the shopping," I said.

Charlotte and I went up and down each street in the Quarter, stopping to peruse the many antiques displayed. There was some amazing artwork to see as well. I wanted everything I saw, and all of it was outside my price range, but I was alright with that because shopping wasn't about buying; shopping was about imagining a world filled with beauty and an escape from some of the harsh realities of life I'd been confronted with. Besides, I had no place to put any of the furniture I admired.

Our day flew by. I felt the surge of relaxation through my arms and legs as we ambled through the narrow streets of the French Quarter, my mind occupied by happy thoughts. These were the streets that felt the footsteps of pirates and rogues from all over the world. The city seemed to collect people with pasts to hide because most New Orleanians didn't care who you were. They just wanted you to fit into the non-judgmental culture of the city, and I liked that.

Charlotte suggested, "Let's have brunch at the Court of Two Sisters. My treat."

"You are kidding, right?" The Court of Two Sisters was one of my favorite restaurants in New Orleans. The food was wonderful. "Can you afford to do this, Charlotte? It'll run us $100 by the time we drink a few glasses of champagne," I said.

"No problem," Charlotte said. "I have something to talk to you about."

Oh shit. Here we go again.

She was setting me up for something. She could always sneak up on me, and even though we'd been friends for years, I never saw any of her surprises coming. She wouldn't consider doing anything to hurt me. On the contrary, she looked out for me, like when she introduced me to Tom, sensing he was the man for me. She was the friend that lured you to a store to purchase a $20 scarf for herself, and then you found out you were going to be a guest on a television makeover show, the type of program where they completely transformed your hair, makeup, wardrobe, and attitude.

"If you're sure," I said, giving into the inevitable.

The Court of Two Sisters had the most amazing atmosphere. White cloth covered tables were scattered throughout a brick-floored courtyard. A fountain emanated trickling water sounds, complementing the smooth music of a jazz trio. Abundant wisteria vines created a canopy overhead, blocking the sun's harsh rays. The restaurant was named for two sisters, Angaud and Emma Camors, who operated a curio shop on the grounds in the late 1800s. Many said they could still feel the sisters walking among the diners, admiring the gourmet creations served. The charm gates at the 613 Royal entrance were wrought in Spain especially for the Court of Two Sisters. Legend had it that Queen Isabella of Spain had them blessed so their charm would pass on to anyone who touched them. I didn't know if the legend was true, but I always touched them just in case it was.

We both ordered a glass of champagne and the soup du jour, turtle soup au sherry, and I waited for the other shoe to drop.

Charlotte looked down at her lap, like an eight-year-old would, searching for words to ask if she could play dress up in her mom's closet. Finally, resolve filled her eyes and she said, "It's about Mandy Morris."

I must have had the most confused look on my face possible. Why would she need to talk to me about her boss's daughter, the party queen of New Orleans?

"What about Mandy?" I asked.

"Alexandra, you know I have worked for the Morris's for more than twelve years. I love my job, and Mr. Morris has been a great boss, and he and I have developed a friendship over the years. He has confided in me on many occasions his concerns about Mandy. I have always assured him that she would grow out of this party phase of her life. Mandy was barely a teenager when I met her. I watched her change from a sweet, young, innocent child into a party monster. Now she has taken a hideous turn I didn't expect and can't understand, leaving Mr. Morris very concerned."

I was still confused. The last time I saw Mandy, she still seemed like the happy party girl I'd always known and tried to avoid.

"What exactly do you mean? Mandy has always been an out of control Paris Hilton clone. What do you mean by taken a turn?" I asked.

"She has gone dark," Charlotte said.

"Dark?" I asked.

Charlotte was finding it difficult to choose her words.

"Just spit it out, Charlotte," I said.

"She has gone Goth. Ever since Bob Broussard was locked up, she only wears black. She no longer hits the party circuit, and she has withdrawn inside herself, staying in her room and reading black magic and voodoo books all day."

"Holy shit, that's quite a change," I said. Bob Broussard, a serial killer known as the Quarter Killer—who'd also murdered his own mother—had been Mandy's best friend. Now he was a guest of the state of Louisiana in a mental hospital for the criminally insane in St. Francisville.

Charlotte nodded her head in agreement. "Mandy's father is concerned she may do something to herself. He has tried talking to her. He even sent her to a shrink. She refuses to discuss what's on her mind. She told him she just wants to be left alone."

"Maybe she's just going through some sort of depression," I said.

"That's what Mr. Morris thought. He imagined she'd snap out of it. But, unfortunately, she is heading in the other direction. Two days ago, he found books about the occult in her room. She's growing darker and darker, and she visits Bob Broussard two or three times per week."

"Bob killed more than seven people. Why would he be allowed to have visitors?" I asked.

"Mandy said the psychiatrists felt his recovery would progress more rapidly if he were able to interact with familiar people," Charlotte said.

"Those doctors need their own psychiatrists," I said. "He was calm that night after he cut his mother's head almost off. He wasn't agitated at all. Bob is a dangerous sociopath."

"I know, and that's what scares Mr. Morris," Charlotte said.

"What does all of this have to do with me?" I asked.

Charlotte hesitated for a moment, returning her eyes to her lap. "Alexandra, he wants you and me to talk to her. He knows how smart you are and thinks you can get through to her."

"Get through to her for what purpose?" I asked. "To persuade her to return to the wild-in-the-streets party girl she once was?"

Charlotte acknowledged my sarcasm with a sigh. "Mr. Morris believes Mandy is searching for purpose and meaning in her life. He believes what you are doing with your blog and your career inspires Mandy. He thinks a positive influence in her life like you could lead her in the right direction. It's his daughter, Alexandra. He's got to try everything he can to help her get on the right track."

"I already have too many irons in the fire," I said. "I don't think I have the time to take on a project like Mandy Morris. You know about my work with Sarah's House. I need to raise funds to provide medical care for the residents and their children. They are in such need. I held a sick baby in my arms yesterday while his seventeen-year-old mother cried because she couldn't afford to pay a doctor to see her. It was heart-wrenching. I'll go with you to talk to Mandy, but I can't commit to do much more than that."

Charlotte smiled. "I knew you'd come through for me. Maybe I can help you raise money for Sarah's House. I think Mr. Morris would help, too."

"To be completely honest, Charlotte, I planned to ask for your help today. But when you brought up Mandy Morris's situation, I didn't think it was the right time. It seemed too much like extortion."

"C'mon, Alexandra, I would never take it that way. We'll help each other."

"Deal," I said.

We dined like the princesses we were always meant to be. We each had a seafood and shrimp Creole omelet perfectly complemented by sweet potato with andouille sausage. Of course, the champagne flowed and the jazz trio played. Charlotte brought me up to date with all of the happenings on *The Walking Dead*. After that, we shopped away the remainder of the day, perusing the many antique shops in the Quarter. We saw a little of everything, even people who looked like they'd walked straight off of the set of *The Walking Dead*. All in all it was an amazing day.

And it completely wore me out. When I reached my condo, I headed straight for a long, hot bath. I put on my most comfortable long T-shirt and went to my blog. Not much news about ACC, but people were burning the blog up with posts about missing girls and serial killers. California figured prominently in the posts. Made sense to me. California accounted for almost 40 million of the total 320 million people in the United States. That was 12.5 percent of the country's population. Not only that, but people went to California from all over the world. They had to have a large number of serial killers operating within their boundaries. Los Angeles County itself had ten million people. They were spread around that cement jungle, the acutely vulnerable mixed with the ruthlessly predatory. Really, it was amazing that there were only 551 homicides in LA County. I wonder what the statistics were for girls who just went missing?

When Tom came home, we sat at the kitchen table to eat our salads and have a glass of wine. He told me about his day planning a trip in the Gulf to track some dolphins they'd tagged earlier in the year.

"I think most people believe the Gulf waters have recovered from the BP oil spill," Tom said. "They haven't and probably won't for a long time."

"Didn't all of the oil get cleaned up?" I asked rather naively.

"Not by a long shot," Tom said. "Most of it settled to the bottom of the ocean where it continues to foul fish and marine vegetation."

"Is there a plan to clean it up at least?" I asked.

"Not really," he said. "They are trying to convince everyone the oil has been cleaned up. But the National Oceanic and Atmospheric Administration's data shows that dolphin deaths are above average since the spill and that infant dolphins have been found dead at six times the average."

"Those poor dolphins. Isn't there a way to help them?"

"That is why we're tracking them. As we learn the areas where they swim, we may be able to divert their migration patterns," Tom said. "I think ROLF should pay a visit to the parties responsible for polluting the Gulf. It is so frustrating to watch the legal process wind on forever in meaningless circles."

"I know how important the animals in the Gulf are to you, and I want to help if I can, but I also have so many other projects going. I can't afford to go to jail again. People are counting on me," I said. "I have to talk to you about something else tonight."

"What?" Tom asked.

"You know I want to raise money to provide medical care for the residents of Sarah's House. Well, I think I've come across a possible way. Charlotte thinks she can get Mr. Morris at Superior Sugar to help—"

"That's wonderful," Tom interrupted me to say.

"Well, I have to do something for her, too. She wants me to help bring Mandy Morris out of the depression she's fallen into," I said.

"Mandy Morris!" Tom shouted. "Why would you waste your time with that party slut? You just said you couldn't help me because your plate is already full. You need to spend any free time you have helping me and the ROLF members."

I recoiled. I had never seen him get angry like that. What was going on? Why didn't he understand I needed to help the women at the shelter?

"Tom, helping the women at Sarah's House is important to me. I've told you how I felt when I held the sick child yesterday. What's wrong with me talking to Mandy?"

"I don't want to talk about it right now," Tom said. "I'm tired. Maybe we should just go to bed."

"Okay. I can't say I understand, but I'm tired, too. We can address this subject in the morning."

"If you insist," he said gruffly.

"Are we having our first fight?" I asked.

Tom looked at me with loving eyes. "No, I just get upset seeing the marine wildlife suffer and die for large corporations to make huge profits. We're a team. I don't really like Mandy Morris, but I see it's important for you to help Charlotte and Sarah's House. I love you! We just have to find a way to take care of all of this together."

I grabbed Tom and hugged him. We made our way to the bedroom. We managed a few kisses, but that was it. We were asleep in minutes.

I was a little disappointed we weren't really arguing because I was hoping tomorrow morning we could have makeup sex.

CHAPTER FOUR
DEATH IN THE FAMILY

I WOKE UP snuggling next to Tom feeling the warmth of his body and his strong arms around me. Instead of jumping out of bed and getting us coffee, I just lay next to him, enjoying the comforting feeling couples share. Tom and I were perfect for each other. We shared a sense of adventure, a love of New Orleans, and a passion for protecting innocent victims of corporate greed. The first night we met, we both felt a chemistry that I wasn't sure about at first, but it turned out to be the real deal. How often did that happen? Now we were inseparable. That is, except when he was pursuing his career as a marine biologist and I was investigating a story for my corporate and street serial killer blog. Were our separate interests pulling us apart? I couldn't let that happen. We needed to find a balance that would allow us to pursue our individual interests without damaging our connection.

Tom rolled over. "Good morning, pretty girl."

My heart always melted when he called me pretty girl. Last night's small tiff seemed distant now. We were in love, and we both knew we needed to nurture our relationship because what we had together was rare and precious.

"Well hello, handsome. Would you like some coffee?"

"Absolutely," Tom answered.

I got out of bed and put the Keurig to work. Almost instantly we were drinking freshly-brewed coffee in bed.

After a few minutes of caffeine ingestion, Tom looked at me and said, "Alexandra, I'm sorry I was inconsiderate last night. Sometimes I let my passion for protecting the environment get the better of me. Those poor dolphins don't deserve what the oil spill is doing to them. I worry about our future. If our priorities don't shift to protecting the earth, we may bring about our own extinction."

That was Tom. Extinction was first thing in the morning. But I knew he needed to explain why he'd been upset. "I know, Tom. I love that you are so passionate. I feel the same way, but my passion extends to the victims of ruthless killers and abusers as well. The women and children I want to help are like those dolphins you are protecting: innocent. If our society doesn't reconfigure its priorities to protect innocent people instead of promoting wealth at any cost, I think we are headed for a different type of extinction."

"You are right, Alexandra," Tom said. "We both want the same things. We can't do everything, but we will do as much as we are able given our limited time and resources, each with our own priorities. Let's not lose our close tie to each other pursuing our goals. I am committed to you, Alexandra."

"Likewise, handsome," I said.

We each had another cup of coffee and talked about our future plans to work together but give each other space as well. *Not bad*, I thought. *All before the second cup of coffee.* Tom and I had just crossed a bridge to a stronger relationship. I could see us going on forever.

I got out of bed and checked my blog. Missing girls dominated the posts. I felt compelled to help the families find these lost souls, alive or not. I had a text message from Charlotte on my phone as well. Mr. Morris had agreed to help raise funds for the medical needs of the center, and Charlotte and I were set to meet with Mandy later today. *My God, that's going to be weird*, I said to myself.

Tom got out of bed, picked up his cell, and checked his voice mail. "Oh no," Tom said. "This can't be good."

"What's wrong?" I asked.

"My mother left me a message to call her immediately," he said. "She never asks me to do anything immediately. My parents are the two most laid-back people in laid-back Northern California."

"Oh, Tom, call her now. See what's wrong," I said. My words were more of a reaction than a suggestion. Tom was already autodialing her number and placing her on speakerphone.

"Mom, what's up?"

"Where are you? How fast can you come home? Tom, your brother Ethan…" she paused, crying uncontrollably.

"What, Mom? What!" Tom screamed.

"Your brother has been killed in a car accident," she whispered, her voice holding all the horror of the news.

"Ethan? Killed in a car accident? Where? How?" he asked, his own voice breaking.

Tom went silent as he listened. I had not met any of his family yet, but I felt like I knew them from the stories Tom shared with me during our endless talks. Ethan and Tom grew up in Northern California. Their parents could be best described as aging hippies. Both were born in San Francisco in the mid-1940s. They were early adopters of the hippie lifestyle; they participated in the Summer of Love and moved to Northern California to get closer to nature. Were it not for their physical resemblance and shared genetic material, you'd never know their two boys came from the same parents.

Ethan was the older of the two. He attended Harvard Business School and Yale Law. He chose the corporate world and lived in Chicago. Ethan was a hard-driven career man who only took one detour from his career path. While in undergraduate school, he got a girl pregnant. Ethan didn't want to take on the responsibility of a wife and a child. The pregnant girl, Sandy, and Ethan went their separate ways. Ethan didn't hear from Sandy or the child until a year ago. Sandy called Ethan out of the blue telling him said she couldn't deal with having a child anymore, especially a teenage daughter. Two days later, fourteen-year-old Constance Sanders showed up on his doorstep. He took her in, maybe driven by guilt, or maybe because it was the right thing to do. Whatever the reason, he gave her a roof over her head and tried to be a father.

Ethan was ten years older than Tom, the age difference creating a chasm between them that they could never close. They had the same parents and last name, but that was about all they had in common. Ethan rarely participated in family gatherings, opting to forgo the warm and fuzzy side of family life. He wanted things, not people, in his life. Lots and lots of things. He had a Mercedes, a yacht, and a New York house in the Hamptons. He was a fabulous lawyer but not much of a family man.

"Mom, don't worry about anything," Tom said. "Where is Constance now? She's on a flight to Sacramento? How did that happen? Okay, good. I'll book a flight to Sacramento right away and call you with the details. I'll take care of everything."

"Oh my God, Alexandra," Tom said, sobbing. "My brother is dead. I can't believe it. He was so young! I know I've told you we weren't close, but…he's my brother. *Was* my brother."

"I'm so sorry, honey."

"Mom sounds devastated. They have a quiet, peaceful life. I've told you that neither are in the best of health, and they're getting old. Ethan's death will be more than they can deal with."

"We should book a flight today and go straight to see your mom and dad," I said.

"I have to check in with my job and let them know what's happened. Alexandra, my parents are too old to deal with wrapping up Ethan's affairs in Chicago. I'll need to make funeral arrangements. His body will have to be brought back to California," Tom said. His voice was on autopilot, the need to make lists and perform tasks to distract himself evident.

"Uh, Tom," I said in the most sympathetic of voices I could muster. "What about your niece, Constance?"

"I don't know. My parents can't take on that responsibility. Maybe her mother has family who will step up. There are a great number of matters to get straight when we get to my parents' house."

He'd just said a mouthful. We already had too many irons in the fire. I had my own one-person public relations firm. I represented Superior Sugar. I was working on a stevia ad campaign to determine if they could establish an alternative market to sugar. I also had my career as an investigative journalist to pursue. My blog had thousands of participants uncovering pesticide poisonings and murders in towns all over the world. I had to raise money for medical care for the women and children at Sarah's House. As of yesterday, I had to help Charlotte with Mandy Morris. *How am I going to manage all of this crap?* Tom needed me, too, so I just had to find a way.

We booked our flight from New Orleans to Sacramento, California, an hour later. The earliest flight we could find left at 6 a.m. the next morning. We packed for every possible circumstance having no idea how long we'd be gone. Tom and I sat in the rear of the plane just like we'd done on our flight home from Mexico. The reality of his brother's death started to sink in. Tom was somber, his cornflower-blue eyes fighting back tears. Still, he wanted to talk. He told me about the good times he and his brother had growing up in California. They were both on their Little League all-star team. Ethan got serious about life in his junior year of high school and decided the simple life wasn't for him. He wanted to make it big in the corporate world. But Tom went the other direction. He wanted to make a difference for our planet, and by the time Ethan had graduated from college, the brothers barely spoke.

"I don't even know my niece," Tom said. "She showed up at Ethan's home in Chicago a year ago. I've never even seen Constance in person. Ethan sent me some photos of her, but I'm not sure I'd recognize her."

Tom brought up the photos of Constance on his phone to show me. She was a thin adolescent with punked-out, multi-colored hair. I counted five colors. She had no visible tattoos but did have a nose ring. I wondered if her tongue was pierced. Tongue piercing was a fad that made no sense to me at all. How could a person with a pierced tongue speak? How could they eat? I guess their reasons had more to do with other skills the tongue could acquire to make life more sharable.

After pensively rubbing his brow, Tom said, "Constance will be with my parents by the time we arrive. I'll have to go to Chicago to wind up Ethan's affairs and then back to Cali. We'll have to send her to boarding school or something like that. Constance has to get a good education. What do you do with a teenage girl, anyway?"

"We'll have to meet her first. Maybe her mother kept her in school. She may be a good student," I said.

Most of what I said to comfort Tom was wishful thinking. It didn't sound like Constance had had a very stable life. There must be some reason why her mother sent her to live with her father, then disappeared. That was just weird. Constance must have been devastated by her mother's rejection.

Tom looked more bewildered than I'd ever seen him. Obviously, he was saddened by his brother's death—and probably shocked, as well. You just didn't expect someone that young to die. He was worried about his parents. He had a career he was serious about and, now, his brother's affairs to wind up. I understood his feeling of overwhelm. I'd just been through something similar. After Sarah was killed, I had to settle her affairs while balancing my career's demands. Overwhelmed or not, we had to deal with this.

Our flight to Sacramento was broken up by a plane change in Dallas. Tom and I chose to walk the airport corridors during our layover. Walking had a meditative effect on us both. Tom seemed to relax a little, and he talked to me the entire time about his hopes and dreams, maybe because he realized how short life could be.

"Alexandra, for the next ten years, I want to continue working for companies able to teach me about plant and animal marine life. Not only in the Gulf of Mexico and the Atlantic and Pacific Oceans, but in all of the seven seas of the world," Tom said. "Then, one day, I would like to have my own ship, just like the famous French explorers, Jacques and Philippe Cousteau. Like them, my dream is to make documentary films to teach the world how to protect and preserve our oceans."

"Wow, Tom, what a wonderful ambition. I remember the Cousteaus' documentaries. I thought it was so cool how they'd go down in the depths of the ocean, showing us this world that was like another planet. Didn't he write books, as well?"

"Yes, they used all forms of media to help people understand the oceans. Imagine how much more powerful the message would be today with the Internet, social media, and YouTube."

"It would be amazing," I said, seeing his vision in my mind.

Talking about his plans transported Tom away from his grief over the loss of his brother and his apprehension of his parents' future care, seeming to bring him great comfort. But I noticed that he didn't mention settling down, getting married, and having children. Not that I was ready to have children now. After all, I had my own career to pursue. I loved the adventurous life Tom and I were living, but someday I would want to settle down and have a family of my own. Did Tom want that, too?

Today was not the day to worry about those plans though. Tom needed me by his side.

The second leg of our journey to Sacramento was pleasant. The weather was nice, and I slept with my head on Tom's shoulder. I was almost sorry to arrive, not wanting to face Tom's grieving parents.

They greeted us at baggage claim. They could have been a postcard for aging hippies. Tom's mother, Rose, had long gray hair in a ponytail down to her mid back. She was slim-figured for her age and rather tall. Tom's father, James, was an older version of Tom. He still had hair, also ponytailed, just not quite as long as Rose's. He was built like Tom, tall and slim, but clearly frail, only a shell of what he must have been in his youth. I could see Rose had been crying, but James looked like the stoic type. Both were friendly but restrained.

After we claimed our luggage, we headed to their car. I fully expected them to have a flower power painted VW van. Instead, they drove a blue Grand Caravan minivan. I guess it was the newer version of a hippie mobile. We crowded our luggage in the rear and headed for their house located outside of Red Bluff, California.

"We feel like we already know you, Alexandra," Rose said. "Tom's told us all about you."

"Just the good parts, I hope," I joked.

"According to him, it's all good," James chimed in.

After the mandatory getting-to-know-you exchange, we addressed the real subject that was on all of our minds: Tom's brother's death and his daughter, Constance. James's voice quavered slightly, and Rose teared up as they shared more details than we cared to know about the accident. Thankfully, Ethan didn't suffer. When the subject turned to Constance, the mood in the minivan changed.

James broached the subject first. "Constance is a handful, always fooling with that damn computer phone."

Rose interrupted to correct her husband, "James, she doesn't like to be called Constance or Connie. She goes by Piper."

"Piper," Tom repeated. "That's not a name. That's a musician. And what do you mean she's a handful?"

Before James could answer, we pulled up to their house, and there was Piper, sitting on the front steps in all her multi-colored glory. She was a small girl with a big presence—I could see that immediately. Just like James said, she was tethered to her cell phone, feverishly pecking away on the phone's virtual keyboard.

A cross-generational, divergent, culture-clash explosion was about to happen.

CHAPTER FIVE
California Dreaming

Piper tore her eyes away from her cell phone to look us over as we stepped from the minivan. She reminded me of a pro golfer surveying a difficult putt on the 18th green. No details were lost to her keen eyes as she sized up each of us. Her innate caution, no doubt a survival skill she'd picked up in her short life, kept her from saying a word.

Rose spoke first. "Connie, uh, I mean Piper, I'm happy to see you've gotten out of bed. Your uncle and his girlfriend are here."

Piper assayed Tom, then me, without speaking. She maintained her perch on the front steps, clutching her phone as we approached the house.

"Did you find something to eat?" Rose asked.

Before Piper had a chance to answer, James added, "Almost two o'clock. You should have eaten breakfast *and* lunch by now. Couldn't eat anything if you were still in bed or had your head stuck in that phone all day."

Piper didn't react except by slightly raising one eyebrow, effortlessly dismissing James's comment.

Tom stood in front of his niece for the first time, his eyes searching her face for signs of his lineage. Apparently satisfied, he said, "Constance, I am Tom, your uncle." He consciously avoided using his name paired with "uncle." *Wise*, I thought, *not to introduce himself as "Uncle Tom" to a suspicious teenager*. Not the image you'd want to create at a first meeting.

Without expressing any emotion, she turned her eyes to me and said, "Who's she?"

"She is my girlfriend, Alexandra," Tom answered, clearly annoyed by Piper's lack of respect.

I watched the tense scene unfold without adding to the drama. Here was this fourteen-year-old girl who'd been abandoned by her mother, had just lost her father to a violent death, and was meeting family members who were really total strangers. How could they think she would just jump up and hug them all? None of us knew anything about her or what her fourteen years of life had been like. What I did know was she had been abandoned by her mother and sent to live with a father with whom she had no connection. Now she was orphaned, having to deal with the expectations of unknown relatives and the cruel hard world. I understood her caution. I'd lost my mother when I was a year older than she. My father's mind, eaten away by dementia, had long since left my mom and me to fend for ourselves. Being vulnerable made a person cautious. I could relate immediately.

"Hi, Piper, I'm Alexandra. I love your hair," I said.

As hard as she tried to fight it, a smile cracked her sullen face, exposing her perfect white teeth, her dainty upturned nose moving with her smile, animating her face.

Our eyes locked. She said, "Thank you," in a soft, easy voice.

James, apparently not much for lengthy conversations, said, "I'm hungry. Let's eat," as he took long strides into the house.

"Me too," Tom added.

"Hope everyone likes Mexican food," Rose said as she shuffled to the kitchen.

Tom and I croaked, "Hell yeah," at exactly the same time, bringing a huge smile to Rose's face. She could tell in the short time she'd seen us together that we were in sync.

It was the first time I'd noticed how Tom and my cadences echoed each other's. Rose seemed to approve of the chemistry between us, which made me like her. We both offered to help her cook, but she turned us down, telling us it was her kitchen, and she certainly knew her way around it.

Tom's parents' home revealed details of his childhood. The furniture was traditional, circa 1980, sporting a couch and recliner. No art decorated the walls. There were scads of photos of Tom and his brother documenting their progression from birth to high school graduation.

After stashing our luggage in one of the two spare bedrooms, Tom and I sat in the family room with James and Constance. James had made us each a drink. I saw Constance studying Tom and me. It looked as though she was trying to make sense of our relationship, but she couldn't quite figure it out. The awkward silence in the room made Tom uncomfortable, something I'd never seen in him. Here he was, sitting in a room with the niece he'd just met, quietly saying nothing, and that made no sense to me. Maybe he needed to talk to his father about Ethan and didn't feel comfortable discussing it with Constance present. *I need to stop referring to her as 'Constance,'* I thought. By God, if she wanted to be called Piper, then, I'd call her Piper from here on. My curiosity was getting the better of me, so I decided to unleash my inner Lois Lane. I put down my glass.

"Piper. I need to stretch my legs. Let's take a walk around the neighborhood."

"Not much of a neighborhood," she said. "We're in the middle of nowhere."

She was right. The Sanders' home was on the outskirts of Red Bluff. Still, I wanted to see the town. I'd never been this far west. "We won't be long," I assured the others, and we took off.

The air outdoors was clean and fresh, evergreen fir trees growing everywhere, their green needles reaching for the sky, a sea of Christmas trees making the town seem festive. Humidity was nonexistent, the air easy to walk through. In the Big Easy, sometimes the humidity was so bad you could swim through the air. But not here; the air was light, yet full of oxygen, not water. Piper and I began our walk around Red Bluff, population 14,000.

"This is my first time in California," I said. "It's beautiful."

"I guess," Piper said.

"I was born in a small town in Indiana. My parents had a corn farm. I couldn't wait to leave," I said. "Where were you born?"

"My birth certificate says Los Angeles. We traveled around some," Piper said.

"I love your name, Piper. It's beautiful and matches your hair," I said. "Who did your hair for you?"

"Me," she said.

She looked at me and laughed. I could tell that she hadn't done much laughing in her life. Her eyes were those of an old soul. There was much more to Piper than her outward appearance revealed. She was intelligent and quick-witted, but she tried to hide behind her quirky looks and habits. It was her eyes that gave her away, revealing a much deeper intellect than her exterior displayed. There was something about this wild child I really liked. I couldn't put my finger on it, but there was something.

We walked for a short while around neighborhoods of similar homes, and then circled back to the house. I was sure the food was ready by now, and we weren't disappointed. Rose was ready to serve chicken fajitas, complete with onions, sour cream, and guacamole. Delicious could only begin to describe it. James brought out some Mexican beer, and I ate and drank until I couldn't move. Piper ate the chicken and cheese but pushed the tortilla aside.

After Tom and I helped Rose clean the kitchen, I set up my laptop on the kitchen table to check my blog. The posts about ACC were waning. Most bloggers posted stories about missing girls and unidentified remains. As I was reading the posts, Piper walked in the kitchen and sat next to me.

"What's this?" she asked.

"My blog site. It's called *Alex's Daily Planet*," I said.

"Like Superman, Louis Lane, and Lex Luther?" she asked.

"You've read the graphic novels?" I asked, adopting the politically correct name for comic books.

"No, saw the movie," Piper said. "So, why are all of these people posting stories of missing girls?"

"People come here to talk about what's on their mind. My blog focuses on two types of serial killers: corporate killers who make products that kill people; and street killers, like the ones who kill strangers to fulfill some bizarre need," I said. "The bloggers' discussions have led to lost girls—young women who have disappeared all over the world. Their relatives are worried that their missing daughters or sisters are dead, the victims of serial killers."

"That's cool," Piper said as she started reading the posts. "Look at all of these posts from LA. There are a lot of missing girls. You should link your blog to more social media sites if you really want to reach younger people."

"I'm not great on the computer," I said.

"Let me do it then," Piper said as she took command of the keyboard.

I watched in awe as she created accounts on Facebook, Twitter, Instagram, Snapchat, and at least ten other social media sites I'd never known existed. Her fingers danced across the keyboard, like a piano virtuosos at Carnegie Hall. She had mad computer skills. Time flew by as she and I worked together reading the posts and adding comments of our own. Soon the hour grew late.

"Constance, it's time for bed," Rose yelled from the family room.

"I hate that name," she muttered. "My name is Piper. Why can't she call me by my name?"

"Sometimes people get stuck in their ways," I said. "She means well. Rose is right, though; it's time to get some sleep. I'm dead tired."

"Alexandra, what's going to happen to me?" Piper asked.

I heard the fear in her voice and put my hand over hers. "I'm not sure, but don't worry. You'll be fine. We can talk more about it in the morning."

I had no idea how to answer her question. From the short time I'd been around Tom's parents, it was clear to me they shouldn't take her in, for her sake as well as theirs. None of us knew where her mother was living, or even if she were still living. Ethan didn't know if he had a a daughter or a son until her mother shipped Piper to him a year ago. Tom knew nothing about Piper's mother. We were going to have to ask Piper about the woman. Surely that would make her worry that we were hoping to get rid of her. I knew what it was like to feel all alone. When my parents died, I had no living relatives. The feeling of being abandoned in this huge world scared the hell out of me. And I was a thirty-year-old woman with a job, able to support myself. Piper was just a child. What must she be thinking? But this was not the time to talk about it. And anyway, Tom and his parents would be the ones making the decisions.

Though I guessed I could help Tom with his part of it, we were too tired to talk about Piper's situation that night. We agreed we needed to sleep. But as I drifted off, she was on my mind—her dancing fingers, candy-colored hair, and sad eyes. I had no answers. I hoped the situation would be clearer tomorrow.

I was awakened by the smell of brewing coffee. I made my way to the kitchen. Rose sat at the kitchen table sobbing. I sat next to her and put my arm around her.

As soon as she felt my touch, her tears started flowing ferociously. I placed her head on my shoulder and patted her back. I felt awkward, not knowing her at all, but she needed to cry. She'd lost her eldest son. There were no words I could say to comfort her. No parent should have to bury their child.

When she stopped crying, I said, "I'm so very, very sorry, Rose. But I believe this life is not all there is. We are all a part of this universe and we never really leave. My mother looks down on me and helps me through hard times. Ethan lives in you, and Ethan lives in Piper."

"Poor little Constance," she said. "What can we do with her?"

Tom walked in. Shortly after, James joined us. As we drank our morning coffee, Tom told us that he planned to go to Chicago to wind down his brother's affairs. That certainly was the logical next step. But the big subject wasn't being addressed, and we all knew it. As we sat there looking at each other, James spoke.

"I'll contact the state today and look into a foster home for Constance. Rose and I can't take care of her. She can stay in the foster home until her mother turns up."

No one said a word. We all just sat there looking at each other. I waited for someone to say something, anything. I couldn't take it anymore.

I looked at Tom and said, "We are not putting that child in a foster home. I know I'm not a member of this family, but I can't sit by and watch her be discarded. I can see your parents can't care for her. Leaving her with them would not be the right thing to do. Tom, she needs to come back to New Orleans with us."

"How are we going to take care of her?" Tom asked. "My job requires me to be away from home several nights a month. She has to be enrolled in school. Taking care of a fourteen-year-old is not easy. That decision has many long-term consequences."

"I didn't say it would be easy. I said it was the right thing to do. My job doesn't require a nine-to-five commitment. I have the freedom to work from home. I don't have to travel, either. I can take care of her. She can sleep on my couch until I can find a larger place," I said.

They all looked at me as if I'd lost my mind. She wasn't my child or even related to me. Yet I was going to take care of her? I guess if I were in their shoes, I'd wonder about my decision, too.

"But, Alexandra, you don't—" Tom tried to say.

I cut him off in mid-sentence. "I don't what? I don't know what it's like to be all alone in this world? I don't know how a teenager feels losing her parents? I don't know how to fend for myself? Tom Sanders, she is coming home with us! Now book your flight to Chicago. You have business to complete. We are done with this discussion. And, by the way...her name is Piper!"

They all rocked back in their chairs and looked at me in amazement. Tom knew not to question my resolve. He knew when I'd made my mind up there was no changing it. His parents had never seen anyone go from sweet to bitch at the speed of light. Once their brains absorbed what had just happened, Rose looked grateful, and James looked impressed. I knew I'd made the right decision.

"Now I'm going to book Piper and my flights to New Orleans. We are leaving tomorrow," I said as I walked out of the kitchen.

I ran into Piper, who'd been standing out of sight listening to the entire conversation. Little tears stained her cheeks. I grabbed her and drew her close to me. She put her arms around me and whispered, "Thank you for not throwing me away."

"Don't worry, Piper," I said. "No one is going to throw you away. We'll figure this out together. You'll love New Orleans. We'll find the right school for you." I stroked her hair, lifting one of the pink sections between my fingers. "And New Orleans will definitely love you."

She smiled back at me. Her smile was tentative but a smile all the same. The first big one she'd had since I met her. Now we had to find a way to make sure it wasn't the last.

I ambled to the bedroom to get my computer to book the flights to New Orleans. Tom entered the room before my computer had time to boot. A silent moment passed between us as our eyes met.

"Alexandra, I am sorry if I upset you a few minutes ago."

"I don't understand why your parents would even consider putting Piper in foster care," I said. "She needs to be living with her family, not strangers."

Tom's face saddened. He slumped onto the bed and asked me to sit beside him.

"What I'm about to say is very hard for me," he said. "My parents are good people, but they are not affectionate people. Kind, I guess, but not warm, and not the kind of parents who love to be with their kids. They met in the mid-1960s at an anti-war demonstration. They have committed themselves to causes all of their lives. When Ethan and I were children, they didn't have any time for us. They both had jobs. In their free time, they joined causes that kept them completely occupied. They didn't attend any of our school or sporting events. They never told Ethan or me they loved us, though I'm sure they must have. They were just emotionally unavailable."

"Oh, Tom, that's so sad."

"I guess Ethan and I adopted their ways," Tom said as he lightly caressed my face with the back of his fingers. "I don't want to live my life like theirs. I want to make my career dreams come true, and I want to have love in my life. It is hard for me to express love. Alexandra, you are the first person I've been able to open myself to. It will take time, but I can learn to show the love that's inside me. We should and will take care of Piper. She needs us."

I placed a kiss lightly on his lips. "Tom, I am so proud of you. Tomorrow morning tell Piper how you feel."

CHAPTER SIX
CONSTANCE

TOM AND I both had a restless night's sleep. Taking in Piper was going to change my life, and the reality of our decision consumed my thoughts. I barely knew how to care for myself. Me, Alexandra Lee, with a teenager to raise. What had I done to myself? She wasn't related to me, and I knew only fragmented details about her life. Most of her life she lived with her mother whom Tom nor I knew nothing about except her name, Sandy Rawlins. We needed to know so much more.

"Good morning, pretty girl," Tom said, the warmth in his voice liberating me from my thoughts. "How'd you sleep?"

"Not very well. How about you?"

"I tossed and turned, worrying about having my conversation with Constance today," he said. I loved that he admitted he was having difficulty exposing his vulnerability. It made me so much more hopeful about the future.

"Tom, that's good that you're thinking about what you intend to say to her, but, here's a tip: her name is Piper. If you want to get off on the right foot, call her by the name she likes. Piper."

"See what I mean? How am I going to be able to get this right? I don't know anything about raising a kid," Tom said. I put a hand on his back. "What's worse is she's an orphan, or she might as well be. Her mother abandoned her and her father is dead. If she were a dolphin calf, I'd know what to do, but not a teenage girl."

"Calm down, Tom," I said. "In some ways she is like an abandoned animal in the wild. She needs much of the same treatment. She needs food, shelter, and someone to protect her as she learns how to take care of herself. Most of all she needs love. You can do that, can't you?"

Wow, where did that come from? Maybe deep inside me I had a nurturing instinct. Maybe it was my mother and Sarah speaking through me. Either way it felt natural, and I liked it.

We put on our clothes and joined Tom's parents in the kitchen. I would have walked through a pit of poisonous snakes for a cup of strong coffee, but there were none to be had. Tom's parents sat at their kitchen table drinking green tea. I'd never had a cup of green tea in my life. *What the hell?* I thought. *When in Rome…*Rose poured me a cup. She offered me stevia to sweeten it with. Funny, I was working on a PR campaign for stevia but had never tried it. I added it to my green tea and, to my amazement, I loved it. I wasn't ready to give up coffee, but I liked the green tea with stevia.

"Where's Constance? I mean Piper?" Tom asked, catching himself.

"She went for a walk," James said. "Said she'd be back in an hour. First time she's been out of bed before noon since she arrived."

"Don't be hard on her, James. She's only been here two days," Rose chastised.

Tom smiled at his mother. She knew how to gently calm his dad down when necessary. "Alexandra and I are definitely taking Piper to New Orleans to live with us. We are going to get legal custody of her and raise her as if she were our child."

"Do you two live together now?" Rose asked as only a mother could.

"No. We haven't really talked about it," Tom said. He blushed a bright Alabama Crimson Tide red and said, "I guess we'll have to move in together. What do you think, Alexandra?"

I was way ahead of Tom. Our future living arrangements were responsible for most of my last night's wakefulness.

"We can look for a larger place to live when we return to New Orleans. We have to provide a proper home for Piper," I said. "My rented condo is nice, but it's too small."

I wanted to move anyway. The place reeked of memories. El Serpiente was killed and Sophia was stabbed there. That condo was a crime scene for a month. *Good luck to the landlord trying to rent it again,* I thought morbidly. Oh well, maybe some New Orleans Anne Rice vampire fans would think it had an atmosphere.

Maybe it was finally time for me to buy a house. I still had money left from the inheritance I'd received from Sarah. I donated the house she left me to the battered women's shelter, so I felt certain she would approve of me using the rest of the money to buy a house, especially now that I would be taking care of a child. She would like that.

Buying a house, moving Tom in, and taking on the responsibility of raising a teenager. Holy shit was my life about to change.

I was getting freaked out when I heard from behind us, "What's the meeting about?"

"Come in and sit down, Constance," Rose said. "Tom and Alexandra would like to speak with you."

Piper shifted her "what now" eyes to me. Her expression reminded me of the look on my face when my eighth-grade guidance counselor marched me to the principal's office for writing the article about the school cafeteria's out-of-date food. They were the ones who'd messed up, but I got in trouble. The episode taught me a valuable lesson: Fair rarely plays a starring role in life's struggles.

Piper sat next to me, much like a tiger cub would move close to its mother for protection when threatened. I gave her a reassuring nod, and all eyes turned to Tom.

"Piper, I don't know the details, but I'm sure your life has been difficult. Certainly, it's been horrible lately. We as a family believe better times are ahead. We have decided you will come to New Orleans with Alexandra and me to live," he said.

Piper's face flushed red. She squared her shoulders toward Tom and said in a combative tone, "You decided? No one talked to me! Don't I have a say in my life? New Orleans? What's in New Orleans?" Piper asked.

Tom was taken aback by her aggressive demeanor. He didn't react right away though and gave himself a moment to calm down and add more compassion to his tone. "Alexandra and I live in New Orleans and we love it. It is a great city. The people are friendly, the food is fantastic, and the music…Most of all, we can give you a stable home there."

Piper recognized the conciliatory inflection in his voice. She crunched her dainty face, squinting her crystal-blue eyes, and asked, "Don't hurricanes go there? Aren't there alligators everywhere?"

We all chuckled a bit. I tried to hide my ear-to-ear smile with my hands, but it was impossible.

Tom thought for a moment before he answered. "Yes, New Orleans does experience an occasional hurricane. But Katrina, which I'm sure you've heard all about, was not the typical storm. The city is much more prepared now for hurricanes anyway. As far as alligators, yes, there are some, but they live in the swamps well outside of the city. New Orleans is much like Chicago or any other city. Native wildlife larger than bugs or rodents have long since fled to the surrounding forests, as they have in every region where humans have built large cities. They don't want to be around us either. New Orleans is a unique city, and you are sure to fall in love with its amazing culture and music. The food is incredible, and the people are warm and friendly."

Piper furrowed her brow, trying to make sense of Tom's words, her eyes a bit glazed over, evidencing her state of overwhelm.

"Where did you go to school in Chicago?" I asked.

"My father sent me to an all-girls' school in the city near his office. It really sucked. The girls were mean. I didn't have any friends. Most of the girls had gone to school together all of their lives. They were rich, snobby bitches. Dad chose it because it was 'the place' to send your daughters. Besides, it was convenient for him since it was close to his office. He dropped me off on his way to work, and our au pair picked me up after school. Dad didn't get home until late at night," Piper said.

"You had an au pair?" Rose queried.

"Sure did. Her name was Flavienne. She was from Geneva, Switzerland. I think my dad knew her before I went to live with him. She took care of the house and ran errands for him."

Tom glanced at me with a knowing expression, one eyebrow raised.

"Young girl from Switzerland. Sounds about right," Tom mocked.

I stomped his foot. He quickly shifted his eyes to me, mouthing, "What did I do?"

Sometimes I wondered about him. He was a smart guy, very loving and sensitive, but he could still say the dumbest things. Poor Piper's father had just been killed, and Tom was implying that the au pair was his girlfriend. She may have been, but this was not the time or place to discuss it. Piper was scared, and she had only known us for one day and we were about to cart her off to a strange city to live. This was the time to show compassion.

Rose took a moment but finally said, "James, why don't you and I go for a drive to town?"

I snaked my arm around Piper's back and rested my hand on the crown of her shoulder. "Tom, why don't you get on your parents' computer and book your flight to Chicago? Piper, you and I can use my laptop to watch some YouTube videos about New Orleans."

I guided Piper toward the room Tom and I were occupying during our stay at his parent's house. It was a large, spacious room for a guest bedroom, painted powder-blue, just like it had been when he shared it with his brother. The bunk beds were long gone, replaced by a queen-sized sled bed, battle scarred from its service to a future marine biologist. We sat next to each other with our backs against the headboard. I placed the computer on my lap and went to YouTube. Piper's eyes were transfixed on scenes of the French Quarter.

"Oh my God. Look at those buildings. They are so awesome," she said. Like her uncle, she loved the uncommon style of the French

Quarter architecture. "Some of these places look like homes. Do people actually live in the French Quarter?"

"Yes, quite a few."

"Is it expensive?" she asked.

"Yes, it is very expensive. But there are places just outside the Quarter that are more reasonable," I said.

Piper took a second, squinted her eyes in a quizzical fashion, and asked, "Where will we live?"

"I've been thinking about that," I said. "The short answer is, I don't know yet. Neither my condo nor Tom's apartment is big enough for three for more than a little while."

Three? How the fuck did that happen? It was one thing lying in bed musing; it was quite another having to answer a smart adolescent's questions.

Piper peered at me with large, imploring eyes. It was a puppy dog look, no doubt one she'd mastered long ago. It worked like a charm. "We can all three look for a place when Tom returns from Chicago," I said.

"Can we look in the French Quarter?" she asked.

I didn't need to discuss living in the Quarter with Tom. I knew he'd want to live there. It dawned on me that as many times as I'd been in the Quarter, I really didn't know much about its history. Maybe Piper and I could spend time learning it. I wanted to know more about her history, too. Tom and I knew squat about her or her mother. Hell, Tom didn't even know much about his brother's life in Chicago.

"Piper, we can look. I don't know if we can afford a place in the French Quarter, but we can look."

Tom sauntered into the room. His flight to Chicago departed the next morning at ten. He'd also made arrangements for the Cook County coroner to release his brother's body to a funeral home for preparation and transport to Red Bluff. His brother's funeral was scheduled two days from today. Tom was anxious to get us all back to New Orleans. Piper, Tom, and I were scheduled to leave the day after the funeral.

Returning to New Orleans would be different for me this time. I had an almost official family again, and I had to admit I was excited. This was a new direction for my life. There was something about Piper I really liked. She had energy and curiosity. Her eyes told me she knew much more than her rebellious outer shell revealed.

James and Rose returned. Instead of taking a leisurely drive, they had gone shopping at a local organic vegetable and fruit stand.

Tom helped them unload the bounty. Rose yelled, "Alexandra, Piper, come see what we have."

Her face was aglow, and her family-trademark blue eyes sparkled, complementing the colors of her Native American turquoise necklace. Clearly, organic food was like Captain Hook's buried treasure to her. We all helped unload the groceries. They were neatly stashed in reusable hemp carryout bags Rose always had in her car. In this part of California, being asked "paper or plastic" was not cool. Especially if your customers were two cottontops stuck in the hippie revolution. *Ironic*, I thought, *how a generation that spawned the environmental movement created more conspicuous consumption that may have accelerated the path to climate change.* Better keep those thoughts to myself.

"Mom, Dad. I am leaving in the morning for Chicago to wrap up Ethan's affairs. Alexandra and Piper are staying here until after the funeral."

"Well, then, I'll cook the best going-away meal for you tonight," Rose said with all of the enthusiasm of a cooking show host. "Tom, would you and Alexandra help me prepare the veggies?"

Rose was masking her sadness, wanting to project a happy persona for Tom and Piper. I could tell she was hurting deep in her heart because she had to put too much effort into smiling to conceal her pain. Sometimes when she thought no one was watching she cried, hiding her face in her hands.

I noticed Piper had disappeared. *No worry*, I thought, *she needs some time to assimilate all of the changes going on.* I knew I did. Rose's kitchen didn't have any new gadgets in it. Every action to prepare the meal was done by hand. We prepared the vegetables for cooking with knives. Rose coached me through the delicate process of peeling the perfectly ripe tomatoes. Tom separated the fresh oregano leaves from their stems. I crushed two garlic cloves, making certain to discard the outer shells. Rose placed a spaghetti squash in the oven. Tom and Rose exchanged stories of the boys' childhood, providing a vocal tour of the stories told by the photos framed throughout the house. I listened to gain more understanding of Tom, but I couldn't help but wonder what Piper was doing. She was still a mystery to me, and my reporter instincts compelled me to learn more.

I excused myself from kitchen duties and walked toward the bedroom. "Piper, are you still here?" I called out.

"Yes. Just shutting down your computer," she answered.

Wow, I thought. She'd been in the bedroom on the computer for the entire two hours we were in the kitchen? I guess that wasn't unusual for a girl her age. Made me wonder, though, I must admit. What was she doing in the bedroom so long? Was I having mommy thoughts? Oh my God, I was. I felt responsible for watching out for her. Maybe I needed to put parental controls on my computer and cable TV box at home. What had I gotten myself into? What I knew for sure was I needed to learn more about her. I entered the bedroom just as she folded the computer together.

"What have you been up to?" I queried.

She cast a wary eye in my direction and answered, "Nothing, just looking at some more New Orleans videos. If I'm going to live there, I'd like to learn as much as I can about it."

I sat on the bed beside her. She was still sitting cross-legged with the computer on her lap. I scooted on the bed and placed the computer on the bed beside me. She watched me carefully, shifting her eyes back and forth from me to the computer. She gauged my movements, wondering if I was going to fire up the laptop to see what sites she'd been visiting.

I placed my hand on her knee. Her eyes locked on mine. She had a deer-in-the-headlights look. Not fear, just wondering what was next.

"Tell me about your mother," I said.

She froze. Except for her labored breathing, she remained completely motionless for a few seconds. Her deep blue eyes watered.

Her face fell. She shifted her eyes to her lap. She whimpered, "No, not now. Not with all of them here. I'll tell you later when we are alone."

I didn't crowd her. She wasn't ready. Besides, Rose announced supper was ready, and there would be plenty of time on the plane to discuss Piper's mother. The smells coming from the kitchen were drawing us in, so we followed our noses, our mouths watering, to join the rest of the family. We had an amazing dinner courtesy of Chef Rose: homemade marinara sauce over spaghetti squash pasta and eggplant parmesan. I dined like a California princess. I didn't realize that healthy food could taste so yummy. Tom and I washed the dishes and crawled off to bed. Tomorrow was going to be a big day for all of us.

I decided I couldn't wait until the flight to New Orleans, so I planned to learn more about Piper and her mother tomorrow.

CHAPTER SEVEN
DYSFUNCTIONAL FAMILY

~

TOM SHOOK ME from a deep sleep. "Hey, Alexandra, wake up. I have to get ready to go."

Slowly I slid down the tunnel to consciousness. We'd only been in California for two days, yet I had adjusted to the two-hour time difference. I guess I needed the sleep. Immediately my thoughts turned to Piper.

"You need to go wake Piper up, Tom," I said. "She needs to tell you what needs to be sent directly to New Orleans from Chicago."

Tom's blurry figure slinked off through the bedroom door. I missed my New Orleans coffee routine. The California version didn't offer enough caffeine. No worry, we'd be home soon, and my morning routine would commence again. Maybe not exactly the same, because now I would have a teenage girl to deal with.

When Tom returned, I'd brushed my teeth and made the bed.

"Piper was hard to wake up," he said. "My guess is she'd been up all night."

Just then I noticed my laptop wasn't in the room. She must have taken it last night, that little rascal. What the hell did she look at on the web? I added that question to the list to ask her today. She'd be trapped with me all day. *Nowhere to hide, little girl,* I thought, my investigative journalist mind in overdrive. She was cagey but no match for Lois Lane.

It was a glorious day to be in Northern California. The temperature was a brisk fifty-two degrees, with clear skies and a high of seventy—perfect weather for a long walk.

After I helped Tom pack for his trip to Chicago, he put his strong arms around my narrow waist. His smoldering blue eyes looked into mine. He lightly brushed his lips across my slightly puckered lips and then over the smooth surface of my face. He gradually slid his hands down to my rear. His lips returned to mine firmer and more forceful as our tongues entwined. My thoughts staggered through my mind like those of a partying teenage girl. *Where is he going with this?* I wondered. I didn't have to think about it long. Soon we were interrupted.

"Alexandra, Alexandra," shouted a voice from the next room—by now a place far, far away. "Come here. I want to show you something." It was Piper. *Oh shit, not now,* I thought.

Tom broke our embrace. "You'd better go see what she wants, Mrs. Mom," he whispered, and I laughed and swatted him.

I guess I'm going to have to get used to this, I thought, still vibrating in my naughty places.

I made my way down the short hallway to Piper's room. There she was propped up in the bed with my computer open.

"Come sit by me and see what I've done," she said.

I scooted next to her. She was on my blog. At least I thought it was my blog, but it didn't look the same. She'd added a section on the left margin below the menu with images of missing girls fading into each other, one after another. Below each photo was a short paragraph detailing the salient facts of each girl's disappearance.

"Not so boring anymore, right?" she asked.

"How were you able to change the format of the site?" I asked.

"Oh yeah, I kinda hacked the site. Hope you don't mind."

I was totally caught off guard. I loved the new addition to the site and didn't approve of her hacking it, but I was impressed by her skills. I feigned anger. "You can't just hack people's sites without their permission."

"Sorry, Alexandra. I thought you wouldn't mind. I only added an RSS feed to help match missing girls with inquiries from your blog visitors. I had to combine feeds from several websites to make them stream into one on your blog. What do you think?"

My mind bounced back and forth like a ping-pong ball between anger at the intrusion and pride at her accomplishment. And what the hell was an RSS feed anyway? Her grin, showing more of her teeth than I'd seen since we met, melted my heart, making me reach out with both arms and draw her in.

"It's spectacular," I said.

"Look how many people have commented," she added.

A quick look at the blog posts revealed a plethora of approvals. It was true; she'd made the site much more interesting. Just like my life with her was likely to be much more interesting. I shouted to Tom, and he made his way down the narrow, darkened hallway to Piper's room. He focused his eyes on Piper first. Then he examined the blog like a stern father reviewing a student's progress report.

"You've been up all night, haven't you?" he asked. "You can't do that when we get to New Orleans. You will be in school. You will have to get your homework done and go to bed by ten o'clock. You won't be able to just do what you want when you want. We will have rules in the house, and you will follow them. You can stay up until eleven on weekends, but you'll have to be up with your bed made no later than ten a.m. You can't be up all night and sleep all day like a vampire."

Piper recoiled from the parental onslaught. "You aren't my father. You can't tell me what to do," she shouted.

"That's where you are wrong. I will be your legal guardian. You will be under our roof and will live by our rules," he said in a raised voice.

Piper's face sagged and her jaw dropped ever so slightly. Her eyelids sunk in despair. Her face, still partially defiant, revealed her unwelcome resignation to her plight. Her shoulders slumped, and her head dropped down. She reminded me of a defendant who'd just been sentenced to life in prison on one of those dramatic TV crime dramas.

Tom angrily wheeled around and stormed from the bedroom without giving her any chance to speak again. I could hear him in the other room throwing around his suitcase preparing to leave. Petite tears worked their way down Piper's smooth cheeks, and she raised her head, shifting her eyes toward mine.

"He's just like Victor," she said.

"Victor? Who's that?" I asked.

"Nobody. Just a friend of my mom's." It was clear to me she didn't want to talk about Victor, and she certainly wasn't trying to compliment Tom. I decided not to pursue the subject now. She'd reacted to Tom's tone like a dog who had been beaten repeatedly, and I wanted to know why.

"Tom is right about having rules," I said. "We'll have to work on his delivery. You did a fantastic job, Piper, making my blog come to life, but you are a beautiful young lady and you have to get your sleep. Agreed?"

"I guess so," she responded.

"Stay right here. I'm going to help Tom pack," I said.

I stepped out of Piper's room and leaned against the white, textured hallway wall. I needed a minute to process my thoughts about what just happened. Why did Tom come down so hard on Piper? It was true, she did need structure, but was this the right time to start? She had just lost her father, and she hadn't had time to grieve. What about Tom? He'd lost his brother and was suddenly cast in the role of a father. Not what he wanted at this point in his life. He had to be struggling with his new responsibilities. Though they'd drifted apart, Ethan was still his brother. There was no point in starting an argument about parenting with him now when he had such a painful task ahead. I'd better let sleeping dogs lie. I'd learn more about Piper while Tom was in Chicago. Maybe I could find a way to get through to her.

When I entered the room, Tom's face was still red. He directed his steely blue eyes to me, making me freeze, not knowing what to say.

"What are we going to do with her?" Tom asked, clearly frustrated. "She's going to be a real problem. No one has taught her any discipline. She's out of control, and I'll not have it in my house."

Tom was venting and I knew it. I didn't think he knew how he really felt, but I couldn't blame him. I was also going to have a little trouble adjusting to our decision to take Piper back to New Orleans with us. I didn't know much about her yet. She seemed defiant and streetwise, and that could be tough to handle. I'd heard enough woe from older friends to realize that a troubled teenager can drive the best parent to distraction, yet at the same time she was fragile and fractured. Had we gotten ourselves in over our heads?

No. We could do it. Piper had nowhere else to go. We had to find a way to deal with this. For all her defiance, she still had hope, so it wasn't too late.

"Tom, you go to Chicago and take care of wrapping up Ethan's affairs. I'll learn more about Piper while you're gone. She seems very confused to me. I don't think we should give up on her. We can make this work."

Tom reached out his arms to me and drew me in tightly to his chest. He held me for a few seconds while I lovingly wrapped my arms around his waist. I felt the emotional conflict in him as he slightly trembled. "Alexandra, I'm scared. I'm afraid our lives will be consumed, and I fear our dreams for the future are lost. I don't want that. Then I also worry that we will fail Piper and she will choose to lead a useless life."

"You're looking too far ahead. We'll get through this," I said. "We'll find a way together. You, me, and Piper."

Tom slowly pushed me back so our eyes could lock together without breaking our embrace. "You are the most wonderful person I've ever known, Alexandra. I am so lucky to have you in my life. Just when I think I can't love you any more than I already do, you do something to double my feelings for you. You are amazing."

He leaned in and pressed his lips to mine. We lingered in our kiss, knowing our connection was solid and could never be broken.

"You'd better get on the road. Don't want to miss your flight," I said.

James helped Tom load his luggage. Rose joined Piper and me in the kitchen.

"We'll be back late tonight," Rose said. "James and I are going to see Tom off at the airport and then do some sightseeing in Sacramento. You two know where everything is, so make yourself at home."

Tom kissed me goodbye and then turned to Piper. He picked up both of her little hands in his. "Piper, I'm sorry for losing it earlier. Things will work out. Have fun with Alexandra. We'll have time to get to know each other better when I return. I love you."

As they drove off into the early morning mist, Piper whispered, "I love you, too."

"So, Piper, where were you born?" I asked. This was my opening salvo into her world. I wanted to peel back her layers and find her core.

"California," she answered, blunting my inquiry. She knew I wanted to know more, but she wasn't ready to give it up. I was fine with her evasiveness, because she was in my world now. After all, I was an investigative journalist blogger, a sport I'd mastered.

"Hey, I know it's early, but how do you feel about going for a walk?" I asked.

"Sure," Piper said in an enthusiastic voice. "I've been at the computer most of the night. Walking sounds great."

Oh, the energy of the youth, I thought. If I'd been up all night, I'd be dead tired. It was a beautiful Northern California June morning. The air was cool and crisp, the sun's rays veiled by a slight mist. Woodpeckers pecked at dead trees, diligently searching for breakfast. Songbirds sang their tunes while a gentle breeze rustled the leaves to provide the percussion for nature's symphony. I grabbed a sweater, and Piper put on a UCLA sweatshirt as we embarked along the winding roads of Red Bluff.

"I see your sweatshirt is from UCLA. Is that a college somewhere here in California?" I asked coyly.

Piper slightly rolled her eyes before turning to me giving me an incredulous look. I knew she was wondering how I didn't know what

UCLA was. But, like every person from California or New York, she believed everyone from any other American state was a dumb hick.

"Yes," she said. "It's in Los Angeles. My mother bought it for me."

"That's nice. Did she graduate from UCLA?"

"I don't think so. That's where she met Victor. I think she gave up on getting a degree after that," she said.

"Really? That's too bad. Do you know what her major was?" I really wanted to find out more about this Victor guy but decided pushing it wasn't a good idea yet. I'd heard very little of his story but was already developing a distaste for him.

"No, I don't know. She was on the dance squad. She told me she marched in the Rose Bowl Parade one year," she said.

"Wow, that must have been exciting. I know your mom's name is Sandy Rawlins. Is Rawlins her maiden name or did she marry Victor and take his name?"

Piper's face turned combative, her eyes as cold as the winter winds blowing through the corn back home in Indiana. "She'd never marry that creep Victor," she said in a harsh tone. "She could have been something if she hadn't met him."

I knew it. Victor was a bad guy. I got the feeling that he was the reason her mother sent Piper away to live with Ethan. I decided to push for more information about her mother.

"So, does your mother work?"

I could see Piper was growing tired of this conversation. She was stressing, her fists were balled, and her arms were crossed. She exhaled heavily. "Mom works at Victor's spa in Los Angeles," she said. "I hated it there. Can we talk about something else?"

"Sure. I didn't mean to pry. I just want to get to know you better," I said. "You amazed me with the way you restructured my blog. Where did you learn to do that?"

"When I lived with my mom, I was homeschooled. One of the ladies who helped homeschool me introduced me to the world of computers. I loved it. I spent hours searching the web, reading articles, and watching tutorial videos about building websites."

"That's cool. So you are mostly self-taught," I said.

"Yeah, you can learn anything on the web. I learned how to write code. It's easy and fun."

When Piper talked about the web, her entire body language changed. Her arms leaped from her side, and her hands drew intricate pictures in the air as she described her learning adventures. She shifted her torso to me as she spoke, open and vulnerable, not closed and protective. Something or someone had instilled fear in her. *She isn't as rebellious as she is cautious*, I thought. She'd learned how to shut down and shut people out to protect herself.

"After a while, Victor restricted my use of the computer," she said. "My mom and the other ladies at the spa helped me sneak around and use it when he wasn't watching. They were scared of him but always did things they weren't supposed to do. We all helped each other sneak."

After that Piper clammed up. She wanted to head back to the house and take a nap. She needed it, too, because her eyes were drooping, and her voice was weakening. She went to bed as soon as we entered the door.

What the hell is going on with her mother? I wondered. Why did the other women in the spa have to sneak around to help Piper learn on the web? *When she wakes up, I'm going to find out who this Victor guy is and what's really going on*, I thought.

CHAPTER EIGHT
PIPER'S STORY

~

MORNING SUN BROKE through the clouded night, casting broken rays through the bedroom window. I reached for Tom, forgetting he was in Chicago, and my heart sunk momentarily. It struck me I was getting used to having him next to me. But even though I was missing Tom, I loved the early morning stillness of Red Bluff. No sounds and no movement except the rising and falling of my own chest.

While Piper slept, I made a cup of California coffee, a.k.a. stevia-sweetened green tea. It was good, but I longed for a café au lait from Café Du Monde in the New Orleans French Quarter, the smell of fresh baked beignets wafting in the air. I missed the warm, friendly daily interaction with the New Orleans' "who dats," a slang term for the city's residents. It was derived from the tune created by the New Orleans Saints fans' favorite chant: "Who dat talkin' 'bout beating dem Saints? Say who dat?" Football was more than just a sport in Louisiana—it was a way of life. In 2009, the city was struggling to find its way back after Hurricane Katrina blew through property and lives. The Saints did the impossible; something they'd never come close to doing before that magical year: They won thirteen of their sixteen regular-season games and went on to win the Super Bowl. The effect on New Orleans was like antibiotics on a bacterial infection. Healing. Buoyed by the victory, the city began its recovery in earnest and never looked back. Smaller but stronger, New Orleans was the number one cultural tourist destination in the United States. Still, the stevia was something I could get used to. The sweetness of sugar without all of the lousy side effects. Very appealing idea.

"Good morning," squeaked Piper's voice from behind me.

Before I could speak, my phone rang. I answered without checking the caller ID, thinking it was Tom.

"Hi, Alexandra," a vaguely familiar voice said. "It's Mandy."

Piper made herself a cup of green tea and sat close enough to me to eavesdrop on my conversation. Her impish ears seemed to grow an inch or two as she tried to catch every word.

"Oh, hi, Mandy, how are things in New Orleans?" I asked.

"Still getting used to not hanging out with Bob," she said, trailing her voice ever downward in deeper and quieter tones like a person hoarse and breathless from a chest cold.

I shivered. No way was I getting into that subject with Piper sitting next to me. "How are Charlotte and your father?"

"They're fine, I guess," she answered, her voice devoid of any hint of enthusiasm. "When are you coming back to the city?"

"In a few days," I answered, wondering where this conversation was going.

"Good. I have a new job I want to talk to you about," she said in an eerie tone reminiscent of a stalker call in a horror movie.

"Where are you working?" I asked.

"Don't want to spoil the surprise. I want to show you when you are back in the city. Call when you get home. Bye for now."

She abruptly hung up. "Who was that weirdo?" Piper asked.

"She's a friend in New Orleans going through a rough time," I said, stretching the friend concept a bit. Piper sensed I didn't want to say any more. She dropped the subject. "Okay, girl, you and I are here alone. James and Rose left early this morning for a meeting with an organic farmer. I didn't catch the details, but it's just you and me for the next four hours. Since you are going to be living with Tom and me, I want to know the details of your life."

She sunk in her chair, becoming even smaller. "What do you want to know?"

"Everything. Where you were born. Were you baptized? What's your favorite color? Have you had all of your immunization shots? Like I said, everything."

Color left her face as she squirmed. "I can't tell you everything. You won't want me to live with you if I do."

"Piper, that's not true. You've got to learn to trust me. We are family now."

"I trusted my mother and she sent me away."

"I'm not sending you anywhere. You're stuck with me," I said. "Since we are on the topic of your mother, tell me about her."

Piper sat back, drew in a deep breath, and exhaled. Her eyes shifted upward and to the right before she looked directly at me. "When I was little, Mom was a happy, fun-loving person. She used to turn on MTV videos and we'd dance and sing along with the stars. We'd do stuff together—go to the bowling alley, to the zoo, or out for ice cream, those kinds of thing. She'd let me fix her hair. You know, mom and daughter stuff."

I knew exactly what she was talking about. I felt a terrible pain for a moment, remembering my own mother-daughter times.

"But a few years ago, we moved into an apartment next to the spa where my mother worked. About twenty other women younger than my mom lived in the same complex and worked at the spa. The spa was owned and run by Victor Ivanovich, a mean man from Russia. Most of the women working in the spa were from Eastern European countries. Victor made sure they worked at the spa every day. They weren't allowed to leave the apartment without Victor or one of his men going with them."

Oh my God, I thought, *that isn't a spa. It sounds like a front for a bordello.* I couldn't tell Piper her mother worked at a whorehouse. I had to find a tactful way to let her know. No wonder she was homeschooled. This Victor guy didn't want the school or anyone else asking questions. How could you have a bordello operating in the open in a city like Los Angeles?

I fought the urge to show repulsion and calmly asked, "What did your mother do at the spa?" I braced myself for an unwelcome answer.

"She was the manager who scheduled appointments and took care making sure rooms were available for the women," she answered. "She bought nice clothes for them and made sure they always looked nice. If she didn't, Victor would get mad and punish her."

"How did he punish her?"

Piper hesitated. Her eyes surveyed the room, trying to look anywhere but at me. She tightly clamped her lips to prevent any words from leaking out. A sinking feeling befell me. *Did he beat her?* I asked myself. She didn't want to answer, but I had to know. I just couldn't let the opportunity to learn about Piper's life escape.

"Piper?" I queried, forcing her eyes to meet mine with my outstretched hands.

"Uh…She, uh…he…uh, he wouldn't give her things. Sometimes he would hit her, too," she answered.

"What would he refuse to give her?"

"Drugs," she spat out, a stream of tears running down her face. Then her voice sped up. "I didn't want to tell you. My mom is a heroin addict. Most of the women who work at the spa are addicted to some type of drugs."

Now she was crying uncontrollably. He face contorted as she tried to form words. They just wouldn't come. I grabbed her and hugged her close to me. "It's okay, Piper. You are with us now. It'll all be okay."

My God, what a miserable childhood she must have had. How did her mother get mixed up in that life? Now was certainly not the time to pursue the answers I so desperately wanted. Piper was too overwrought—understandably so. How must she be feeling? Her crack whore mother threw her out; her career-driven, emotionally unavailable father was killed; and now she had to move to a strange city to live with people she didn't even know. My heart ached for her. I hoped Tom and I could deal with all of this in a way to make her feel loved.

"Hi, everybody. We're home," Rose yelled as she entered the front door.

Piper wiped her eyes, composing herself quickly before she headed to her bedroom. She'd learned to conceal her emotions well. She had probably led a "see and not be seen" life for as long as she could remember. I didn't blame her for not wanting to interact with Rose and James. They were nice people but, like most people of their type, lived for their most recent cause, emotionally secluded, avoiding intimate relationships. Ethan was like his parents. Driven by his career, he'd been consumed with his own world, excluding all others. I saw a little of this trait in Tom, too, and it scared me, because I was close to my family and wanted to be close to my future family as well.

"Alexandra, let me tell you all about the organic farm we visited. They use no fertilizers or pesticides. They rotate their crops to avoid depleting the soil of vital minerals. They have free-range chickens, given no antibiotics, who lay large brown eggs. The owner told me most eggs labeled in the supermarket as free range are a fraud. The chickens are cooped in small cages and allowed to roam a small area for one hour a day."

"Wow, I had no idea," I said. James ambled to the couch to sit down, giving Rose the chance to have the spotlight.

"They also have cattle on the property. They graze on grass. Most cattle ranches pen the cattle in small areas. They feed them number two corn, not the type of corn you see at markets. It's a genetically modified version that barely resembles the corn we all know."

"Does corn fed versus grass fed make a difference?" I asked.

"Oh yeah. Grass-fed beef has the proper ratio of omega-3 to omega-6 fatty acids. Corn-fed beef causes your arteries to clog. Grass-fed beef doesn't lead to clogged arteries. Your heart remains in tip-top shape with grass-fed beef."

"If that's true, why don't they feed all cattle grass instead of corn?" I asked.

"It's all about money. The industrialized farm conglomerates maximize their profits by using the smallest amount of land possible. Placing the largest number of cattle in small areas without grass and feeding them corn. Letting cattle roam free on fields requires large amounts of land. It could still be profitable, but the corporations want to squeeze every penny they can out of each cow."

The way she laid things out reminded me of Tom. *This is where he got his "lecturing" manner*, I thought. Somehow it made me feel more affectionate toward him. We don't choose our parents, and his were flawed, but still better than many, and certainly better than Piper's.

My thoughts were interrupted by my phone ringing. My heart jumped when I saw it was Tom.

"Hello, how's it going in Chicago?" I asked.

"Hi, Alexandra. There are some very disturbing details coming to light," he said. "I don't think Ethan's car crash was an accident. I ran across his phone when I collected his personal belongings from the police. Go in the bedroom or go outside. I don't want to alarm my parents or Piper. I need to play a message from his phone for you."

I casually walked out the front door toward the street. I could tell by the smile his mother gave me she thought we wanted to have phone sex or something just short of it. James didn't budge.

"Okay, I'm outside," I said.

"Listen to this message. It's from Piper's mother, Sandy," Tom said as he played the message.

A woman's voice speaking in a whisper-like, secretive tone said, "Ethan, I've got to say this fast. Be very careful. Victor is coming after Constance. I told him she ran away last year. He's found out I sent her to you in Chicago. He wants her back here. Don't let him—"

"Who the hell are you talking to, bitch? Give me that damn phone." Then there was the sound of a slap, and the phone went dead. That was the end of the message.

"I don't know who this Victor guy is, but he sounds dangerous," Tom said.

"I've found out a little about him," I said. "He was Sandy's boyfriend or something like that. She lived with him in an apartment complex next to a spa. I think the place was really a front for something else entirely. I'll tell you all about it when you get back."

"I'm at the airport now. Ethan's body is on its way back to California. I've arranged everything. We will have a short ceremony tomorrow, and when it's over we are heading back to New Orleans on the first plane out. If this Victor guy is coming after Piper, I want to be on our home turf."

"What makes you think your brother's car wreck wasn't an accident?"

"I found out it was a one-car accident. He was going over one hundred miles per hour and ran off the road. My brother never drove fast even when we were teenagers. So I claimed Ethan's car from the impound lot, and I took it to a mechanic. He discovered the car's computer was tampered with. Some son of a bitch murdered my brother, Alexandra!" His voice broke.

"Tom…"

"Hey, they're calling my flight. I'll see you when I get back. Don't worry, I can deal with this. I'm just angry. I'm arriving in Sacramento at nine tonight. Borrow my parents' car and pick me up. We can talk about our plans on the way from the airport to my parents' house."

"Okay, darling. I'm so sorry. I'll be there."

When I went back in the house, Rose was regaling Piper with the virtues of organic farming. Piper sat across the table from her with glazed eyes, listening with silent numbness. When Rose finished, I shared the news about Tom's return and Ethan's funeral, having some trouble keeping my manner calm, still digesting the news I'd just heard. I was stunned that Ethan had been murdered. What was the matter with the world? It seemed that everywhere we turned, there was murder.

My faux calm was matched by theirs. I still wasn't sure what they felt or how much they were hiding. I thought it odd that parents who'd just lost a child could be so removed from the pain of the loss, not participating in making the funeral arrangements. They seemed content to remain bystanders and let the grief roll over them like a wave at the beach, just anxious to get it over with and get back to their lives. Maybe that was the only way they could cope with it.

I enjoyed the quiet time on the way to the Sacramento airport. I had time to think about what had recently transpired. Sandy worked at a whorehouse disguised as a spa. Her boyfriend, Victor, owned the place and kept the women secluded in an apartment complex that he probably also owned. The women appeared to be mostly from Eastern European countries. This situation stunk. I'd seen a report on television about women who were tricked into coming to the United States with promises of jobs and new lives only to end up as prostitutes, or worse, slaves. Now Victor wanted Piper back. Why? Did he want to turn her out? Make her a prostitute? What about Sandy? When did she become a heroin addict? So many unanswered questions caused my mind to race, seeking in vain to find answers to these questions.

I parked at the Sacramento International Airport. This airport was built from mostly recycled materials and is a marvel of efficiency. The only complaint I heard while waiting at baggage claim for Tom was that there was no cell phone waiting lot. Many wanted to just drive by baggage claim, pick up their loved one, and be on their way. They didn't want to pay for parking in the lot as I did. So they parked at an Aarko convenience store a short distance from the airport to wait for a call to pick up their loved one. *We are so lazy and spoiled in the US*, I thought. But I had bigger worries on my mind than convenient parking.

My heart jumped when I saw Tom walking into baggage claim. I ran to him, jumping into his strong arms. He held me close, whispering, "I missed you," in my ear. I felt a chill run down my spine, and we lingered for a full minute holding each other. It was like a battery recharge.

We began our journey to Red Bluff in the silent darkness of the cool California night, cold by New Orleans standards. The temperature was in the fifties, a cloud cover blanketing the sky, and no celestial body's light penetrated the darkness, not even the moon.

"Ethan was murdered because of Sandy. I think whoever she was mixed up with killed him trying to kidnap Piper," Tom said. "We've got to find out more about these people. When they learn we've taken Piper to New Orleans, they'll be coming after us next."

CHAPTER NINE
SUSPICIONS

Tom and I contemplated every possible scenario to find a reason Victor or his people would kill to get their hands on Piper. She was just a little girl. Did she see something they wanted to keep secret? Why would they wait a year to go after her? Was it only that they wanted her to work in the spa, turning tricks like the women from Eastern Europe? Did they want to sell her to some pervert from another country? Whatever the reason, they weren't getting her, and Tom and I vowed to protect her no matter what the cost.

When we arrived at Tom's parents' house, everyone was asleep—everyone except Piper, that is. She was on my computer in her bedroom. I knocked before I entered, resisting my urge to rush in and catch her doing whatever it was she was trying to hide. I didn't know how long I could contain my curiosity, especially since we'd found out about Victor's intent. When I entered she asked me to sit beside her. She was on my blog site.

"Can you believe all of the young girls that have gone missing all over the United States?" she asked. "I wonder if someone is taking them and hooking them on drugs like Victor does."

"How do you know he's the one who gets them hooked on drugs?" I asked.

"I saw so many of them come and go over the years. When they first got to the United States they were innocent, small-town girls. They didn't speak much English, but I found a way to communicate with them anyway, and learned about their lives in their home countries. Over time they got hardened by what they had to do for Victor. He made them have sex with men. At first he just offered them booze. They'd get drunk at the end of the night and make jokes about the men that weren't very funny. You know."

I didn't know. I wondered why her mother let her listen to that stuff. "Sometimes they'd cry. Soon the booze wasn't enough to help them escape the misery of their lives, so they turned to drugs. Victor always had an abundant supply handy."

"Do you think he's dangerous?" I asked, forcing the question from my lips. I didn't want to scare her, but I had to know more about this asshole.

"Oh hell yes he's dangerous. Some of the girls refused do what he told them to do and they disappeared. He told us all he sent them home, but my mom told me he *took care of them*. All of the women in the spa said they were murdered and their bodies disposed of at sea." She said this in a flat voice, as if every fourteen-year-old knew about stuff like this. I felt so bad for her but was also glad she was telling me.

I could see Piper was uncomfortable talking about Victor, her mom, and the spa. I suspected her mother had a larger role in the shady operations of the spa than she knew or cared to admit, so I decided to drop the subject.

"Piper, I'm interested in hearing more about this, but we all need to go to sleep now. We're having a short funeral service for your father tomorrow. Then you, Tom, and I are heading to New Orleans. Shut down my computer. I'll charge it in my room."

"Suits me fine," Piper said. "I'm so bored with Red Bluff. I've watched lots of videos about New Orleans. I can't wait to see it."

I really wanted to get in bed with Tom. I wanted to feel his arms around me, his warmth. I crawled in bed naked next to him, and like always, we were instantly in sync, his nakedness next to mine. Sex was out of the question. We were too loud together for that. We both just wanted the maximum amount of skin-to-skin, connecting, bonding. As I spooned behind him, he said nothing except, "Mmm." We fell into a sweet sleep, the kind where you feel you smile all night.

Few people attended Ethan's funeral. Not surprising, considering both Tom and Ethan had moved away as soon as they graduated high school and his parents spent most of their time out of town pursuing their various causes. We loaded in the Sanders' car and headed to the Sacramento International Airport. On the way I was surprised again how little the family talked about Ethan. Most of the conversation was about how farm life in this country had been ruined by industrial farming. Tom withdrew inside himself around his parents. I guess growing up with a family who cared more about larger causes than immediate family issues made Tom keep his concerns to himself. He didn't say anything to his parents about Ethan's death or Sandy's voice mail. This disconnect created an air of tension for me. My family discussed almost everything. Once again, I wondered what our relationship would be like.

The flight to New Orleans was pleasant—that is, as pleasant as flying could be these days. Piper played on my computer the whole way. She was fascinated with my blog. She and I answered many of the bloggers' questions. Piper was turning into a sharp detective, too. She theorized about the missing and the nameless bodies, trying to connect the dots. I was impressed.

Tom and I didn't have time to talk any more about the potential danger we were all in, acting as though nothing had happened. Tom decided to spend the first night in New Orleans at his place, and Piper and I went to my condo. Traveling all day wore us all out, so we crashed early.

I was up at morning light. Before I did anything I made a cup of good old New Orleans coffee. God, was it delicious! I sat at my computer on a mission, knowing exactly how to find out about Victor Ivanovich. I sent an email to Sophia Garcia, an Interpol agent

I'd befriended in my pursuit of ACC. I knew if this Victor guy was connected to any international crime, Sophia could find out.

Soon Piper joined me. She wanted a cup of coffee and was hooked with the first sip. Piper was slowly becoming my shadow. As I watched her follow me around, I couldn't help but think she had to be disoriented having no parents, just me and Tom. I'd known her for less than a week, and I was already attached to her. I just needed to know more about her, but she wasn't the most open child I'd ever met. How could she be after coming from such a disturbed environment? But I had a feeling she was one of the smartest and most interesting young ladies I'd ever know. My Lois Lane brain couldn't stop scheming of ways to find out everything about her, and investigating Victor's background was the first step.

"How would you like to go to the Café Du Monde in the French Quarter for some café au lait and beignets?" I asked.

"I don't know what any of that is, but you said French Quarter and I'm all in," Piper responded.

I texted Tom, inviting him to join us. He passed, needing to go to his job and let them know he was back in town. Tom loved his job more than anything. It was more than a job to him; it was a calling. After meeting his parents and seeing how they raised him, I could see how he ended up so passionate about the environment. He was fortunate to have a job that allowed him to be flexible. Sometimes he stayed in the Gulf for two weeks without coming home. Other times he would be free to do what he wanted for a week or so. It suited him.

Piper was amazed by the sights and sounds of the New Orleans French Quarter. Having grown up in LA, she'd never seen classic European style architecture like the buildings that permeated the Quarter. As we parked, she witnessed the city coming alive. Shock and amazement filled her radiant blue eyes as we walked down Bourbon Street passing bars open at eight in the morning. Every bar had customers sitting on well-worn stools, drinking their nutrition-free breakfasts. Characters of all types and sizes littered the street. She said it reminded her of Venice Beach only more fairy-tale-like and exaggerated. She absolutely loved it. When we arrived at the Café Du Monde, we took our place in the customary line that wound down the street. The beignets reminded her of small, puffed-up versions of the funnel cakes she'd tasted at her only visit to Disneyland on her eighth birthday. As we went through the line, she ordered a café au lait but passed on the beignets. She guzzled down the café au lait while she watched table after table devour snow-topped beignets. She went back for seconds on the coffee and quickly sat back down at our table so her eyes could dart all around to take in the entire, exaggerated flock of humanity. We sat quietly, sipping our coffee and watching the procession of visitors mixed with locals sashaying through the streets.

After a few minutes of people-watching, I asked her more about her life with her mother. "Where did you live before the spa?"

"In a little apartment near my mom's job in West Hollywood. It had yellow walls in the kitchen and a mural outside on the front of the building," she said with a sad smile. "Mom worked in a law office as a secretary while she attended UCLA. That's how she met Victor. He was a client. They started dating when I was ten, and within a month she quit her job at the law firm and went to work in the spa. We also moved to the apartments Victor owned next to the spa. I was taken out of school and homeschooled after."

"When did Sandy start using drugs?"

"She was really pretty, but she always had a problem with her weight, and it bothered her. She loved sugar. She ate cakes and ice cream every night. Sometimes she would go into the bathroom and I could hear her throwing up. I heard Victor tell her that he could give her pills that would help her with her weight problem. She jumped at the chance, especially since Victor offered it. She would do anything to please him. I could always tell when she tried to quit the drugs. She would start eating a huge amount of sugar again. Finally she got off of the pills and went to heroin."

"Who took care of you?" I asked.

"The other women in the spa were like a second family to me. Many of them had children back in their old country, and I was like their surrogate child. They spent time tutoring me. One lady was a math whiz. She taught me algebra and calculus. I spent time on the

Internet learning just about everything. I couldn't go outside the apartment complex without escorts, so the Internet was the only entertainment I had."

"Where is Victor from?"

"He is Russian and proud of it. All the girls say he's Russian Mafia," she answered.

"He sounds like an evil bastard," I said as she nodded in agreement.

We left the Café Du Monde and strolled around the French Quarter. The shops were open. As we passed by, our eyes were stabbed by the brightly colored T-shirts, gadgets, and souvenirs displayed in each shop. Every second door was a bar or restaurant blasting out jazz, zydeco, or some other unique sound native to New Orleans. People stood in doorways dancing by themselves or with each other. Some were holding daiquiris, some were holding children. All were having fun. The aroma common to all large city downtown streets was masked by the smell of Cajun cooking swirled streetward, filling the nostrils of all who passed.

"Is it always like this?" she asked.

"Yes. This city is always ready to pass on a good time with people from all over the world," I said.

We stopped in Jackson Square and marveled at the talented street artists. Each artist painted with a unique style that added to the gumbo of art that is New Orleans. As we gazed at an artist's abstract version of the Quarter at night, a tour group walked by. I stared at the tour leader, dressed all in black. A large wide-brimmed hat with a thin lace veil partially covered her familiar face. It was Mandy Morris. I whirled around, turning my back to her. *What the hell is she doing leading a tour group? Weird*, I thought. I grabbed Piper, shuffling her to one of the many horse and buggies waiting to take tourists through the Quarter. I thought it best to avoid explaining a zombie version of Paris Hilton to Piper, though she most likely would have welcomed the meeting. This wasn't the time. I'd call Charlotte tomorrow to find out why a Goth version of Mandy Morris was leading a tour group through the French Quarter. My focus remained on finding out about Piper's life in Los

Angeles. What was Sandy in to? Why was Piper so streetwise? Then there was this mysterious Victor guy.

The clickety-clackety sounds of the horse's hooves on the pavement quickly spirited us away. It was a real treat to see the city from this perspective. Piper admired the decorative iron-work accents adorning the swarm of balconies that complemented the breathtaking French architecture. She was wowed by the buildings, but I couldn't erase the scene I'd just witnessed. Mandy Morris, a tour group leader. What the hell was going on? I had to know more.

Piper's voice pierced my thoughts. "Can we live here?" she asked. "I see people living here. I love this place. I didn't know anything like this existed. I want to be here all the time."

"We can look for a place near the Quarter," I said. "I don't think we can afford a place actually inside the Quarter itself, but we can look."

"Oh, thank you, thank you, thank you!" Piper screamed at the top of her lungs, causing the buggy driver to momentarily turn to look at us. Others walking alongside us barely noticed. That was part of the charm of the city. No one bothered you.

Tom called as we considered our lunch options. "Alexandra, where are you?" he asked.

"We're in the Quarter," I said.

"Go back to your condo right now. I'll meet you there. A woman claiming to be Sandy, Piper's mother, called my dad asking to speak to Constance. He told the woman Constance went to New Orleans to live with us. I don't think it was Sandy. My dad shouldn't have told her where she was."

Suddenly I felt vulnerable. Piper read my face like a card shark at a poker tournament in Vegas. "It's Victor, isn't it?" she asked.

"No, it was Tom. He asked us to meet him at the condo." Piper studied my face for a millisecond, totally unconvinced by my feigned nonchalant demeanor, before she grabbed my hand and led me toward the car.

In full military march, she said, "We'd better go then and see what he wants."

CHAPTER TEN
TIME FOR CAUTION

PIPER FIXED HER eyes on the road ahead making no small talk or asking anymore about Tom's call. I insisted we stop at Whole Foods on our way back to the condo. After we raided their buffet, I received an email from Sophia on my phone. I knew I'd have to sneak past Piper's observant gaze to read it. Nevertheless, I peeked. There were a great many attachments, and Piper glued her eyes to me like a hawk perched in a tree watching a field mouse. I had about the same chance as the mouse, so I thought it best to wait until I was on my computer to read it all.

Piper sat across from me at my kitchen table eating her Whole Foods curry chicken and vegetables and chattering away about the sights and sounds in the French Quarter. I opened the email from Sophia. She was in Paris recovering from the life-threatening wounds she'd received at the hands of El Serpiente in this very condo. She said she'd be returning to active duty in one week. She asked how I ran across Victor Ivanovich. She'd circulated his name around Interpol's Paris office and discovered a great deal about him.

She wrote, "Be wary of this guy, Alexandra. Victor Ivanovich is a Russian currently residing in Los Angeles. He is associated with a group of criminals commonly called the Saratov Mafia. Some say he is the leader. His group is involved in human trafficking, money laundering, drugs, and bank and credit card hacking. He has never been convicted or even arrested for any crime. Even so, he is under investigation by Interpol for human trafficking in the US, Romania, the Czech Republic, Belarus, Latvia, and several other countries around the world.

"His organization guarantees young women in these countries education and employment in the fast-growing American spa market. Most are not formally trained in any spa services such as massaging, skin care, or hair care. He recruits girls from poor families living in small towns who are unable to pay for their daughter's education. He pays for transportation, including airfare, to the States. He picks them up from the airport and their families lose touch with them with the exception of emails and occasional calls on holidays and birthdays. The girls are told they have to work to pay back the money put out for their trip and education. Most of the girls come from cultures where heavy vodka drinking is accepted. They are given all the vodka they want. Eventually they are introduced to special gentlemen as 'dates.' The vodka is a gateway to their transition to sex and drugs. They are trapped in the life with no way out. Open the attachments to see a photo of Victor."

I opened the photo attachment and nearly had to catch my eyeballs before they rolled off the table. I saw a clean-cut handsome man in his early forties. His chiseled jaw and high cheekbones framed striking green eyes and a welcoming smile. His hair was a bit tousled, black with gray streaks running above his ears on both sides. He appeared to be about six foot two with broad shoulders, fairly narrow hips, and muscular legs. He was damn near perfect. He could have had a career as an underwear model or a model for romance novel covers. Then it hit me. This was the man checking me out in the Court of Two Sisters at brunch with Charlotte. I broke out with chill bumps. Victor was in New Orleans.

His dossier said he was educated at one or more of the six institutes of the Russian Academy of Sciences in Saratov, Russia. He graduated with honors and worked for a while as a contractor for the military and the KGB. The Interpol dossier ended abruptly with the statement, "Nothing more is known about the subject."

A second email from Sophia read:

Alexandra,

The Interpol agent who is responsible for tracking Victor Ivanovich's movements is Alric Jaeger. He will be in New Orleans by the time you receive this email and will contact you shortly. He's keen to get Victor.

All the best,

Sophia

Tom used our secret knock at the door. *Rap, rap, rap, rap…rap, rap.* I let him in. His cheeks were red, and his eyes bulged more than normal. Small beads of sweat collected on his forehead. He carefully locked the door behind him and kissed me lightly on the lips. Before he could speak, my phone rang. Why was Detective Demetre Baker from the NOPD calling me?

"Hello, Detective Baker. I haven't heard from you in a while. What's up?" I said.

Baker, not much for small talk, said, "Alexandra, you need to get here right away. Bring your boyfriend, Tom Sanders, and his niece, Constance, with you. Oh," he paused, "be careful. Watch your back." He hung the phone up without another word.

I left Piper sitting at the kitchen table and grabbed Tom's hand to lead him to the bedroom. I filled him in on what I'd learned from Sophia, and I told him about seeing Victor when I went to breakfast with Charlotte. I dug in the bottom of my underwear drawer to retrieve my pistol and holster. Tom watched as I strapped it around my ankle. When we returned to the kitchen, Piper had read Sophia's entire email.

Piper hung her head and shook it side to side gently. When she looked up at Tom and me, she had a terrified look on her face, but what she said was, "I am so sorry for bringing trouble into your lives. Victor will come for me. I've placed you both in danger." I wanted to hug her. This was an amazing kid.

"Don't you worry about Victor," Tom said in a voice full of authority, safety, and strength. "We'll deal with him New Orleans style."

What the fuck? Tom was not from New Orleans. What did he know about dealing with people New Orleans style? He was from namby-pamby California. At least I was a farm girl. Then again, he'd been here for five years or more. He'd probably learned a trick or two. And this was his niece, his murdered brother's surviving daughter.

He was right. If Victor was coming to take us on, we had the home-court advantage, and we would use it. Besides Californian, Indianan, or New Orleanian, we were Americans. We didn't run. *Bring it, Victor!* I thought.

We were escorted into Detective Baker's office when we arrived at the precinct, and he greeted us at his door. He had his coat hung neatly on the coat rack in his office, his holster and gun clearly visible against his crisp white shirt and bright black and yellow New Orleans Saints tie. He'd thoughtfully brought in a third chair so we would be comfortable. Baker introduced himself to Tom and Piper, firmly shaking each of their extended hands.

"Have a seat," he said. Baker opened a large file strategically placed in the center of his desk. I could see many of the same documents Sophia had sent me, only he had twice as many as I had received. "I'm going to cut straight to the chase," he said as he widened his eyes. "You are all in danger. Sophia told me she showed you much of Interpol's file on Victor Ivanovich, but what she didn't tell you is Interpol believes he is responsible for more than forty-seven contract killings over the last ten years."

"Forty-seven killings?" I gasped. "Why isn't his ass in jail?"

Baker looked at me, turning his palms face up, raising his shoulders nearly to his earlobes. "Slippery bastard, I guess. We've got to talk about something else. A German Interpol agent named Alric Jaeger has traveled from Paris to go after Victor. Sophia called me on the DL to warn me about this Jaeger guy. He doesn't always play by the rules. He's got a personal thing of some sort going on with Victor Ivanovich. Seems his folks were treated poorly by Victor's parents during World War II. Sophia wanted me to give you a heads up before you met with him."

"Oh great, we've got to rely on a crazy to protect us from a crazy," I said.

Baker looked at all of us as if he were addressing a room full of newly condemned criminals. "Oh, he's not here to protect you. He's here to catch Victor Ivanovich breaking the law and bust him. According to Sophia, he doesn't worry about collateral damage. She said he's sixty-five years old but acts more old school than that."

A text came across my phone from Charlotte. Mandy told me she saw you in the Quarter today riding in a horse-drawn buggy with your new ward. She wants to take us all on her tour tomorrow. You in?

Oh shit, I thought she didn't see me. With all of this Victor stuff going on, I didn't really want to go on a tour with Mandy Morris. But then again, I'd promised Charlotte and Mr. Morris I'd help with Mandy. I'm sure Piper would jump at the chance to learn more about the French Quarter, so I sent a text back. Fine. What time should we meet?

Nine-thirty in the morning at the Café Du Monde.

Holy shit, what kind of tour was Mandy qualified to lead? Bars and beds where I've blown and banged? I made myself laugh out loud and blushed as Tom and Piper stared at me.

Detective Baker showed us to the interrogation room down the hall from his office. After making the introductions, he excused himself, saying, "Sorry I can't sit in, folks. There's a killer preying on working girls in the city. Of course there always is. They are such easy targets for crazy bastards."

Memories flooded my mind. This was the same interrogation room Sarah and I sat in so many months ago answering questions about her ex-husband's attack on us. Now she was gone and I was back here to talk about another murderous maniac. *What the fuck is wrong with the world?* I wondered. At the table in the center of the room sat a completely bald man, about six feet, four inches tall with a muscular build. His face was weathered, making him appear older than his sixty-five years. His teeth were a yellowish brown from smoking cigars, consuming way too much coffee, and who knows what else. He spoke with near-perfect English after he'd looked us all up and down.

"So this is Constance Sanders," he said, looking directly at Piper.

That was weird. How did he know her name? Why did he focus on her? I thought he'd been chasing Victor internationally. "Nice to meet you, Mr. Jaeger," I said. "Is this Victor guy coming to New Orleans to kill us?"

"Why, heavens no, Ms. Lee. Victor never gets his hands dirty. He contracts out his dirty work."

"What the hell does he want?" Tom asked.

"He wants the girl. You see, I have infiltrated his organization. She has something he wants," he said as he turned and looked directly into Piper's eyes. "I would like her to tell me what she has that he wants so badly."

Piper's expression never changed. She narrowed her gaze, shaking her head side to side, saying, "Haven't the foggiest." She was convincing, but I'd been with her long enough to know she was hiding something. I didn't study Lois Lane's methods for getting to the bottom of a story for nothing. I was fine with her not opening up, because I didn't trust this Alric Jaeger guy at all. He looked down his nose in a condescending fashion as he spoke to us. He was a user. He couldn't care less what happened to us as long as he got Victor.

"What should we do to protect ourselves?" Tom asked.

"Just go about your normal everyday lives. He won't try anything here in New Orleans. If you were in LA he might, but not here. My sources tell me he needs the little girl's cooperation."

Jaeger's words set Piper's face on fire. I grabbed her forearm to stop her from going across the table and popping him in the nose with one of the dainty hands balled into fists under the table. She didn't like this guy, and neither did I.

"So what's your plan?" Tom asked.

"I have contacts here in New Orleans who can track Victor's movements. He has to work through local folks. Some of the very people he'll talk to are our informants. We'll know what he's up to before he can make any moves. He's not as smart as he thinks he is. Victor is an egomaniac who thinks he can outwit me as long as he chooses. He thinks his charm and good looks open any doors that need opening, and the ones he can't charm, he bribes. Those he can't bribe, he kills. Victor's time is running out just like all of the rest of those Russian Mafia thugs from the underbelly of Europe. You see how Putin acts on the world stage? Distributing pictures of himself with his shirt off, claiming he's not afraid of bears. They are all the same: bullies who only pick fights with the weak. Crimea, Ukraine, it's all the same. Had it not been for an unusually harsh winter, Germany would have overrun Moscow in World War II. Then there would be no Victor and no Putin either." His nostrils flared as he lost himself in his diatribe, rewriting history to suit his prideful boasts.

I hadn't come here for a history lesson, especially from the likes of him. Jaeger wasn't the type of person who inspired confidence. He was talking about Victor not being from New Orleans as if Jaeger himself was born and raised here. This was probably his first trip to New Orleans. He seemed to be the kind of guy who thought he was ahead of everyone else in the race, when in fact he was being lapped. If he was so much smarter than Victor, why hadn't he busted Victor in the last five years? What the hell was all of that World War II crap about anyway? That war ended in 1945 with Hitler's Germany getting their asses handed to them. Where had he been for the last seventy years? Still licking his wounds?

Tom didn't mention anything about his brother's death in Chicago. He must have gotten the same vibe from Inspector Jaeger: he wasn't to be trusted. As we left the precinct, Piper said in a squeaky little voice, "He needs to get a grip."

We all laughed, shaking our heads in agreement. But it was clear trouble was brewing, and somehow or another Victor and Jaeger were going to collide. I only hoped we weren't in the middle. Tom's feeling was we weren't in any imminent danger. He suggested renting a movie, popping some popcorn, and killing a bottle of wine to ease the tension.

"Wow," Piper said. "I'm going to like it here. Sometimes the ladies at the spa would do things with me, but never my mom. Not in the last few years. She was too busy running after Victor or shooting her drugs. And my dad, when he wasn't at work, was with the nanny." Her voice was empty of emotion by the end of her speech, but I could feel it anyway.

I felt terrible for her. So neglected and starved of affection. Once the popcorn was popped, the movie was in, and the wine was poured, I said, "Well, little Miss Piper. How would you like to go on a tour of the French Quarter tomorrow with my friends Charlotte and Mandy?"

Her eyes popped wide open. "Can we? I love the Quarter. I can't wait."

CHAPTER ELEVEN
A DIFFERENT WORLD

MORNINGS IN THE condo with Piper living with me were different, especially when I woke with the urge. The one that stirs in the reproductive parts of the body. The one that kicks reason to the curb or persuades me to go along with lustful acts. I sidled close to Tom who'd rolled onto his back. I tried to stop myself but just couldn't. I dove down under the covers allowing my shoulder-length hair to trail down his chest to rest on his stomach. I slowly bathed him with my tongue, feeling him grow as I worked until he filled my mouth. Tom stirred, running his fingers through my hair and grabbing the back of my head to set the pace of pleasure he needed. The fire building in me flashed out of control, and I needed more. I needed to take him. Burning inside, I mounted him with the grace and speed of a gymnast. Soon our rhythms synced together, building to the point of no return. I bit my lower lip, fighting to confine the scream looking for a way out between my clamped teeth. Both mine and Tom's volcanic eruptions were marked only by clenched, spasming muscles and a deep, guttural *UUUUUUUHM!* I rolled off Tom to catch my breath, the roaring fire gradually subsiding to a manageable flame.

"I'll get the coffee," Tom said.

I muted a giggle as well as I could, feeling like I'd just gotten away with doing something I wasn't supposed to do.

Today was the day Piper and I were going to tour the French Quarter with Mandy Morris as our tour guide. What a bizarre turn of events. The last time I was with Mandy in the Quarter, we had partied at the Cat's Meow and sang karaoke. Her best friend and boyfriend, the murderous Bob Broussard, drugged me and took me home. Instead of killing me, he watched me sleep, finally deciding I wasn't the type of victim he needed to kill to get his rocks off. And now I was going on a tour with her. But that would be the way things were in New Orleans. Everyone had a good and evil side to their personality, I supposed. The problem here was you couldn't tell where good ended and evil began. They were mixed together like chicken and sausage in jambalaya.

Tom and I drank a cup of dark roast coffee together in bed. When I felt like my legs would carry me, we went to the kitchen. Piper was seated at the table feverishly fingering my computer keyboard. She quickly exited whatever program or site she was interacting with when we sat down.

"Good morning," I said. "How did you sleep?"

"Okay, I guess. When are we going to tour the French Quarter?"

Before I could answer, there was a knock at my door. Tom cautiously looked through the peephole before opening the door, saying, "Hello, Zach. What are you doing here so early in the morning?"

"Good morning, Tom. I am so sorry to bother you and Alexandra, but I need to talk to both of you right away."

I shouted to Tom, "Tell him to come in and have some coffee."

Zach hollered back, "Is it okay if my sister comes in, too? She's in the car."

"Of course," Tom and I said in unison.

I didn't even know Zach had a sister. Why would they show up at my condo this early in the morning? Something must be up. I excused myself to the bedroom, reached into my underwear drawer, and strapped my .38 to my ankle. My floor-length nightgown more than concealed the weapon. *Is this necessary?* I asked myself. *Do I really need my gun?* Maybe not, but I wasn't taking any chances. I'd learned blind trust could be very costly. After all, Zach had disappeared in the past without good explanation, leading me to believe something more was going on with him than he was willing to share. Before Sarah's death, I could let erratic behavior slide by, but not anymore. I was no longer naive. Besides, it wasn't just me I had to worry about. I had Piper to protect.

Zach introduced his sister, Maddy, to us. She was an attractive girl with raven-black hair and iridescent blue eyes accented by eyelashes that must have been at least two inches long.

Pleasantries exchanged, Zach cut right to the chase. "Alexandra, I think it best Piper not be a part of this conversation."

"No problem," she said, scooping my computer up and heading to my bedroom.

Oh shit. As she disappeared down the hall, I hoped I'd pulled the sheet and cover up. I listened for a teenage "EWW," but didn't hear one. I guess I made the bed well enough.

When Piper was safely in the bedroom with the door closed, I spun around, and all eyes planted themselves on Zach.

"Please, everyone, don't say a word until I finish. I'll answer any questions you have when I'm done," Zach said as we all nodded our consent. "Alexandra, I know you met with an Interpol agent named Alric Jaeger yesterday."

"How the hell—" I said before Zach cut me off.

"Please, just hear me out first."

"Okay," I said with my bottom lip stuck out and a pouty tone in my voice.

Zach's sister moved closer to him and put her left hand on his right forearm and gently patted him, showing her support. "Maddy and I grew up in foster care. Our parents died when we were toddlers. I hated the family I was living with, so at fourteen I ran away, but Maddy stayed. She was only eleven, and I didn't want to leave her, but what choice did I have? I couldn't take care of her. I hitch-hiked my way to Los Angeles and lived on the streets, selling myself for money.

Alexandra, you know I'm gay. Gay men party harder than anyone else in the world. There is a gay party event in a different state at least once a month. I met a very rich guy who took me in when I was only fifteen as his trophy. He bought me fine clothes and spirited me around the US to party after party. Most of the parties went on for two or three days at a time. I drank vodka and did every type of drug you could imagine. Eventually I got hooked on cocaine. I dumped the guy and came back to New Orleans to search for Maddy. Problem was, I was an addict. I needed money and I needed drugs, so I found a way to buy my drugs. I became a mule for drug cartels supplying the Dixie Mafia."

"Dixie Mafia?" Tom said. "I've heard of them. They are some badasses mixed up in drugs and prostitution."

"That's right, and much worse—murder. I brought cocaine from Colombia and transported cash out of the country. My luck ran out when I got busted in the Miami airport with a brick of cocaine. Instead of arresting me, Alric Jaeger, who was working the case for Interpol, made a deal with me. He allowed me to work off my charges by snitching on the Colombians selling the drugs."

"Sorry, Zach," Maddy interrupted. "Tell them about Jaeger's close ties to the Dixie Mafia."

"Oh yeah, his ties went back to the Ronald Reagan/George H. W. Bush administration when the White House and the CIA were using a retired airline pilot from Baton Rouge, Barry Seal, to work undercover to smuggle large amounts of cocaine into the US from Colombia. Seal hooked the CIA up with the Dixie Mafia. They weren't mafia like the Italian Costa Nostra you see on television. They weren't that organized. The Dixie Mafia is a loosely related group of criminals in the Southern states who dealt in prostitution, gambling, drugs, and other criminal enterprises. Jaeger's connections at the CIA introduced him to some of the worst guys in the Dixie Mafia. He used them and they used him."

"I'm sorry, Zach, but I just have to interrupt. How does all of that stuff involve us and why are you here?" I asked.

"Patience, Alexandra. I'm getting there. With the help of Maddy, I got off of the drugs. Jaeger decided to discontinue working with me when Barry Seal was gunned down by the Colombian Medellín

Cartel in the streets of Baton Rouge. Then one day I backslid. A former boyfriend introduced me to heroin, and I was hooked immediately. I loved it. Once again, I needed money for drugs, so I turned to my contacts with the Dixie Mafia. They hooked me up with the leader, Kirksey McCord Nix Jr. He was running a lonely-hearts scam on gay men by placing personal advertisements in national gay magazines. When lonely, desperate men responded to the ads, Nix played on their compassion by saying he was having financial difficulties and needed money wired to me or another one of his pawns. Sadly, he received hundreds of thousands of dollars from the scam, preying on those poor, lonely men. I received money and drugs for helping.

"Maddy got me off drugs again and I quit helping Nix. It was too late; the scam got busted by the feds, and someone in the Dixie Mafia called Jaeger for help. He stepped in to cushion the blow for Nix and the rest of the guys. He told me I had to go back to work for him or I'd go down with the rest of them. I had to help. So you see, Alexandra, when I disappear, I'm doing something for Jaeger."

"So why are you here in my kitchen telling me this now?" I asked, disgusted with the whole sordid story he'd just told.

"Because you, Tom, and Piper are in grave danger."

I knew we were in danger because Victor most likely murdered Ethan. But I chose to play dumb, using my God-given investigative reporter talent to make Zach tell me everything he knew.

"I know Victor wants Piper to go back to Los Angeles, but why would he hurt us?" I asked.

"There are greater forces at work here. Jaeger told me Victor traffics in girls from around the world. He puts them to work in all convention cities, like Las Vegas and Orlando. He wants to expand his prostitution ring into New Orleans. The Dixie Mafia doesn't want the competition, and you can believe me when I tell you a war is coming. I don't want you to be caught in the middle. For some reason, Victor wants Piper back in LA. Jaeger wanted me to pass messages to the Dixie Mafia advising them of Victor's moves. He's encouraging the war to get to Victor. He really hates the guy."

"Why would you put yourself in such a precarious position?" I asked.

Zach looked at me with beleaguered eyes, much like a caged dog exhausted from trying to escape. "Jaeger threatened to get me prosecuted for my involvement with the Dixie Mafia gay men scam if I didn't help him. I've been clean for more than two years. I don't want to get mixed up with those thugs. I don't have a choice. I am taking a big risk telling you all of this."

Maddy patiently sat by her brother's side, not making a sound until she could no longer contain her emotions. Suddenly, the words she was holding in burst from her mouth like a crowd of Christmas shoppers rushing through the doors of Walmart on Black Friday.

"He's trying to warn you, dammit! He doesn't have to be here risking his life and freedom for you. He's just trying to help," she said as tears welled in her reddened blue eyes.

"Okay," I said. "Thanks. I just wanted to know the bottom line. What are you telling me to do?"

"You need to get out of town for a while. Why don't you go to your farm in Indiana to lay low until everything blows over?" Zach said.

Blood rushed to my face as my heart pounded in my chest. I felt my fists ball up instinctively. I narrowed my eyes at Zach. "We aren't fucking going anywhere. New Orleans is our home. Piper, Tom, and I are a family. New Orleans is where we live, and New Orleans is where we'll die if we have to. We won't run and hide. That's not what Americans do. Not after 911, not after Katrina, and certainly not after some Russian Mafia asshole threatens our family. Let the bastard come after us. We'll be ready, right here, right now, in our city."

Tom rose to his feet, began pacing, and said, "You're damn right we'll be ready. We'll fight the devil himself if that's what it comes to. We are staying put!"

Zach bowed his head. "You are right, Alexandra. My deal-making with Jaeger just prolonged my misery. I just felt like I needed to tell you what you're up against. If you want to fight them, Maddy and I are with you until the end."

Maddy gave me her contact information before she and Zach left my condo. We decided to proceed with our lives, a little more cautiously but not frozen in fear. We talked about getting better locks, not letting our guard down, and one of us always being with Piper. Tom was adamant about that—not that I disagreed. For some reason, Piper was in the middle of this, and we needed to protect her. Then Tom went to work. Piper and I dressed in shorts, comfortable cotton tops, and walking shoes and headed to the French Quarter.

Charlotte, always Miss Punctual, sat at her favorite table by the sidewalk. She nibbled bird-style on a beignet while she sipped her black coffee. As usual, tourists and locals mixed among the tables in Café Du Monde. Piper once again avoided the beignets but guzzled the café au lait. Piper and Charlotte really hit it off, and I saw how charming Piper could be with strangers. She steered the conversation toward Charlotte's life history, avoiding revealing her own. We were so engrossed in our conversation, we didn't notice the pale, blond-maned figure dressed in solid black approach the table.

"Hi, Charlotte. Hi, Alexandra. Hi, dhampir," the sullen figure uttered.

I looked up to see a morose version of the person formerly known as Mandy Morris, party queen of New Orleans. She wore a floor-length black dress with lace trimming complemented by an even blacker bonnet-style hat accented by a black veil covering her pale face.

"Good morning, Mandy," Charlotte said without the slightest surprise in her voice. "You already know Alexandra. I'd like you to meet Piper."

"You really think I look like a dhampir?" Piper asked. "I always wondered if I were a mixed breed."

Mandy fixed her gaze on Piper, smiling brighter than she'd probably done in months. Mandy and Piper thoroughly inspected each other, making no sound for a full minute.

Finally, I broke the silence. "What the hell is a dhampir?" I asked, not quite sure if I'd said the word correctly.

Piper responded with the quickness and vigor of youth. "It's a young female offspring of a vampire and a human...Duh! *Vampire Academy?*"

Mandy nodded her approval. "I can see you will enjoy the tour today. Alexandra, as a New Orleans resident, you ought to keep up with current popular literature of the bloodsucking persuasion."

Whatever. "What exactly are we going to tour?" I asked.

"I am taking you on a haunted French Quarter tour. You'll see the places where ghosts have been spotted by tourists and locals."

"Awesome," Piper said. "I've read about ghost tours. I want to see Marie Laveau's house."

Before she spoke another word, the rosy color drained from her petite face, and her mouth flung open. She turned to me to say, "Victor is sitting at that table in the center of the room."

CHAPTER TWELVE
A HAUNTED WORLD

As I TURNED to look, my eyes met his. His photo didn't do him justice. He was truly a handsome man, his bright green eyes visible from across the room. Had I not known he was an evil bastard, I might have thought him the most handsome man I'd ever seen. He was definitely the same guy I'd seen at the Court of Two Sisters. He mouthed, "Hello, Alexandra Lee."

Holy shit! He knew my full name. I'd seen this tactic before. Bart Rogan tried to scare me by showing up at a bail hearing using my name before we'd met. I knew he was trying to intimidate me, and just like Rogan he was a bully and a beast. His type couldn't be reasoned with because they only knew the business end of a strong left hook. Or, if necessary, a bullet between the eyes. I looked away and instructed Piper not to even glance his way again.

"Have a seat, Mandy. I'll buy you a coffee," I said.

She declined, saying, "We should go now and begin our tour. Don't want to disappoint the spirits. Disappointed spirits are angry spirits. And angry spirits are mean."

Great, I thought, *a live asshole here and dead assholes on the tour.*

Not exactly the day I had planned. It was a good idea to leave Victor by himself wondering if his plan worked. Let him stew.

As it turned out, we were dressed perfectly for the day ahead. Mandy was taking us on a walking tour of the Quarter. She began by taking us to the house of Marie Delphine LaLaurie, long considered a must-see spot in New Orleans.

Madame LaLaurie lived at 1140 Royal Street, in a house befitting a person of means, with her second husband, Jean Blanque, a prominent banker, merchant, lawyer, and legislator.

A kitchen fire revealed her heinous crimes when rescuers discovered she'd been torturing and killing slaves for years. Firefighters and eyewitnesses reported several men had eyeballs poked out and genitals mutilated. Women were chained to beds and mutilated, their abdomens sliced so their intestines could be wrapped around their waists. Other victims had amputated extremities. Some said another man's joints were dislocated in order to force his limbs into positions resembling those of a crab. The good citizenry, led to an attic full of mutilated slaves by survivors of her attacks, formed a mob to track down and punish Madame LaLaurie. Unfortunately, she escaped through a back door to spend her remaining days in France.

Mandy spoke in a low guttural tone as she related the history of the mansion to us. "Many visitors to this house report seeing spirits in chains wandering the halls, some horribly disfigured." Oddly, she had a slightly upbeat lilt to her voice as if she was taking a ghoulish pleasure in the story.

Piper hung on every word, snapping picture after picture of the house. She ooohed and aaahed her way through the next three houses we visited. Mandy told stories of brutal murders, suicides by hanging, and every sort of human depravity imaginable all with the same bass, gleeful tone in her voice. She sounded like the recorded voice you'd expect to hear welcoming all who dared to enter a haunted house on Halloween.

We made our way to 941 Bourbon Street, the location of Lafitte's Blacksmith Shop. It was a bar that claimed to be the oldest in the country. It served the pirate Jean Lafitte and his older brother, Pierre, during their respites from smuggling excursions in Barataria Bay near the mouth of the Mississippi River. Jean Lafitte worked his way out of trouble by helping the fledgling United States government defeat the British in the war of 1812. Patrons had seen ghosts of swashbuckling pirates and fully outfitted soldiers walking throughout the premises well into the late hours of the night. "They don't seem to be dangerous, just thirsty," one regular patron of the bar commented.

Onward we trudged to a building I knew too well. Mandy smiled at me as we entered. "This is the condo owned by the infamous Quarter Killer," she said. "He is credited with murdering and mutilating at least seven women, eight if you count his mother. Many of his victims were stabbed to death in the bathtubs, allowing them to bleed out without detection. The Quarter Killer currently resides in the Louisiana State Hospital for the criminally insane in Jackson, Louisiana, a short, two-hour ride from here. Some say the murdered gather here at night awaiting his return. Maybe revenge is their motivation."

Holy shit, she just creeped me out to the max. This was where Tom and I consummated our relationship. Right here on this balcony on Mardi Gras night. Mandy failed to mention that she regularly went to visit Bob in the asylum. How weird was it for her to tour us through this place? Weird or not, I couldn't help but tingle remembering Tom entering me for the first time on the balcony.

Piper loved the place and the story. "Tell me more about this Quarter Killer guy," she said. "This is the finest place in the Quarter."

Mandy cast a coy glance my way and answered, "Maybe another time. We have to move on now. Disturbing the spirits' privacy isn't a good idea."

The more we toured, the more Piper came alive, hanging on every morbid word out of Mandy's mouth. Electricity seemed to bolt from her eyes as we stood outside of the house on the corner of Ursulines and Royal, formerly belonging to Jacques St. Germaine. She grabbed my arm with excitement before Mandy uttered a single word about the house.

Mandy directed her words to Piper, "This house used to belong to a young man from the picturesque South of France. He immigrated to the United States in 1902. His immense wealth gained him immediate social status in New Orleans. He was invited to society diners where he only drank one certain red wine he brought with him to each soiree. He never touched the food, delivering an unforgivable social insult to his hosts. His stay in the city was cut short when he attacked a young woman with his teeth, biting her viciously. The New Orleans Police raided this very house and were shocked to find a vast collection of wine bottles filled with his private label mixture of wine and human blood. Traces of human blood were found throughout the house. Ever since, he has been known as the Vampire of New Orleans. Some say he never left the city and still stalks the streets at night quenching his thirst."

Well, I thought, *New Orleans is a food city. I guess there's something for everyone.* Piper, Charlotte, and Mandy were so engrossed in the grisly stories of murder and mayhem that they didn't notice the two men stalking us during most of the tour. I kept an eye on them, studying their faces, clothes, and mannerisms. Clearly they weren't from New Orleans. No one in the Big Easy wore dress slacks and wing-tipped shoes walking the streets of the Quarter for hours. I kept my purse strategically slung over my shoulder giving me easy access to my loaded .38.

After the tour, I took Piper to see the artists in Jackson Square painting their masterpieces. She walked from one to the other asking questions while admiring their work. The musicians took a shine to her as she danced to their music doing a teenage jig, most likely one of her own creation and unrecognizable to me or anyone else. The men following us had disappeared. I wondered if they were lurking somewhere along the narrow streets in the Quarter preparing to ambush us. I stayed vigilant the entire trek from Jackson Square to our car, ready to display my Annie Oakley quick draw abilities. My eyes darted side to side each step of the way as Piper prattled on about the sights and sounds she'd experienced during the day. She had fallen headlong in love with the Big Easy, begging me to buy a place in the French Quarter for us to live.

My mind kept spinning, working to figure out how those overdressed stalkers knew where to find us. Did Mandy set us up? Too many unanswered questions circulated through my weary brain. Once in the car, my muscles relaxed—until my phone rang, making me nearly jump out of my skin. It was Detective Baker again.

"Alexandra, I need you to come to the precinct."

"When?"

"Now," he said.

Piper and I walked into the familiar confines of the police precinct, still dressed in our haunted tour clothes. I felt a little underdressed and certainly overexposed. Who could I trust? Victor was in the city, Zach and inspector Alric Jaeger had some type of clandestine relationship, and Mandy was just plain weird. Walking into the interrogation room did nothing to ease my fears. Jaeger sat next to the two men who'd followed us all day. What the hell was going on here? Piper sat at the table and scooted her chair closer to my side, butting against my chair. She hooked her arm in mine as she looked across the table at the assembled trio.

Baker looked at Jaeger and nodded.

"Ms. Lee," Jaeger started. "As you know, we are investigating a group of criminals from Russia doing business in the United States. Our information confirms Victor Ivanovich has business with you. At our last meeting, the girl said she had no idea what Victor wanted from her. Does she remember now?"

I cast my eyes toward Baker, who sat in silence, motionless. "I have no business with Victor Ivanovich, and neither does 'the girl.' And for your future reference, her name is Piper. Who are these two guys, and why did they follow us all day?"

"Fair enough," Jaeger said. "These 'two guys,' as you put it, are CIA contractors. We work together from time to time. They are interested in the activities of Mr. Ivanovich and his associates. They are not at liberty to discuss any of the details of their investigation with you."

Once again Jaeger managed to piss me off within a few minutes of sitting across the table from him. The CIA duo sat like robots without batteries, completely expressionless. Jaeger continued, "We want you to cooperate with us. Work with us to nab Ivanovich."

I just couldn't take it anymore. I couldn't listen to one more word from this pompous asshole. "We aren't getting in the middle of your war with Victor. We just want to be left alone. This young lady is my responsibility, and I'll use whatever means necessary to protect her. She is not a pawn in your pseudo law enforcement game, and neither are Tom and I. So leave us the fuck alone."

I looked at Baker, who was using all of his willpower to suppress his smile. It didn't work. He turned and winked at me as we left the room. Jaeger and the two robots had their hands raised to their chins, calculating their next moves in whispering tones. Their anger wasn't concealed any better than Baker's amusement at the conversation we'd just had.

I needed to talk to Tom, so I asked him to meet me at the condo. If Tom, Piper, and I were going to stay out of the fight between these Godzilla-sized assholes trying to interfere with our lives, we had to act now. When Tom joined me at the condo, he'd just gotten off a call with Hector Gonzales, the member of ROLL with whom we were jailed in Mexico. Tom seemed agitated by the call.

"Alexandra," Tom yelled as he burst through the door, "we need to go to Mexico right away. The hybrid corn companies are persuading the Mexican government to allow them to plant their Frankencorn in South Mexico. Hector needs our help to stop this travesty."

Piper calmly sat at the kitchen table never looking at Tom. Instead, she watched me carefully to gauge my reaction. I knew how passionate Tom was about environmental transgressions by large multinational corporations, so I treaded lightly.

"That's horrible," I said. "Hector must really be upset. But I don't think we should leave town right at this moment. You know what's going on with Victor and that Jaeger guy. Now some CIA guys are involved."

"We'd be safer in Mexico. We could get out of their reach with Hector's help. We can't just quit living because some prick from Los Angeles threatens us. Can we?"

"No. We don't have to quit living our lives, but you said it yourself—we are safer here on our own turf. We don't know what he could do to us in Mexico. We might be sitting ducks. Our plan was to make our stand in New Orleans. This is our city, and it will protect us," I said.

"That was our plan, but I can't just turn my back on Hector. I promised to help him. Alexandra, I am ready to fight these bastards, too, but they are demons living in the shadows. Who knows how long it will take to get them off our ass. What we need to do is flush them out, just like we did with Rogan."

"Okay, but we have to be smart about it. We have the power of the press on our side. I'll contact Jess Johnson at *The New Orleans Times* to see how she can help. In the meantime, I need to catch up on my public relations campaign for the stevia company. I've come up with a slogan I want to run by Mr. Morris tomorrow. 'Stevia, processed by nature, not by chemicals.' What do you think?"

"Pretty good. Why don't Piper and I stay at my place tonight to give you a little time to work?" Tom said. "You haven't had a minute to yourself since we returned from Mexico. We can talk about Hector and his problem tomorrow."

I looked at Piper to see how she felt about it. She nodded her head in approval, saying, "Can we watch another movie and pop more popcorn?"

"Damn straight we can," Tom said. "We'll even order a pizza."

"Perfect," Piper said. "Pepperoni?"

"You know how they process that stuff…? Oh, never mind. Pepperoni it is," said Tom.

"Okay, it's settled. You two keep your eyes peeled for Victor tonight. I'll work on my presentation for Mr. Morris after I call Jess Johnson to get input on Victor Ivanovich. I'll check out my blog to see if anyone out there has information about him. If he's a shadow demon, the light will fry his ass like water did to the Wicked Witch of the West. We'll get him before he can release his flying monkeys."

Piper laughed at the *Wizard of Oz* reference. "I can so see Victor in a witch's costume riding a broom. Maybe if he stays in New Orleans long enough, we could persuade Jacques St. Germaine, the Vampire of New Orleans, to bite him and suck the vodka blood from his veins." We all laughed until our sides hurt.

Once alone in my condo, I called Jess. She asked me to come to her office early in the morning. After the call, I got to work on my presentation, keeping my gun within reach at all times. I knew Victor came from a culture of death dealing. He trafficked in young women, hooking them on drugs and forcing them to prostitute themselves. He wouldn't hesitate to kill me if I got in his way.

Tomorrow we were going on the offensive.

CHAPTER THIRTEEN
AN OFFENSE

THE MORNING COFFEE rallied my blood, forcing me out of bed early. With the aid of my caffeine-charged energetic warriors, I was ready to battle the day. Battle was what I had to do, too. I dressed in a business suit, complete with stylish pumps and my .38 strapped to my leg, to go to Jess's office. The television broadcasted the news of another prostitute's body found murdered on the streets. *Must be the work of the serial killer Detective Baker mentioned*, I thought as I put six additional rounds in my purse for my .38. Navigating through security was a breeze with my near-celebrity status at the paper. Prominently displaying my press credentials and my security badge, I followed the familiar path to Jess's office. Upon entering, I stopped to read the plaque above her desk with my favorite quote:

The only thing necessary for the triumph of evil is for good men to do nothing. —Edmund Burke

Jess was the sage of *The New Orleans Times*. She'd seen good and bad times in New Orleans. Larger problems than mine crossed her desk daily, and if anyone knew how to handle the coming storm, she did.

"Sit down, girl," Jess said. "You are here to talk about that child you took in and the people who are after her. Demetre filled me in on all of the details. You've got a mess of trouble on your plate. These are bad folks."

"They scare me, Jess."

"Nothing wrong with being scared. It's natural. What's important is what you do with that fear. Do you run or do you fight?"

"Run?" I said. "I'm not going anywhere. I just want to figure out the best way to fight the bastards."

"That's my girl. I figured you'd say that. I've done some research into Victor Ivanovich. He's the real deal. After the fall of the Soviet Union, lawlessness ruled. Strong, mean criminals fought for control of illegal money-making schemes. Victor was just a teenager at the time. He was smart, and he allied himself with a ruthless group from the former KGB. He schemed and murdered his way to the head of the organization, body by body. No one messes with him, largely because he has always been smarter than the rest of the Russian Mafia guys. He's a twenty-first-century criminal, assembling a team of hackers whom he's stashed at one of his strongholds in Moscow. They break into government computers around the world, including computers belonging to major corporations and banks, stealing money, credit card information, and personal identities. He hacks other mafia group's cell phones to stay ahead of them."

"He's in New Orleans now. I saw him at the Café Du Monde yesterday," I said.

"Victor is here in person? That's interesting. I knew he had thugs here already, but I didn't know he'd come himself. That's not his usual style. There must be some compelling reason for him to be here."

The corner of my mouth turned down, and I closed my eyes, creating tiny crow's feet at the corner of each eye. Anguish pulled my heart into a flurried rhythm because I knew what he was here for. He was here for Piper, but I just didn't know why.

"Jess, how do you know Victor's thugs are in New Orleans?"

"My sources tell me he's making a move on the Dixie Mafia's control of prostitution in the city. Some of the working girls have been approached by his men. Yesterday, a Dixie Mafia street pimp's body was found floating in Lake Pontchartrain, his throat cut ear to ear. No one else would dare do that. The Italian Mafia and the Dixie Mafia have an understanding: They don't mess with each other's property. War is coming to our city, Alexandra, and it won't be pretty. Bodies will drop on both sides."

Great, I thought, *like raising a teenager wasn't hard enough. Now I have to worry about being in the middle of a mafia war.* Suddenly my .38 revolver seemed small. Even a combat tank seemed small in the face of all of this shit. But what could I do? I had to fight them.

I left Jess even more resolved to protect Piper at all costs. It was a cloudy day, scantly misting rain. I looked skyward to the heavens, allowing the rain to bathe my face with nano-drops, to ask my mom and Sarah to look out for me. Maybe it was a coincidence, or maybe it was a sign, but the cloud cover broke and the sun's rays shone through. I took it as a sign and headed to meet Charlotte and Mr. Morris at Superior Sugar's corporate office, confident that I could defend my family and my home.

We convened our meeting in Superior's conference room. Their large-screen projection capabilities were perfect to demonstrate the PR program I had planned. "Stevia, sugar's healthy alternative." "Expand your food choices with stevia, not your waist." These were but two of the many options I presented to Mr. Morris. I was surprised to hear that such a busy man had read every word of the research paper I had written and emailed him in advance of our meeting. The thesis-style report detailed the health benefits of stevia. Mr. Morris homed in on the benefits for diabetes, a disease he'd battled all his life. My father fought the same battle and lost, suffering from dementia and then a stroke, his doctor attributing both conditions to sugar. I was pleased to see that Mr. Morris loved all of my ideas and would take them to the board of directors at their next meeting.

After the presentation, Mr. Morris confided in me what he'd already told Charlotte. He was planning to sell his interest in Superior Sugar and spin off the stevia company for himself, feeling he couldn't continue to sell what he'd learned was poison. Sugar in moderation wasn't horrible; it was the proliferation into so much of our food that was causing the trouble, and he had helped with that proliferation. As a result, guilt and diabetes had gotten the better of him. Mr. Morris believed sugar contributed to Mandy's erratic behavior as well, so he wanted to get away—and lead others away—from sugar's destructive rampage through the American body. His attitude reminded me of Sarah's need for redemption. Maybe he felt the pursuit of the dollar had clouded his judgment and detached him from his humanity.

Holy shit, this is more like a therapy session than a meeting, I thought. I applauded his change of course. I'd lost close to thirty pounds and felt wonderful since I'd restricted sugar and other simple carbohydrates. I didn't cut them out of my diet entirely, but I did make sure to only eat them occasionally. America needed to change, and I was happy to be a part of that change.

I couldn't help but notice that Mr. Morris and Charlotte were really close. *What's going on there?* I wondered. *Stop it, Alexandra*, I chastised myself. Those gossipy thoughts weren't fair. They were both single, and their business should be private. Besides, I had bigger issues to occupy my thoughts.

I weaved my way through the slow-moving traffic of the Central Business District, or CBD as we locals called it, my progress momentarily halted by one of the many traffic signals. A homeless man sprayed my windshield with Windex despite my protestations. I rolled my window down to give him a couple of dollars for his effort. As I was distracted, the passenger door opened and a man slid next to me in one swift motion. I barely had time to process what had happened before he jammed what looked like a cannon in my ribs and said, "Take the next right."

"What are—"

"Shut up and do what I tell you to do," he growled in a deep voice. He looked to be in his late fifties, with greased, black hair, and was maybe five foot, eight inches tall. His gut extended over his belt line. Old school tattoos, no doubt acquired in prison, accented his don't-fuck-with-me demeanor. He guided me to a parking lot and ordered me into a waiting car. I was desperate to escape, but his gun was very convincing. He gave me no time to think, prodding me until I numbly climbed in, two more rough types on either side of me as he drove to the French Quarter. *Oh my God, Victor wants to kill me himself,* I thought. The car stopped in front of a strip bar on the lower end of Bourbon Street, and the two brutes escorted me inside. We passed a lone girl spinning on a pole beginning her act. She winked at me as I was zipped past her to an office in the rear of the building. She must have thought I was a new girl, and if I wasn't so terrified, I might have been flattered. I was thrown in a chair in front of a balding, menacing man disgustingly covered with ugly tattoos and cheap gold chains.

He stared at me without saying a word for what seemed like an eternity, then said, "So you are Alexandra. I've heard about you. I've even read your blog. I brought you here 'cause you need to do something for me."

No, Alexandra, don't do it, I told myself. But I just couldn't help it. "I'm not doing a damn thing for you except kick you in the balls if I get the chance."

He and the other two men in the room broke out in loud, guttural laughter. "Damn, she's got more stones than that guy we had in here. We had him by the balls 'cause of his drug problems, but he wouldn't cooperate until we threatened to nab his sister. He caved like a mud house in a hurricane."

I knew they were talking about Zach. So that was how they got him to cooperate; they threatened Maddy. They could threaten me all they wanted, but I'd never make any deals with these demons. They were just like Rogan and those Colombian cartel monsters, thriving in the shadows. Deals with demons like these only lead to misery and death. Look at poor Zach. No matter what he did for them, he couldn't get control of his life and off of their roller coaster.

They didn't search me, and my gun was strapped to my leg. I'd at least take one of them with me before I went. When they quit laughing, the big asshole behind the desk rocked back in his chair, putting his hands together to form a ten-finger pyramid. "Just listen to what I have to say before you get your panties in a wad."

I nodded.

"We haven't been formally introduced. Some call us the Dixie Mafia. We are just a bunch of guys working for a living. Our bosses run our group from the prisons. You see, sooner or later we all end up in a prison. If we haven't done what we were supposed to, we have lots of accidents in jail, some fatal. Our big boss is in Angola State Prison, and he isn't happy about what's going on these days. You know that Russian prick Victor Ivanovich wants to move in on our territory. He did the same thing to us in Mobile, and our boss wants to stop Victor from ruining our good thing."

"How does any of this involve me?" I asked.

"You work with the newspapers and the cops. All you need to do is report the truth about what's going on. We'll clue you in and you report it. Check out the information as much as you want. Just report it in the paper and to the cops. You see, the cops don't have a clue what's really going on in the streets until lots of bodies drop, especially when it involves our kind of people. Then they get around to figuring it out. This Russian prick is the one killing the street hookers in New Orleans. It's the same shit he pulled in Mobile. First he tries to get the girls to work for him. If they refuse, he kills them and makes it look like a serial killer is on the loose. Who's going to be the wiser? The cops don't care about working girls. Neither does the public. It scares the shit out of the girls, and they look to us for protection. They'll switch sides if we don't protect them. That's the game, babe, kill or be killed."

"So what proof do you have?" I asked. My journalistic instincts were kicking in. I had compassion for the unfortunate victims, but this could be a major story. I felt guilty for a few seconds, like I was profiting off of the girls' plight. But that was what journalists did: report the truth. Shedding light on these dark dealings would help them more than anything else I could do.

"We've got some girls who will talk to you and the cops and some videos you should see. We'll give you the video, and you handle getting it to the right people," he said.

"Let me be crystal clear," I said. "I'll make no deal with you." I hesitated for a moment to let those words sink in. "But if you give me evidence of crimes against these girls, I'll bring it to the police and report it in my blog and the paper. Understand, we aren't on the same side. You are predators just like Victor, and if I get the chance, I'll come after you, too."

They didn't laugh this time. They all looked at me with sinister eyes. The man behind the desk sat up straight and leaned toward me. "Okay, bitch, for right now, the enemy of my enemy is my friend. We'll give you the proof. No deal necessary."

One of my fat, greasy escorts brought me a disk before he drove me to my car, blowing me a kiss as I exited his vehicle. Oh my God, the anti Prince Charming just blew me a kiss. I'd just taken a trip to another dimension. Though I projected a tough image, I was scared shitless. My legs shook so much that my knees almost clanged together. I'd just been in the shadowy underbelly of New Orleans. I had known it existed but had no idea it was right under my nose.

So what was on this disk? Should I go straight to the police station and give it to them? No way. Not until I had a copy for myself. The cops would never let me copy it once they had it.

I felt like I couldn't go to my condo because it might not be safe. I went to the only refuge I knew, Sarah's House. Susan was surprised to see me but as always was the perfect hostess, offering me coffee. We sat together chatting and drinking our coffee as she updated me on who was new and who had left. She was so excited to see me she went on and on about the broken lives of the girls who'd come and gone. She asked if I would meet the new girls since they'd heard her talk about me.

"Susan, I'd love to spend some time with each of the new girls, but first I have a favor to ask. May I use your computer to copy a disk?"

She led me to her desk. "Use this one. It's the newest we have."

I copied the disk for the police and uploaded the contents to my private cloud account. Mission accomplished, I said, "Now introduce me to the new residents."

She took me to the common area room. There sat many of the girls I knew and a couple of new ones watching TV and chatting while others played with their kids. Susan introduced me to the whole room, and one of the new girls sidled up to me, her accent unfamiliar to me.

She said she was from the North and had only been in Louisiana for a month. She was petite, well-groomed, and intelligent, and she stood out from the rest. I wondered how someone as much on the ball as she was could end up with some jerk who abused her. Not an unusual story, though. Love was blind.

"Your accent sounds unusual to me," I said.

"Maybe because my grandparents were Romanian. They immigrated to the United States after World War II. My parents were shopkeepers. They worked long hours, so I spent most of my time growing up with my grandparents. My grandmother spoke Romanian to me much of the time."

"Do you still speak Romanian?" I asked.

"A little," she said.

It was getting dark, and I didn't want to view the disk at Sarah's house—it wasn't safe. I needed to get home, so I said my goodbyes. I thought there was something funny about the Romanian girl's story, but I decided to look into it more tomorrow. I was pretty anxious to see the contents of the disk. Hoping my condo was safe, I hurried home, locking my car's doors and scanning my rearview mirrors for thugs.

CHAPTER FOURTEEN
Lighting the Shadows

I drove past my condo twice, my head swiveling in every direction to see if any unusual cars or activity stood out. It all seemed normal, so I parked, went in, and secured the door behind me. For the first time I wedged a chair against the door as an extra measure of security, freaked out by all of the seedy characters trying to commandeer my life.

I checked in with Tom to make sure all was well with him and Piper. They were eating popcorn watching the *Twilight* movies. Piper took the phone from Tom to tell me the story reminded her of the French Quarter Vampire. I laughed and told them goodnight.

I'd forgotten all about food today. Thank goodness I had some cage-free brown eggs in the fridge. After eating, I placed the disk in the computer to watch the video. I felt like a scream queen in a horror flick waiting to see something that would hypnotize me and turn me into some sort of zombie. What I saw was nothing like that at all.

I watched a car with an Uber driver sign on the windshield and both sides of the back bumper pull up to an obvious prostitute in the French Quarter. After some conversation, she got in the car. Then the car drove off. Nothing pointing to Victor in that clip. As I watched three more clips, the scene repeated itself. An Uber vehicle pulled up, picked up a streetwalker, and took her away, and it was the same Uber vehicle every time. Maybe he was working for Victor. Maybe that was the connection the scary guys in the strip joint were trying to expose. I decided to take a copy to Detective Baker tomorrow morning.

I turned to my blog retrieving all of the entries from the Mobile area. There were scads of women who turned up missing or dead around the same time last year. I wrote a post explaining I was doing a story on the missing women of Mobile and invited all who had information to contact me.

Bushed from a long day, my gun and I headed to bed. I hoped to have responses from Mobile tomorrow morning. I felt I needed to learn how Victor operated to fight him.

I arrived at the police precinct at eight-thirty, shortly after Detective Baker got in. He brought me to the coffee room for a huge cup of Community coffee before we started our conversation. Both gassed up on caffeine, we took the short walk to his office.

"What can I do for you, Alexandra?" he asked.

"It's about what I can do for you," I said. "Here is a video from a confidential source showing what I believe are your murdered working girls being picked up by the same Uber driver. I'll venture to say they were never seen again after their ride."

Baker popped the DVD into his computer. He watched it carefully and said, "You aren't going to tell me where you got this disk, are you?"

"No, but it's yours to keep. I only have one request," I said as I batted my eyelashes at him. "I want you to let me watch you question the Uber driver."

"I can't officially promise you that, but maybe I could carelessly leave the door to the observation room open when I'm questioning him. Do you think this Uber driver is our killer?" he said.

"I think your killer is Victor Ivanovich, and the Uber driver is his accomplice. Do you have to involve Jaeger in this?" I asked.

"No, not really," he said. "Right now, it's still an investigation of a serial killer preying on prostitutes. We have no evidence pointing to anyone else. I'll bring this Uber driver in for questioning. I'll let you know when I get him."

Tom was dropping Piper off at my condo at nine-thirty. I was running a little late, so I ran some red lights on my way home. Maybe if I stopped twice at some others, my traffic signal karma would balance itself.

When I got home, Tom and Piper were there. Piper went on and on about the *Twilight* movies. I wondered if it was the vampire part or the love story that got to her. Maybe it was the part about the vampires being a family.

She asked if Mandy could take us on the haunted cemetery tour. She wanted to see Marie Laveau's grave. Marie, a Creole woman, was the voodoo queen of New Orleans. Tom begged me to let him go to Mexico, and I finally agreed since I needed to go to Mobile to follow up on some leads from my blog.

"So it's settled then," Tom said. "I'll head to Mexico for two days and you can stay overnight in Mobile. We'll meet back here. You know, Alexandra, we also have to go to your farm in Indiana to choose a contractor to remediate the poisoned well."

"I know, I know," I said. "But can't it wait until I get to the bottom of the prostitute murders? There's more to that story than has been reported. They may not be dying at the hands of a serial killer after all."

"Okay, we'll make plans to deal with the farm after Mexico and Mobile," Tom said.

I chose not to tell Tom about the Dixie Mafia encounter or what Detective Baker and I had discussed. He wanted to help Hector in Mexico so badly, I didn't want to do anything that would make him cancel his trip. Maybe the right thing to do was to get out of town.

Has Detective Baker picked up the Uber driver yet? I wondered. Maybe the Dixie guys were wrong. Maybe the Uber driver *was* the serial killer. I could just be making too much out of the Victor thing. After all, he hadn't really tried anything yet. Maybe Jaeger was playing me. He could be working Zach and the Dixie guys to use me and Piper as bait to smoke Victor out. Was I in over my head? All of these thoughts swirled through my mind as I made reservations for a hotel room in Mobile.

"Hector told me some of the small farmers from Northern Mexico have mobilized against the industrial farm companies using the genetically modified corn plants. They are joining Hector's efforts to stop the spread of the Frankencorn to Southern Mexico. They tell stories of water they use for irrigation from streams and ground aquifers containing pesticides and herbicides. They can prove the pollution was caused by runoff from the Frankencorn fields. Worse yet, the pollution in the water is killing their crops," Tom said.

I couldn't help but notice how animated Tom's face became as he spoke about Hector's activism. His eyes twinkled like the stars in the night sky. He leaned forward like a ski jumper about to launch from the ramp. He emphatically punctuated each sentence with symphonic hand gestures. Even Piper noticed; she cast me a wry smile. *This is your family, Piper*, I thought. *Intense but lovable, and now my family, too.*

Tom waved to Piper and me as he sped off to work. How could I stop him from doing what he was born to do?

My thoughts were disturbed by a *rap, rap, rap* at the door. I looked through the peephole to see a man dressed in a suit with a sheriff's deputy badge around his neck. He had a wad of papers in his hands. What now?

"Are you Alexandra Lee?" he asked as he looked past me into the condo. "Is Tom Sanders here?"

"Yes, I am Alexandra, but Tom Sanders isn't here," I said.

"Does he live here?"

"No, he doesn't. He's my boyfriend, but he has his own place."

"Can you give me his address?" As he wrote down Tom's address, I tried to read the title on the legal documents in his hand, but I could only see the caption:

Sandy Rawlins
vs.

Tom Sanders
Petition for Custody of Constance Rawlins

Oh shit, she was taking us to court to get Piper. This had to be part of Victor's plan. We might be in some deep shit now. After all, she was Piper's mother.

I called Tom on his cell and told him not to go home yet or show up at work. I wanted to tell him about the custody suit in person, but we had to move fast to counter Victor's move, so I told him about it over the phone. I made an appointment for me and Tom to see my lawyer, Mr. Swartz, and a specialist he brought in to help, Joshua Clark. Mr. Clark was well known in legal circles in New Orleans, having a reputation as a ferocious and cagy litigator. He had dark brown hair, an athlete's build, and a handsome face, his dazzling smile hiding his tenacious demeanor. I sat Piper down and told her what I'd been able to read in the process server's hands. She loved her mother and would gladly live with her here in New Orleans but refused to go back to Victor. She agreed to come with us to see the lawyers, but she remained in the waiting room as we met with them. We told them the entire story of how Piper ended up with us. Joshua put his hand on his chin and rocked back in his chair, squinting his eyes a bit.

"Hmmm, so you weren't served with any papers?"

"No, not yet," Tom said.

"Here's how we'll proceed then. I will draw up custody papers for you to sign. I will ask a judge to give you immediate temporary custody pending a hearing. Since Constance is living with you, the judge will probably sign them. That will protect you until the complete custody case can be heard. I must warn you, though, it's only a temporary order. Mothers are given strong preference in custody cases. You'll have to show she's not fit to care for Constance. So go get me some evidence I can use in court."

I asked Piper to join us in the conference room. She clung to the bottom of my shirt with both hands as we entered the room. I asked her to tell Mr. Clark about her life with her mother in California. She talked about the good times before Victor and how full of life her mother was every day. There were parties, bowling trips, and picnics in the park.

"Then the dark times came," she said. "My mother met Victor. He made her laugh when they first met. He gave me piggyback rides. She fell in love with him. He asked her to work at his spa. She strained her back lifting a massage table and started taking pain pills. Victor furnished her with all the pills she needed. Before long, she was hooked. Then, the pills weren't enough. Heroin took their place. My mother was no longer my mother. She was a zombie doing whatever Victor wanted."

"How did you come to leave your mom and go to live with your dad in Chicago?" Clark asked.

"She and Katerina, the woman who tutored me, took me to the bus station late one night, and that was it. I was on my way to my father, a man I'd never met. I tried to call my mom's cell phone many times, but she never answered. I even called the spa and asked for my mom or Katerina. None of the ladies would get them to the phone. Finally, I gave up."

"Where do you want to live?" Swartz asked as Mr. Clark studied Piper's face.

"I love my mom, as messed up as she is. But I want to stay here with Alexandra and my uncle."

I couldn't help myself; I burst into tears, grabbing Piper and hugging her as tightly as I could. She wrapped her tiny arms around me as we cried together. This poor child had seen too much in her short life. The only family she'd had was a kaleidoscope of drugged-out sex workers in a brothel and an emotionally unavailable father who wanted a career, not children. She needed a family who could take care of her and show her love, not drug addicts she had to care for.

"Are you willing to tell a judge everything you just told me?" Clark asked.

Piper unbuckled from me and raised her watery blue eyes to Clark. With hesitation she said, "Yes, I will." I could tell she liked him, his reassuring manner calming her.

Swartz and Clark said they would get the necessary documents for us to sign within an hour. We went to a Starbucks near the office to pass the time. After we signed the documents, Clark took them to a judge and returned with a court order giving temporary custody of Piper to Tom and me. The order set a full custody hearing date three months from today. I was certain if Victor were behind this litigation, he would not be happy that we'd won round one, but Joshua Clark's confident manner made me feel like we had a fighting chance.

Tom took Piper to work with him, and I went to see Detective Baker. As she stretched her arm to its full length to wave goodbye, I noticed a stamp on the back of Piper's left hand, like the ones you got at the door of a nightclub. *Hmmm*, I wondered, *where did that come from?* This was not the time to conduct an interrogation. I'd wait until I got her alone.

Baker wasn't at the precinct, so I sat in the lobby of the police station, making a great effort to be patient, which does not come naturally to me at all. The police precinct was almost as good a people-watching venue as the Las Vegas Airport. I witnessed daytime drunks stumble by, trannies who'd tried to scratch each other's eyes out priss through, and pickpockets who weren't quite ready for prime time skulk as they were paraded to a cell. The NOPD handled each and every one with professional compassion. These were the street people of the Quarter living in the dimly-lit spaces. The people the police kept away from the tourists and from each other. Outcasts in many ways, and yet also our people—inhabitants who made up the fabric of our pirate city. The cops were honoring a retiring sergeant on his last day of work, and risqué jokes flew through the air as gag gifts were given.

Detective Baker strolled in, dragging a handcuffed, scrawny man sporting a wispy wannabe beard. As he passed, Baker bobbed his head, alerting me that this was the Uber driver. I'd been in this precinct enough to know the protocol; they were on their way to the interrogation room. I'd lucked out, because the retirement party allowed me to slip into the viewing room unnoticed.

Baker questioned the Uber driver about his driving patterns. The driver seemed normal enough; a little on the weaselly side, but normal.

As the questions narrowed to the dates of the prostitutes' murders, Baker threw photos of the dead girls in front of the driver. Color left his face as he pushed back from the table, creating distance between himself and the photos as if touching one would get blood on his hands he could never wash off.

"Are these the working girls who've been murdered?" he asked. "Oh fuck. I recognize them. I gave all of them a ride. Hey, you don't think I killed them, do you?"

"Did you?" Jaeger asked as he barged into the room unannounced.

"No way, man. I just gave them a ride. The same lady booked the trips every time, and I brought them all to the same hotel. She was a really hot lady with short blond hair."

Baker looked at Jaeger, a little shocked at his brashness in breaking into the interrogation room uninvited, before bearing down on the driver. "Can you describe her to us?"

"Dude, I can do better than that. I wanted to show my buddy how hot these girls were, so I snuck a picture of her with my phone."

As he pulled his phone from his pocket, Jaeger jerked it from his hands. Jaeger and Detective Baker looked at the picture together for a minute before Jaeger left the room with the phone in hand. Baker resumed his questions, trying to get more details—a name, method of payment, etc.

"I sent the picture to your phone and mine," Jaeger said as he re-entered the room.

"I'll get forensics to run it through facial recognition to see if we can get an ID," Baker said.

God, I wanted to see that photo. *Patience, Alexandra, patience*, I told myself. Baker continued his questioning of the driver for another hour and a half. As he concluded, he turned toward the glass, knowing I was on the other side, and motioned me to his office. I scurried down the hall. It was excruciating waiting for Baker to come in. I wanted to see that photo.

"Here's the picture of the woman who paid the Uber driver," Baker said as he cupped his phone in his hand allowing me to view the photo.

"Holy shit!" I blurted. "I know that face. She's one of the new girls at Sarah's House."

"I'm going to pick her up," Baker said. "Want to meet me there?"

I was out of the door and on my way to Sarah's House in a flash.

CHAPTER FIFTEEN
Impostor

Gotcha, Victor. We blocked your little legal maneuver for the time being. Next I'll bet the impostor at Sarah's House is working for you. We'll bust her. She'll tell Jaeger everything you put her up to doing and your ass will head off to jail, I thought as I sped toward the shelter. What else could she do? The Uber driver's testimony together with the photo he snapped with his cell phone camera nailed her. Her choices were to cooperate with the police or do some really hard time.

I saw red flashing lights everywhere as I approached Sarah's House. Oh my God, I hope nothing has happened to Susan. If they hurt her I'd...I'd. Hell, what would I do? I wasn't a killer. I couldn't do the things they did. At least I didn't have to worry long. Susan was standing outside the center speaking with Detective Baker when I drove up.

"What's going on?" I shouted across the narrow walkway leading from the parking places to the cluster of police cars parked next to an ambulance.

No one answered me because they were watching the paramedics place someone in the ambulance. As I took a few more steps, I recognized the girl with the unusual accent, the one whose picture the Uber driver had taken, lying on a gurney. She wasn't moving as they slid her head-first into the ambulance.

"Susan, what happened to her?"

"I'm not really sure. She left today just like she did every day to go to work and returned around three-thirty. Today she got back a little early, but other than that she came and went just like usual. She sat down to watch television with some of the other girls. Suddenly, she went into convulsions and tumbled to the floor."

"She didn't look like she was breathing when they pushed her into the ambulance," I said.

"The paramedics did what they could to revive her, but she hasn't taken a breath for more than five minutes. I don't think she is going to make it," Susan said, finally breaking down in a pool of tears. "This is horrible, Alexandra. Our residents and their children are terrified. The violence they've seen in their homes has followed them here to our sanctuary. All of these flashing lights, people gathering, traffic backing up to see what's happening…we can't have this!"

Poor Susan. She wrung her hands as she paced aimlessly. I just hoped the scene would clear soon. She was right; the center's residents didn't need any more trauma in their devastated lives. The women were cowering in the corners and behind doors, their curiosity about what was happening battling their desire to hide. The children were huddled next to their mothers, trying to understand or make sense of the chaotic scene. I wondered what effect this horror would have on their lives. Did they already associate flashing police lights with dad beating mom? Would this send them into a panicked state?

My heart sunk as I realized I may have been responsible for raining this suffering down on these poor souls. This had to be connected to Victor and the Dixie Mafia. Nausea captained my churning stomach and steered my thoughts into a sea of guilt. I looked at the lifeless body on the gurney, lamenting my involvement in this whole sordid episode. At that moment, I felt anger flare up from the core of my being. This wasn't my doing. This was part of the evil that resides alongside each of us every day, and we couldn't defeat it by ignoring it. We had to fight it. I had to fight it. Then those words flashed through my mind. The ones displayed on Jess Johnson's wall:

The only thing necessary for the triumph of evil is for good men to do nothing. —Edmund Burke

Not on my watch, I thought as Detective Baker took me aside to tell me the cause of death was not apparent from a cursory examination of the body. He'd called his forensic team to the scene to go through the entire house looking for evidence. Baker asked the paramedics to place the body in the ambulance until the coroner arrived to ease the tensions among resident women and children. He suggested I leave to allow the police to do their job. Before I got in my car, Jaeger pulled up. He stopped the paramedics before they closed the door to the ambulance so he could get a look at the body. Satisfied it was the same girl as in his photo, he walked slowly over to me. He pulled out his phone to show me the photo saved on his phone, not knowing I'd already seen it.

"Have you ever seen this girl before?" he asked, handing me his phone.

I fingered the wrong icon on the phone and pulled up his text messages. Holy shit. He'd texted the photo to Clint, the Dixie Mafia thug. He'd given Clint and his redneck gang a three-hour heads-up to track her down. Did they kill her? Jaeger must have told them she was the one murdering their working girls. Why else would he send them the photo? This must be his misguided plan to smoke Victor out in the open. Would he go that far or be that stupid?

"Yes, I have. I met her here at the shelter a few days ago. We spoke for a brief while. She introduced herself to me as Tiffany. Maybe the center's director knows her full name."

"Tiffany, huh? Sounds like a stripper name. They must take in strippers and hookers at this place?" Jaeger said, casting a glance at the front of the center.

What a prick. I wanted to kick him in his insolent German balls. He had no idea what these women had been through. But here he was with his pious attitude, and all the while he was consorting with the Dixie Mafia. Detective Baker was right. I needed to watch out for this guy, because he was nothing but trouble.

If it weren't bad enough having Jaeger stomping around, Child Protective Services drove up. Two ladies in discount clothing store attire approached Detective Baker and Susan. Oh shit, this couldn't be good. Baker looked my way and waved his hand, shooing me away. Susan mouthed, "It's okay."

I was torn between my desire to stay and offer moral support to Susan and my journalistic instincts compelling me to track down Zach. I wanted to find out more about Clint, the Dixie Mafia, and Jaeger. If I stayed, what was I going to do? Tell Child Protective Services that this was my fault because I'd put these children in the middle of a turf war between a Russian syndicate and the Dixie Mafia? Not really a good idea, and besides, this entire situation wasn't going to get any better until I got to the bottom of it all. How did I get myself into this shit anyway?

Zach was easy to find. He texted me right back that he was at the gym working out with his sister. Why was it all gay guys were ripped and gorgeous? Did they have some type of hot gene that straight men didn't have? Of course not; they just paid more attention to their appearance. Zach and Maddy met me in the parking lot. They both had cheek-to-cheek smiles on their faces, no doubt induced by the endorphins released by their workouts as well as the fact that they were finished. We agreed to adjourn to PJ's Coffee Shop two blocks from the gym.

PJ's is a New Orleans original, kind of a mashup of Starbucks and Bourbon Street. The first store opened close to Tulane University. Students met there to discuss music, dating, and anything else other than school. PJ's claim to fame was that they bagged their fresh roasted coffee the same day they ground it. Just like on Bourbon Street, you were likely to see every type of person imaginable in PJ's.

"You're here to talk about the woman at Sarah's House, aren't you?" Zach said.

"As a matter of fact, I am. Not just about her, though. I want to know all about Jaeger and the Dixie Mafia."

Maddy eyed me with growing impatience. "Can't you see he's trying to get away from those people? They've had control of Zach's life for more than ten years. Why do you want to drag him back into this mess?"

Zach patted her arm. He maintained his composure and spoke in a low serene voice. "Maddy, I got myself involved with these thugs. Alexandra had nothing to do with it. She's not trying to hurt me."

Maddy sat back in her chair. She took a sip of her mango frozen lemonade, allowing her pulse to slow and the redness to leave her face. I understood her frustration. She was just being protective of her brother. She wanted him left alone; we had that in common. I didn't want to be dragged into a turf war, but neither Zach nor I had a choice. We had to fight to get them off our asses. If I had to fight, I was going to use everything at my disposal to stop the bastards. It seemed like good and evil were always at war around me, and I had to choose a side. Bystanders became collateral damage; disposable pawns in a deadly game of chess.

"So you know about the woman being killed at the center?" I asked.

"Killed? She was killed? Oh shit. You've got to be kidding. No, I didn't know she'd been killed," Zach said, abandoning his serene tone.

"Did Clint or any of the other Dixie Mafia have anything to do with her death?" I asked.

"No. No. I really don't think so. Jaeger sent them a picture of her. They used their street sources to track her to the center. They were going to follow her tomorrow and kidnap her. Their plan was to force her to tell them Victor's scheme for New Orleans. They were going to video it for Jaeger. The whole thing was supposed to be a trap for Victor. Someone else must have killed her, maybe Victor himself."

"Jaeger used her as bait, and the bastard got her killed. He really doesn't care who gets hurt, does he?"

"None of these guys care who gets hurt. They are all killers. Let me give you a little background on the Dixie Mafia. I've already told you how they used me in their scheme to bilk gay men out of money. Well, some of the money from the lonely hearts scam allegedly went through the bank accounts of a law firm in Mississippi. The two partners in the firm were eventually elected to public office. Attorney Pete Halat became the mayor of Biloxi, and his law partner, Vincent Sherry, was elected judge. Halat convinced the mastermind of the scam, Kirksey

McCord, that Sherry stole some of the money. McCord ordered a hit on Judge Sherry and his wife, Margaret. Both were gunned down in their home. McCord was given a life sentence for murder, and Halat was sentenced to eighteen years in jail for conspiracy to commit racketeering, obstruction of justice, conspiracy to obstruct justice, and conspiracy to commit wire fraud. These guys will stop at nothing to protect their turf."

Maddy wrung her hands. She put her right arm around her brother as she closed her eyes and sighed. They looked pitiful to me. It triggered my mother's words to ring through my ears over and over as I watched them fret about their perilous future. "When you make a deal with the devil, the devil always collects." She was right, too. Zach knew he chose to get involved with the Dixie Mafia thugs and made his deal, and now he was suffering the consequences. But it occurred to me that evil didn't have to win. We all had power over our lives. *When evil leaves its shadowy world and enters our lives, we have to fight,* I thought. Fight with every fiber of our being, because the deal wasn't forever. It had a beginning, so it must have an end. It ended when you chased the shadow demons back to their dark world.

"Jaeger wants Zach to do something for Clint," Maddy said. "I think it's a bad idea. I want us to run away. Go to another town and start fresh."

Zach and I turned, and our eyes met as soon as Maddy finished. He knew what I wanted, and he knew I wouldn't leave until I found out what they'd asked him to do. She'd let the cat out of the bag, and now he had to tell me.

"Jaeger told me Victor wants to dominate the drug business in New Orleans. He is trying to make a deal with a supplier. Victor's supplier is a competitor to the Dixie Mafia's supplier. Jaeger is using two CIA contractors to set up a deal with the guys Victor is talking to about supplying the drugs. These two guys tell everyone they are CIA, but they aren't. They are independents that the CIA uses from time to time. They aren't any cleaner than the Dixie Mafia. Jaeger wants me to go to Colombia and bring back heroin."

"Colombia!" I blurted. "Who are you dealing with in Colombia?"

"I don't know any names. All I know is Jaeger calls the group the Scorpions."

Holy shit! That was El Alacran's cartel. He's the one who kidnapped me in Colombia and stuck my hand in the scorpion cage. He murdered Camila, cutting her head off and showing it to me. He was Bart Rogan's guy. Jaeger was playing with fire and so was Zach. There wasn't a version of this story that Zach would survive. He'd either be murdered by Clint or Victor or get caught in the crossfire. No matter what, he'd be killed.

"Maddy, you said you want to start fresh. Where do you want to go and what would you like to do?" I asked.

"Anywhere away from these animals." She closed her eyes for a brief moment then locked eyes with mine. "I have always been into health and fitness. Healthy eating and exercise transform a person's brain. The American diet contains too much sugar and processed foods, and it's riddled with pesticides. Zach's drug addiction began with his over-con-sumption of sugar. His brain became dopamine dependent, the chemical in your brain that creates that good feeling associated with all pleasures—drugs, sex, and comfort food. I've always wanted to be in the organic food business because eating right changes people's lives. I don't care where I live; I just want away from these human predators."

I looked at Zach. He nodded his head in agreement. "Zach, play along with them for now, but keep me informed about what they are asking you to do. Don't you dare meet with any of the Colombians. I know how dangerous they are. There may be a way out of this for all of us."

I left Zach and Maddy sitting at PJ's. They were trapped. I knew who I needed to talk to, so I headed back to my condo to make the call.

CHAPTER SIXTEEN
CALLING ON FRIENDS

"I'D LIKE TO speak to Sophia Garcia, please. Yes, I can hold."

I needed help dealing with all of this. Staying in New Orleans was working so far. Piper was still safe. *Oh shit*, I thought. *I'd better call Tom and make sure nothing had happened to her or him.* As soon as I talked to Sophia, I planned to call Tom.

"This is Sophia," a voice said on the other end of the phone.

"Oh my God, Sophia. It is so great to hear your voice. Did you return to active duty?"

"Sure did. Doctor says I'm fit and ready for action. Good thing, too, because I was going crazy sitting in this office. I'm not a desk kind of girl."

"No, you are not," I laughed, remembering her chasing the Serpent down the street a few months ago. "Sophia, I need your help. Before you answer, let me tell you what's going on. Jaeger is working with a gang of goons called the Dixie Mafia trying to smoke out Victor, the Russian Mafia creep, by starting some type of gang war. He knows Victor is after Tom's niece, and he's using her as bait. Detective Baker is helping as much as he can, but his hands are tied. Can you come to New Orleans and help me?"

"Jaeger has too much seniority on me. They will never let me come on an official basis. But New Orleans is such a beautiful town, and I'm ready for a vacation. It'll take me a few days to do all of the paperwork, but I'll get there one way or another," she said.

"Thank you," I said, and I meant it with all my heart. How wonderful. She was just the person to have my back. I thought about my planned trip to Mobile. It wasn't really a good idea to leave New Orleans right now. When I called Tom, he said he and Piper had scads of fun at his office, and it lifted my spirits to hear that those two were bonding. It was quitting time, and Tom said he'd get us some food on his way home. Before we could say our goodbyes, someone beeped in on the other line.

"Hello, this is Alexandra."

A low, sultry voice spoke softly. "Hello, Alexandra, this is Mandy Morris. Am I disturbing you?"

Oh no. I didn't want to get trapped in a telephone conversation with a person from another dimension. Mandy was hard enough to take when she was a normal New Orleans party slut, but now, as a Darth Vader impersonator, she was more than I could deal with. But I had promised Charlotte and Mr. Morris I'd help try to bring her back to reality. *So what the hell?* I thought.

"Oh, hi, Mandy. No, this is a good time," I lied. "What's up?"

"I wanted to invite you and Constance on another tour with me. She was so interested in vampires and voodoo, I thought she might enjoy the cemetery tour. We'll visit Marie Laveau's grave. It's one of our most popular tours."

"Sure," I said, gritting my teeth. "We'd both love to take that tour with you."

"By the way," she said, "you may want to give Charlotte a call. Daddy's not doing too well." After dropping that bombshell, she hung up.

What the hell? I thought. I immediately called Charlotte. She told me Mr. Morris had been diagnosed with cancer just this afternoon. No one except immediate family had been told. Mr. Morris had given explicit instructions not to tell Mandy until he knew more detail, and Charlotte and I wondered how she'd found out. Someone leaked it to her, but who? Charlotte and I made plans to meet tomorrow for lunch at my condo. She said she'd pick up some salads on her way over. I could tell from the tone of her voice things were more serious than she let on.

I got on my blog site. The pattern of missing girls was unmistakable. I knew many of them were lured into drugs and prostitution. Apparently human trafficking like this had been going on for some time, but the public was just becoming aware that Americans were being trafficked right here in the United States. Right under our noses, young girls were being prostituted and murdered. Their pimps on the street were being replaced by highly sophisticated organizations from the US and abroad, and Victor was one of the big players in the game. Millions if not billions of dollars made their way into the pockets of these low-life pigs. Now they wanted Piper.

Tom and Piper were a welcome sight. I felt an instant connection to Piper because we'd both lost our parents at about the same age. But now it had grown into much more, and I really loved the little thing. She and I just clicked. Oddly I felt more like a mother to her than anything else. My feelings were weirding me out because I didn't really want children at this point in my life. I was too career-oriented. She'd opened my eyes to the joy of unconditional love of someone who is dependent on you for protection. I knew I loved Tom, or at least I thought I did. He seemed to love her, too. Could we really turn into a twenty-first-century version of a family? Maybe.

Piper interrupted my warm thoughts. "Can I use your computer? My phone's almost dead."

"Sure," I said. "Take it in the bedroom. I need to talk to Tom."

I told him all about the day's events. He was happy to hear we'd discovered Victor's spy at Sarah's House, but not happy to hear of her death. Tom mourned the death of any creature, even one who had allowed evil to dictate her path. He told me he'd booked his flight to

Mexico and was scheduled to leave in two days. He offered to cancel, but I insisted he go. I knew how much it meant to him to help Hector. We had to go on with our normal lives as well as we could. Who knew how long it would take to kick Victor out of New Orleans? Right now, going on with our lives included Tom and I sleeping together. We had unbelievable sex once again with clenched teeth to muffle our sounds.

Charlotte came over the next day for lunch. She told me Mr. Morris had been diagnosed with colon cancer, and he had to go through treatments in Houston at MD Anderson Cancer Center. He'd asked her to go with him. I could tell there was more to their relationship than employer and employee. I believed she was in love with him, and she was worried that he might be too sick to save, so I spent time comforting her. She made me promise again to try to salvage Mandy. It killed me, but I promised.

Piper and I took Tom to the airport the next day. He was so excited to go help Hector. He made me promise I'd be very careful while he was gone. I promised, but I was lying through my teeth. *Sorry, Mom, no way I am going to sit back and wait for Victor to get Piper.* I wanted to stop him, and so far, so good; my plan seemed to be working. He was blocked at the center, and Jaeger and his Dixie Mafia friends were blocked from using Piper or Zach as bait.

Piper was immensely excited when I told her about touring the cemeteries with Mandy. She immediately went online and looked up all of the places the tour visited. She babbled on and on about how Marie Laveau was a real voodoo lady. Marie could do magical things, including preventing and curing illness. Piper wanted to draw an X on Marie's tombstone because according to the legend, all who did had a wish granted. I was afraid to ask what her wish would be.

Piper and I went to see Detective Baker at the precinct after we dropped Tom off at the airport. Just like the last time, Piper sat in the waiting room getting a good dose of people-watching. Her phone was fully charged, so she was good for awhile. Detective Baker showed me into his office and closed the door behind me.

"I don't want Jaeger to walk in while we are talking," Baker said. "We've gotten the coroner's report in on the death of the woman at

Sarah's House. She was poisoned, and not just with any poison either. She was poisoned with aconite. According to the lab rats, aconite is a plant found in Europe and Asia. It is not generally used in the United States. It looks like parsley when sprinkled on food. Death comes quickly. I would say she was poisoned at the center or shortly before she got there. Our search warrant of the center turned up nothing. We interviewed all of the women, and no one saw anything unusual. No men came to the center or met her in the parking lot."

"You don't think anyone at the center poisoned her, do you?"

"We just don't know at this point."

I told Baker about my conversation with Zach. He wasn't surprised to hear about what Jaeger was up to. He'd pegged Jaeger as a guy who was obsessed with getting Victor, because it was personal for him, not professional. His face lit up when I told him I'd asked Sophia to come to New Orleans. He'd worked closely with her on the Bart Rogan case. I always thought he had a sweet spot for her, too. I asked Detective Baker if he could recommend a firing range for me to practice shooting my .38 caliber handgun. I'd always shot guns on the farm back in Indiana but figured I needed to be sharp with everything that was going on around me.

"I know the perfect place. It's owned by a good friend of mine. I'll go with you and give you a few pointers. They have plenty of .38 rounds there, so we won't have to stop to buy any. They call me 'Dead Eye' around here," he said with a smirk.

I was glad he was going with me. I was anxious about what Victor's next move was going to be. Ethan dead…Tiffany, or whatever her name was, dead…Mr. Morris dying…it was too much in a short period.

Piper and I met Baker at his friend's firing range. I was a little rusty at first but soon was back in my farmgirl form, hitting near the bull's-eye with each shot. Since Baker knew the owner, he allowed Piper to fire some rounds, as well. She learned her way around the gun but didn't come close to the target. By now I was exhausted. Besides, now that Tom was gone, I wanted to corner Piper and probe her more on her life with her mom and why Victor wanted her so badly.

We picked up a couple of plates of shrimp etouffee and went to the condo. I didn't waste any time sneaking up on the subject of Piper and her mother. I'd learned from my journalistic endeavors that if you wanted to ferret out facts, you often had to ask direct questions.

"So, Piper, you said you did try to call your mom on her cell phone after she sent you to your dad's house in Chicago?"

Piper looked at me sheepishly. "I wasn't supposed to. She and Katerina gave me strict orders not to contact either one of them."

"Did you?"

"I tried. I called mom's cell phone over and over. It usually went to voice mail. I'd leave messages begging her to call me. I wanted to go back to LA to live with her. She didn't answer or call me back. I know it was the heroin. She must have been out of it. Eventually, the phone was disconnected. I tried to call Katerina, but she never would answer, either. Then my dad was killed, and you know the rest."

"I've noticed you are quite good with computers. Where did you learn?"

"Katerina taught me quite a bit to get me started. From there I learned on my own. I loved working on the computer. Mom and Katerina made me hide what I knew from the other girls. I stayed up all night long almost every night surfing the web. I discovered the dark web. I learned to use the Tor browser and others to go to sites you can't get to using your regular browsers. I saw several of Victor's porn and prostitution sites."

"How were you able to get into those sites?" I asked.

"Once I started surfing the dark web, I found sites that taught hacking," Piper replied. "I learned HTML and other code the web uses to create sites. I found it easy, maybe because I loved it so much. Once, when Victor pissed me off really bad, I hacked one of his sites and shut it down. He crapped his pants trying to figure out who did it."

"So Victor has his own programmers?" I asked.

"Oh yeah. My mom and Katerina were afraid if he knew what I was able to do, he'd send me to Eastern Europe or Moscow to work with his hacking group. They said I was a hacking prodigy. I think that's why my mom sent me away. She'd messed her life up with heroin, and I guess she didn't want Victor to make me become one of his hackers in Eastern Europe or a prostitute. Victor was going to make me do one or the other. No one got a free ride. I am so scared, Alexandra, that he'll hurt you or Tom to get me. I love you and want you to be safe."

It all started to make sense to me. Victor must have discovered her hacking abilities, and he wanted her to do his dirty work. He wanted to ship her to a country with corrupt law enforcement and turn her into a criminal. His sick mind calculated she could only make a few hundred dollars on her back but she could make millions with her mind. He probably would do anything to get his hands on her. How often would he get a chance to have a computer prodigy working for him? Especially one so young, so easily controlled? No wonder he was willing to go all in to get her. I was beginning to think better of her mom for sending her away. Victor would have used Sandy against Piper and had her just where he wanted her.

"Don't worry, baby. We'll figure something out." I didn't know if I was trying to convince her or myself. I didn't feel too optimistic about her mother. Victor had doubtless punished her severely.

I couldn't talk to Piper about that. I was already regretting letting Tom go to Mexico. I needed him here with me to face Victor's attack on our family. I knew this was going to get ugly.

Piper didn't look reassured. Her eyes darted back and forth as if she were looking for a place to hide, her mouth curved downward. She was scared and so was I, but I dared not show her how scared I really was. To break the heavy mood, I changed the subject to Mandy and her invitation to take us on the cemetery tour. Not my idea of a happy subject, but Piper perked right up as soon as I mentioned the haunted tour. This was something she really wanted to do, so I phoned Mandy to set it up.

"Mandy, when would you like to take Piper and me on your cemetery tour?"

"Alexandra, I am so happy you called. As a matter of fact, I'm taking some of my friends on a tour tonight. Would you and Piper like to join us?"

I looked at Piper, and she was bobbing her head up and down in exaggerated agreement. "Tonight would be perfect!"

"Great. Meet us at the Lafayette cemetery at ten tonight," Mandy said. "Lots of movies are shot there. She'll love it. We'll save the best for last, the St. Louis Cemetery, where Marie Laveau's grave is located."

Piper dug in her clothes until she found some black pants and a new black T-shirt emblazoned with the Grateful Dead's logo, a gift from Tom's parents, I concluded. I watched her eat the shrimp from the shrimp etouffee, pushing the rice aside. Her animated face glowed with excitement at the thought of touring the haunted cemeteries of New Orleans.

We joined Mandy and her friends at the first cemetery, and we had to sneak through a broken section of a rusted gate to get in. Once inside the city of the dead, we strolled around brick and plaster structures listening to Mandy explain the burial practices of the city. All of the tombs were above ground since the water table in New Orleans would float any caskets buried below ground back to the surface. Mandy's friends were all dressed in black, eerily similar to each other. They resembled an army of morose cadets. Their appearance unnerved me but thrilled Piper. As we walked through the graveyard streets, I couldn't help but think of how each of these lives once contributed to the fabric of New Orleans. We made our way to the St. Louis Cemetery and trouped to Marie Laveau's grave. A solemn figure kneeled beside the white plaster edifice, dressed in black as Mandy's friends were. She was praying. As we approached, the figure turned to face us. It was Amanda, the young girl I'd comforted in the jail in Mexico. What the hell was she doing here? After touching her lips with two fingers and moving them toward us, she resumed her prayer. I watched in astonishment as each of the members of our group made the same gesture to her. Mandy began her diatribe about Marie Laveau's life as Amanda joined the group. After a five-minute history lesson, Mandy walked up to Marie's grave and made an X mark. I was transfixed watching each one of her friends do the same.

I turned to comment to Piper how uneasy this scene made me, but she wasn't there. I looked all through the group but couldn't see her.

I called her name. She didn't answer. Then I raced through the group yelling, not caring how loud I was being, when I hit my knee on a tombstone.

She was gone. So was Amanda. I screamed "Piper!" loud enough to disturb the dead. Still, no answer. Mandy and her group, once alerted to the problem, spread out to help me look for her. I was in a state of panic. I couldn't believe it. Piper was gone.

Maybe she sneaked off to pee or something. Then I saw it, lying on the ground by a mausoleum, the pink case glowing in the dim light. Piper's cell phone. *Maybe it isn't hers*, I thought. I picked it up to look more closely. It was definitely Piper's cell. My face turned as white as the dead's. I called the only person I thought could help.

"Detective Baker, help me, please! This is Alexandra Lee. Piper is gone! I think she's been kidnapped!"

CHAPTER SEVENTEEN
DESPERATE SEARCH

I GOT ALL of the members of Mandy's black brigade to pair up to look for Piper. Each pair walked along a different paved path between the graves, calling Piper's name. Three police units rolled up and corralled our group together. One of the officers stayed with our group while the others took up the search. Detective Baker arrived and stayed with us, allowing the other officer to join the search. As Baker questioned me, a police van's lights illuminated Mandy and her group.

Detective Baker spun around to face Mandy and her friends. "Please go with these officers in this van to the precinct. Your cooperation will greatly assist us in finding the lost young lady. Thank you."

I found Detective Baker's calm demeanor oddly sedating. "What would you like me to do?" I asked.

He requested that I give him a detailed history of Piper and her recent activities. I told him everything leading up to Piper coming to stay with us, some of which he knew. I repeated the conversation she'd had with me earlier before we joined Mandy for the tour. Detective Baker and I both agreed that Victor seemed to be the most likely person to have taken her. I paced back and forth in the cemetery parking lot for two hours as the officers conducted their thorough search. Piper was not there.

Detective Baker asked me to follow him to the precinct. When we arrived, the other officers had just completed their interrogation of Mandy and her friends. We ran smack into Jaeger. How did he know to be here? According to the interrogating officers, none of the tour group had any helpful information. Nobody had seen her get taken. Nobody had seen any suspicious people or heard sounds of a scuffle. It was unnerving how quickly and quietly she'd vanished from a group of people with not one person noticing. Of course, these weren't the best witnesses in the world, but what about me? I should have kept an eye on her. I'd known the danger. Guilt raced through me, but I forced it away. It wouldn't help.

The realization set in that Piper was gone, and I had to keep my wits about me to help find her. Tom needed to know. He had to come home and help us look for her. I called his cell over and over again to no avail. *Damn him and his ROLL organization*, I thought. Why wasn't he here when I needed him? *Calm down, Alexandra. You've been through worse than this.*

"Bring her into the interrogation room," Jaeger said to Detective Baker.

Baker gave Jaeger one of those you've-got-to-be-kidding looks, rolling his eyes to the top of his head. Jaeger wasn't fazed. He acted like a machine on an assembly line, doing the only thing he knew how to do, pursue Victor. Jaeger had the bedside manner of a vampire, flat-toned and cold. His questions were his fangs trying to suck information out of me. I was in no mood for his insensitive German attitude, so I kept my answers short, giving only the least amount of information I could. Jaeger didn't give a damn about Piper.

Satisfied he'd gotten all he could from me, he walked out of the room. Baker stood up and asked me to follow him to his office.

"Alexandra, I don't want Jaeger to hear this," Baker said. "Jaeger is heading up the search for Piper. Piper's disappearance isn't technically a NOPD matter yet. She hasn't been gone long enough for the missing person's unit to get involved, and there's no evidence of foul play, either. No crime, no police. My hands are tied."

My face fell. No way I could trust Jaeger to find Piper and bring her home safe. I needed to take charge myself. "I understand," I said. I knew what I was going to do as soon as I left the police station. I needed to go into the shadows where the demons live. I, like most people, went about my daily life ignoring the dark underworld of the city. That world reeked of crime, dirty dealings, murder, and treachery.

"Alexandra, I'm afraid there's more bad news. There are serious problems at Sarah's House for Battered and Abused Women. We are executing a search warrant this morning at the center, and I'd like you to stay away from there."

I slumped in my chair searching his eyes for an explanation. "Search warrant? I thought you'd already searched the center? What are you looking for? Why do I need to stay away?"

"I can't tell you the details now. Wouldn't be right. Besides, it would just put you in more danger than you are already in. I'll fill you in after we execute the warrant. I just need you to stay away for now. You need to focus your energy on finding Piper. Maybe you should go see Jess Johnson. She's got more contacts on the street than anyone I know. The problems at the center are police matters now."

Just as my head was about to explode, I received a text from Charlotte.

Alexandra, can you meet with Mr. Morris and me today? It's really important.

I'm really tied up. Can it wait until next week? I texted back.

No, sorry. We need to meet with you today.

Oh shit, now what? Charlotte was not one to insist unless it was absolutely necessary. Okay. I'll meet you at Mr. Morris's office at 2 p.m.

Maybe Mandy knew where Piper was and she'd told her dad? Wild thoughts were cascading through my mind. I had to slow my brain down and keep it on track. What I really wanted to do was trade my pistol for an army tank and start blasting away at Victor, Jaeger, and the Dixie Mafia.

I bolted out of the police station to my car. The sun was up and the city was coming to life. I was headed to the bowels of the French Quarter. Clinton Cunningham and I needed to talk. If he was involved in Piper's disappearance, I was going to beat her whereabouts out of him.

I walked into his strip club on lower Bourbon Street like a gunfighter swaggering into a saloon. Even though the day's sun was only three hours old, a stripper was on the pole and customers were in the bar. The smell of old, stale liquor and cigarette smoke stung my nostrils. I trouped past the bar directly to Clint's office. There he was, butted up to his desk as close as his fat gut would allow him to get. He didn't flinch when I entered. He just lit the cheap cigar in his mouth.

"I've been waiting for you to get here," he said. "Take a load off."

I sat across the desk from him and sneered into his cold, criminal eyes. "Where the fuck is Piper?" I barked.

A slight smile lifted his jowls. "What makes you think I know anything about her?"

Angry, murderous thoughts filled my mind, and I said, "You and the other shadow demons who prey on the desperate and the vulnerable know when someone who lives in the light gets dragged into the darkness where you dwell. If you didn't take her, then you know who did."

"You are right. Usually I know everything that happens on the streets of this city. But with so many new players in the game now, some of my channels are blocked. I don't know where she is. Victor may have her. Word on the street is he wants to ship her out of the country when he gets his hands on her. I can tell you he hasn't taken her through the airport or I'd know."

"You need to find her," I said.

"Or what?" Clint said. "You don't come in here and threaten me, you little bitch. If I snap my fingers, you'll end up as gator food in the Atchafalaya swamp. And…you wouldn't be the first."

I paused before I spoke my next words. I didn't care that I was on his turf. I looked him directly in his lifeless eyes and said, "New

Orleans is about to read about the Dixie Mafia's history of crime and their current depraved activities. They'll learn about the hookers you put on the streets, the cops you own, and the drugs you distribute. What do you think your boss in the penitentiary will think of that?"

Clint drew in a deep breath and sneered at me with contempt. "Okay, bitch. I'll put my feelers out. But I'm not risking any of my guys to get her back for you. I've got my own beef with Victor. If the little girl gets caught in the crossfire, it's not my problem."

I stormed out of his office, slamming the door behind me. I went straight to *The Times* to see Jess, the most street-connected newspaper editor in the US. As always, I walked past security directly into Jess's office.

"Detective Baker told me about the young lady's disappearance," she said as I entered. "Sorry to hear about it. Would you like a cup of coffee? I'd sure like another one."

We retrieved our coffees and scooted back to her office. "I have run the traps on the street, Alexandra. All I can tell you right now is that the Dixie Mafia doesn't have her. They are freaked out by Victor moving in on them. He's a vicious killer. He and his Russian Mafia are trying to control prostitution and drugs in all of the major convention cities. He's in Orlando, Atlanta, Los Angeles, and Nashville already. Maybe more than that."

"Do you know where he's staying?" I asked.

"Why? What are you going to do? Walk up to him and threaten him? He'd laugh in your face. You've got to go about this smarter than that."

"Jess, I really don't know what to do. That's why I'm here. Can you help me?"

Her normally stern demeanor softened. "Yes, child, I can help. Victor is in the Marriott Hotel in Baton Rouge. He is smart, Alexandra, and he knows he has to have some politicians in his pocket. He always combines brute force with political influence to move against his prey. He's spreading some money around the Louisiana legislative halls, working the unscrupulous politicians in BR just like lobbyists do."

"Do you think Piper is with him in Baton Rouge?" I asked.

"Not very likely. If he's taken her, he'd have already shipped her away from Louisiana. Give me a day or so and I'll find out exactly what happened to her."

Oh shit, I thought. In a day or more she could be on her way to Eastern Europe to be Victor's super hacker. *I don't have a day to wait*, I thought. But what could I do? Jess was right. I couldn't go to Baton Rouge to confront Victor. He would just laugh in my face or worse. No, I had to wait for Jess to scour the city. If Piper were still in the city, Jess would find her.

Time was flying by. I had to hit the road to meet Charlotte and Mr. Morris. Holy shit, I was still in the same clothes I wore to go on the cemetery tour. I needed a shower and a change of clothes. As I sped across the downtown streets, I tried Tom's cell again. Straight to voice mail. Something was wrong. No way he would ignore my calls.

I must admit having a shower and clean clothes calmed me a little. When I arrived at Superior Sugar's office, I noticed some changes. Two of the three flags hoisted on the poles in front of the building were flying at their normal height. The Superior Sugar flag was at half-mast. I asked the security guard if someone had died but received no answer, only a somber look and a slow escort into Mr. Morris' office. Charlotte stood facing the window, gazing into the distance. She caught my reflection in the glass and spun to greet me. My eyes met her reddened eyes. She'd been crying. Did she know about Piper? Did she know something I didn't?

"What's wrong?" I asked.

"Please sit down," Charlotte said. "I've asked one of the staff members to bring us coffee."

We sat with our coffee in a deadly silence until Mr. Morris spoke. "Alexandra, I have been told my cancer is stage four," Mr. Morris said. "It's much worse than they originally thought. I have to undergo dangerous treatments that I might not survive."

Tears streamed down Charlotte's face. She hunched her shoulders forward and she cried openly as I sat stunned by the news. Mr. Morris still looked so healthy. He looked the same today as he did the last time we met. Charlotte, on the other hand, looked like she hadn't slept in days. She wasn't her elegant, always perfectly put together self.

"I am going to fight it as hard as I can," Mr. Morris said. "My doctor is putting me through an intense round of chemotherapy treatments in Houston. He's also ordered me to reduce the stress in my life, so I've decided to step down as president of Superior Sugar. My brother, Garrett, will be taking over. Charlotte told me you met him in Vegas at the Processed Foods Show. Charlotte and I are going to develop the stevia company. Will you help us?"

"Mr. Morris. I don't know what to say. I am so sorry to hear about your illness," I said. "You can count on me one hundred percent."

"Things are moving quickly. Our lawyers are working on the paperwork to put Garrett in charge of Superior Sugar. The stevia company is being spun off, and I will own all of the stock in that company. My doctors have opened my eyes about sugar and its effects on the human body. I've learned that when we eat too much sugar and other simple carbohydrates, our bodies produce advanced glycation end products, a mouthful abbreviated to AGEs. These AGEs are byproducts of sugars and proteins reacting with each other. They careen through our bodies damaging all organs on a cellular level. AGEs help cause cancer, heart disease, Alzheimer's, inflammation, and kidney damage, just to list a few. I can't be a part of that plague anymore."

I assured Mr. Morris I would help in any way I could. I stayed with Charlotte for a while to make certain she was alright. She didn't want to have anything to do with Superior Sugar if Garrett Morris was going to be in charge.

"He's a pervert, Alexandra. He gambles, goes to underground dog fighting matches, and likes young girls. He's always been a sick bastard," she said.

I remembered Jess Johnson and my old boss, Mr. Jenkins, warning me about him. I didn't need any more trouble in my life than I already had. I needed to find Piper. I left Charlotte and worked my blog to try to develop leads on Piper's whereabouts. I blogged until I fell asleep, nearly knocking myself out when my head hit the keyboard.

I went to bed and fell into a deep sleep. It was one of those nights where my dreams were so real I thought I was awake. I dreamed I chased Victor down a dark road that ended in the swamps. He got out of his car and ran through the mud by the water's edge. A huge gator popped out of the water and grabbed his leg. The gator rolled as he dragged Victor into the swamp. I froze and watched him disappear into the murky water. *Good riddance*, I said to myself as he sunk beneath the surface. When I finally woke up, it was morning, the sun beaming through the bedroom window.

I grabbed my cell. No call from Tom, but there was a missed call from Detective Baker. Maybe he'd found Piper. "Detective Baker, this is Alexandra. Did you find Piper?"

"No. No leads on Piper. We are trying to find this Amanda person you saw at Marie Laveau's grave. Without a last name, it's proving to be difficult," Baker said, trailing his voice down to a low tone. "Alexandra, there's something I need to let you know. I wanted to tell you myself. I just arrested Susan McAllister, the center's director, for murder."

CHAPTER EIGHTEEN
LOOKING FOR ANSWERS

"SUSAN ARRESTED? THERE must be some mistake," I said. "Susan would never hurt anyone. She is one of the most caring and loving people I know."

"How well do you know Ms. McAllister?" Baker asked.

"Well enough to know she'd never kill anyone," I said.

I dressed, my mind panicked, searching to make sense from the words I'd just heard, and drove to the police station. I felt like I was living in some type of alternate reality. Susan arrested for murder, Piper kidnapped, Tom not answering my calls, and Mr. Morris sick with cancer. What the hell was going on? Even though Detective Baker warned me not to, I drove to the center first. Susan's office had been ransacked by the police search. I tidied things up before I went to the family room to talk to the residents. I assured them that they were all safe and that the recent events weren't going to affect them. I only hoped I was telling them the truth.

When I arrived at the police station, Detective Baker was waiting for me in his office. There was a dark-haired woman sitting in his office with her back to me. I stopped at his door thinking maybe I was intruding until I heard the woman speak. *That voice, I know that voice,*

I thought. It was Sophia, the Interpol agent who'd battled Bart Rogan with me. She was a sight for sore eyes.

"Sophia!" I screamed.

She stood, turned around, and flashed the broadest smile I'd seen in many months. Sophia threw her arms around me and hugged me tightly. I trembled with joy, feeling the warmth of a trusted friend in this time of need. She would help me work my way through all of this. I knew she would. At least that is what I told myself as tears of joy eased their way down my cheeks.

"Sophia, you look good. Are you okay?" I asked.

"Yes, the doctors in Paris say I am completely healed. It's so good to see you, Alexandra. Detective Baker was just filling me in on your problems."

"That's why I'm here. Detective Baker, how in the world could you ever think Susan McAllister could be guilty of murder?"

"Sit down, Alexandra. I'll tell you what we've found. We received a tip that Ms. McAllister poisoned Tiffany at the shelter. The tipster said she kept the poison in her car. I obtained a warrant and found a vial in her glove compartment. The lab advised us that it contained pure aconite, the deadly poison also known as wolf's bane. It's the same one I talked to you about earlier. Though the autopsy report isn't final, the coroner's conclusion is that Tiffany was poisoned with aconite."

"She's being set up. I know she wouldn't hurt anyone," I said.

Sophia listened, raised her eyebrows slightly, and brought her hand to her mouth. "What do you know of Ms. McAllister's past, Alexandra?"

"Very little. I know she came from a broken home. She has dedicated her life to helping abused women."

Baker leaned forward in his chair. He grabbed his computer mouse in his right hand and clicked on the screen. "There's a great deal you don't know about her. Let me read the background report our investigators have compiled. Susan McAllister was born in Alexandria, Louisiana in 1948. Her parents were Marty, a.k.a. Martha, and David McAllister. She attended Catholic school until her graduation from high school in 1964. Her father, an oilfield roughneck, was arrested six times for domestic battery, mostly from beating his wife, Marty. The couple stayed together despite their troubles. In 1964, two days after Susan's graduation from high school, her father died. The coroner's autopsy revealed he was poisoned with aconite. Marty McAllister was arrested and found guilty of murder. She served twelve years in the Louisiana Correctional Institute for Women in St. Gabriel, Louisiana. Susan moved to Baton Rouge a few miles from the prison to be close to her mom."

"That doesn't mean anything other than she's had a rough life. Just because her mother poisoned her father doesn't mean she is guilty of poisoning a woman she barely knew," I said.

"You are right, Alexandra. It doesn't prove her guilt. It does prove she was aware of the effects of aconite as a poison," Baker said.

"What possible motive would Susan have for murdering Tiffany?" I asked Baker.

"I can't tell you everything our investigation has revealed. But I can tell you we interviewed all of the people at the center. Some told us Tiffany complained to Ms. McAllister about the living conditions at the center. She intended to complain to the Department of Family Services in Baton Rouge. She was killed before she could lodge her complaint."

"Something is terribly wrong," I said. "There is no way Susan did this. Has her bond been set? I want to bail her out."

"The judge has refused to set bail in this case until he gets more facts. She will be given a hearing to determine what the bail amount will be if granted at all. So, for the present, she isn't going anywhere," Baker said.

"Can I see her?" I asked.

My exasperation must have been evident. I was wringing my hands together. Sophia put her hand on mine and spoke to Detective Baker. "I'll go with her. Can you arrange a visit?"

"It's highly irregular, but I'll see what I can do," Baker said, shrugging his shoulders.

Baker said he'd call us when he had arranged the visit. Sophia and

I went to Starbucks to catch up with each other. Sitting with Sophia calmed me a bit. I needed a break from all of the craziness going on. It gave me time to tell her all about Piper and her disappearance. She was amused to hear that Mandy Morris was dressing in black and leading haunted tours of cemeteries. Sophia thought it very odd that I hadn't heard from Tom, and she promised to find out what she could about him through her police connections in Mexico.

"I know Victor is behind everything that has happened at the center, Sophia. I have brought all of this trouble down on the heads of Susan and the residents. They are innocent bystanders, collateral damage as the Dixie Mafia calls them. I must find a way to stop Victor. If he has Piper, I'll never see her again. I can't let that happen."

"Alexandra, we have another problem, too. Jaeger is obsessed with trapping Victor. I think he wants Victor dead. Victor is the grandson of Nikolai Ivanovich, a Soviet intelligence officer during World War II. He was responsible for expelling thousands of Germans from of Russia because he suspected they were Nazi sympathizers. More than a thousand died during the trip. Jaeger's entire family perished on the train. Only an infant at the time, he was the lone survivor. He wants revenge, and he considers punishing Victor his responsibility to his family."

"Oh, great! He's lived his life brooding about how to even the score with the Russians. He's putting my family in the middle of his seven-and-a-half-decade grudge fight. He's as bad as Victor."

"Yes. I'm afraid you are right, Alexandra. At his age, I guess he feels he has nothing to lose," Sophia said with the caring compassion of a nurse treating wounded soldiers on the front lines. Sophia was an odd mix of seasoned police hardness and Colombian softness. She was the type of person who could wrestle a cartel member to the ground and handcuff him, then rescue his cat from a tree. She possessed a delicate balance of fire and ice bubbling under her smooth, tan Colombian skin.

"Sophia, I know you are here on your vacation time. Would you like to stay at my condo? If I can't bail Susan out of jail, I'll have to move into the center. That way if Piper comes back to the condo, she won't think I abandoned her. I know my condo may bring up some bad memories for you and I completely understand if you don't want to stay there."

"I'd love to stay there. I've long since put getting knifed by El Serpiente behind me. If we are going to get Piper back and run Victor out of town, we need to have all of our bases covered. No telling how long this will take to play out," she said.

Two hours passed and Detective Baker hadn't called. Sophia and I cruised to my condo to settle her in. I grabbed my computer to check my blog. An anonymous blog post from Mobile told a story about Victor moving into the Alabama Gulf Coast. He infiltrated the locals, using his own hookers to recruit others. Those that didn't sign on with him met a brutal end. She attached a photo of one of Victor's lead girls that had been sent into Mobile. There was no mistaking that face. It was Tiffany. Her name in Mobile was Blaze. Her post was clear evidence that she was tied to Victor. I showed the post to Sophia.

"We have to get this to Detective Baker," I said. "We can print it out after I get my things together. Maybe we'll get more information when others read the post."

I packed some clothes to tide me over while I stayed at the center. It took me longer than normal to pack. I'm usually a throw-a-few-clothes-in-a-bag-and-head-out kinda girl, but not today. I had no idea how long I'd have to stay at the center. I'd learned legal matters have a life of their own.

I returned to my computer to print the post, but the site wasn't up. I tried to surf back to the site but kept getting an error message. Maybe it was me. Sophia also tried to find the site, without any luck. She attempted to navigate to it on her smartphone, too. It was becoming painfully obvious that the site had crashed, and I had a sinking feeling that Victor's hackers were behind it. Try as we might, we couldn't find it. The site was gone.

I still hadn't heard from Detective Baker. *He must be having trouble getting me in to see Susan*, I thought. I couldn't wait any longer. I asked Sophia to try to find out what she could about Tom in Mexico. I was lucky she came to help me. With her Latin American contacts, she would have a better than average chance of finding Tom. She cranked up her phone before I even got to the door, and I headed to the shelter. Susan getting locked up had to have frightened the hell out of the residents, and they were going to need some explanations.

When I arrived at the center, I was almost attacked by the women, asking me if Susan was responsible for Tiffany's death. I tried my best to reassure them, but I had to be careful. I didn't have any real facts. I hoped that telling them everything was going to be okay would get them through the night.

Some of the new girls expressed their skepticism. "Are we going to be okay here? Are the police coming back to question us? Is this place safe for our children?"

I looked over the room at the scared faces before I spoke. "Please, everyone just calm down. This shelter is a sanctuary for all of you. You are safe here. I will stay as long as needed to make certain you are all taken care of. This is a time to pull together for the benefit of each other and your children. Why don't we have a pizza night? I'll spring for pizza for everyone." I barely got the words out before the kids shouted in agreement. It seemed to calm the room. Good old pizza therapy. Always worked for me.

Most of the ladies talked to me one on one. A couple of the newcomers expressed their concern about staying at the center but decided to hang in there with us. I was relieved we didn't have a mass exodus. The newspaper would have pounced on a story like that, and it would have been devastating to the center's future. As it was, I was going to have to deal with the neighbors' cries to relocate. I didn't need any sensationalized stories with headlines like "Murder Causes Battered Women to Flee." My damage control seemed to be working.

I walked into Susan's office and shut the door behind me. I needed to think about the situation I'd placed myself in. Now I was committed to staying at the center while Susan was away. How would I be able to look for Piper and take care of the center at the same time? I was feeling overwhelmed, like the world was crashing down on me. *Why did I take on all of these responsibilities?* I asked myself. I had reached my dream life. I was a successful journalist with a hot boyfriend and a steady income. What led me to become a makeshift mother to a young girl and a caretaker of a facility for battered women? What did I do to myself? *Well, Alexandra, that's not what you do. That's who you are,* I thought. *You were raised with a loving family who showed you unconditional love. Your mother gave the last years of her life to allow you to go to college. Your father showed you as much tenderness, caring, and love as was possible, considering dementia was controlling his mind. You have created the twenty-first-century version of a modern family. Tom and Piper are your nuclear family. Susan and the center's residents are your extended family.* "You are a family woman!" I said out loud.

I looked around the room, and for some reason saying it out loud made me look at the world differently. My family was under attack, and I needed to fight to protect them. The feeling boiled inside me. I felt anger stream through my thoughts as I clenched my teeth. I asked myself, *How do you fight the ones trying to hurt your family?* The answer was completely clear. I had to go after them. I had to seek them out, force them from the shadows, and eradicate them. Sure they were dangerous, but so was I.

I surfed the web for the telephone number of the Marriott Hotel in Baton Rouge. I entered the hotel's digits in my phone and pressed Send. I pushed so hard I nearly broke the glass.

"Thank you for calling the Marriott. How may I assist you?"

Through clenched teeth, I said, "Please give me Victor Ivanovich's room."

"My pleasure," the operator said.

As the phone rang the room, I felt my stomach churning. I was afraid for sure, but I wanted to confront this demon.

"Hello, this is Victor."

"Victor, this is Alexandra Lee. When can we meet?"

"Oh, hi, Alexandra. So nice to talk to you. I'd love to see you. Let's have lunch tomorrow at Gino's Restaurant in Baton Rouge. Can you meet me there at noon?"

Of course I knew all about Gino's Restaurant. Everybody who'd ever been in Baton Rouge knew it. It was the finest Italian food in the city. "I'll be there," I said and hung up.

CHAPTER NINETEEN
LION'S DEN

~

I WAS AWAKENED by the sound of my phone. It was Detective Baker. He'd finally arranged for me to visit Susan at central lockup. Holy shit, it was eight o'clock in the morning. I'd slept late a second time. Baker had arranged for me to meet Susan at nine, so I had to get a move on to make it in time.

After my shower I looked in my closet, completely perplexed about what to wear. Should I dress for central lockup or for Gino's and Victor? I opted for the dressier look. It might sound odd that I'd be thinking of my appearance, but the reason was simple: all day I would be representing my family, who was in danger. I didn't want to be treated as a lesser person by the police or by the criminal. Dressing well was my way of declaring I was important and should be treated with respect.

The New Orleans Central Lockup was a miserable place. The battleship gray walls and bars were cold, hard reminders of the world away from the world I was entering. I felt like I was going to a secret place where society hid its trash so the tourists wouldn't see that part of the city. It was clean yet smelled dirty. And it was quiet except for the blare of police radios and the clanking of bars. As I entered a holding area, I heard the loud metal against metal of the steel bars closing behind me. It felt final, and I felt like I'd entered a world where I was no longer a person. I was a numbered unit to be guided to my assigned spot and then processed out again.

As I was escorted to a small room with a table and a few chairs, I heard a deputy say, "McAllister, walk this way."

Susan walked into the room. Her makeup-free face was pale, much like Tiffany's except Susan was upright and not on a gurney. Color had abandoned her cheeks, and her eyelashes were brownish gray, her pallor matching the walls. She walked zombie fashion as if she had been hypnotized. I stood to hug her tight but, before we embraced, the guard stepped between us, instructing me not to have physical contact with the inmate.

"Susan, I am so sorry this has happened to you. How are you feeling?"

She sat across the table looking at me with hollow eyes. "Alexandra, I didn't hurt anyone. They say I murdered Tiffany. Why would I hurt Tiffany? I love all of those girls. Tell them. Tell them, Alexandra. I love those girls."

Tears ran freely down her face and dripped on the metal table where she'd rested her arms. Her chest heaved, drawing in a deep breath, which created a rattling sound as she exhaled. She wiped her eyes with her limp hands but couldn't stop the unbridled flow.

"Do you have a lawyer?" I asked.

"Lawyer? No, I don't have a lawyer. I never had any need for one. The center has been my whole life. All I have to my name is about $1,000 in a checking account. I don't think that's enough to hire a lawyer. Some of the other ladies in here tell me the court will appoint a lawyer for me."

"No way," I said. "I will get you a lawyer tomorrow. Don't worry, Susan, I'll find a way to get you out of here. Do you have any idea how the bottle with the poison got in your car?"

"No. I only use my car for errands and to take the girls to the medical center. I keep it locked when I'm not in it. I have no idea how the bottle got in my car. Thank you, Alexandra, for helping me. I don't know what to do. I feel so lost. I am scared I'll be put in jail for a long time even though I didn't do anything. Who'll take care of the center?"

"Susan, don't worry about the center. I will stay there until we get this cleared up. I have to leave now. I'll have a lawyer contact you tomorrow. Don't worry, we'll get through this."

"Thank you, Alexandra. Thank you for your strength. It's been a long time since I felt this kind of fear."

Oh my God, Susan was totally out of it. She was lost in that place. I didn't know how long she could remain sane in there. I felt so bad, believing I'd brought this down on her. Now I had to go see that bastard Victor in Baton Rouge. What could he want with me? If he wanted to meet me, he didn't have Piper yet.

I guess that is good news, I thought.

The drive to Baton Rouge was beautiful. It was a lovely summer day. When I crossed Lake Pontchartrain, I saw a ten-foot alligator searching for lunch. Funny. Was this some type of omen? Was Victor the gator looking for me to lunch on? Or maybe it was the gator from my dream and I should invite it to come with me.

I had news for Mr. Ivanovich. I wasn't going to be anyone's victim. I reached down and patted my ankle holster. I felt better for a second, but then my thoughts wandered to Tom. Was he okay? I knew he was in Southern Mexico. Maybe he didn't have cell reception in that part of the country. Thank God Sophia was in New Orleans. With her Interpol and other law enforcement contacts, I felt confident she would be able to find Tom no matter where he was.

As I entered the city limits of Baton Rouge, I remembered how different it was from New Orleans. I attended LSU to get my journalism degree, which seemed like a hundred years ago. Baton Rouge was much more conservative than New Orleans. Then again, anywhere in America was more conservative than New Orleans. But by national personal behavior standards, Baton Rouge was liberal. There were more bars—as well as places that masqueraded as restaurants, selling more alcohol than food—than in any other capital city. Drive-by daiquiri shops, hard liquor in every store including pharmacies, and festivals galore with vendors selling beer to all old enough to buy it enchanted the Baton Rouge landscape. Residents were conservative in their political views but not in their partying habits. LSU football game day merriment rivaled Carnival in Rio. Food, fun, and football summed up this river city.

I was greeted at Gino's by a stunning hostess. She scanned me in an instant and said, "You must be Alexandra. Let me show you to Victor's table."

Impressive, I thought. Victor's table was situated in a private room in the rear of the restaurant, complete with a white tablecloth and candle. Victor was on the telephone, and he immediately terminated the call and stood to greet me as I entered the room. He was more strikingly handsome than I'd remembered from my two brief sightings of him in New Orleans, and he moved like a jungle animal. His powerful shoulders were discernible under his sports coat. His thick black eyebrows framed the clearest iridescent green eyes I'd ever seen. He smiled, exposing a perfect set of teeth contrasted by his naturally tan skin, partially covered by a scruffy shadow beard. Just like I thought the first day I saw him, I'd never seen a more handsome man in my life.

"Alexandra, please sit down. Let me order you something to drink. Would you care for a vodka martini? I believe it's your drink of choice."

Holy shit. He knew what I drank. His voice was smooth and hypnotic with a slight European accent. I almost wanted to drink with him, his cologne wafting my way. Subtle but alluring. I felt an attraction to this monster, forgetting what he really was. No wonder Piper's mother, Sandy, fell for him. He was close to perfect.

"No, I'll just have water."

The Miss America look-alike hostess left us to retrieve the drinks. "Why don't you take a few minutes to look over the menu," Victor said.

I'd eaten at Gino's when I was at LSU. It served the finest Italian food I'd ever eaten. Mama Marino, an immigrant from Sicily now well into her eighties, still supervised the preparation of each of the authentic dishes. I settled on shrimp champagne, described as fresh shrimp, sautéed with butter, green onions, and the chef's special champagne sauce, and pasta. Victor ordered marinara pasta with homemade Italian sausage. This would be an enjoyable feast under different circumstances.

"So, Alexandra, you were born in Silbee, Indiana on a corn farm. You must find New Orleans much different from your hometown."

I stiffened, startled that he knew where I was born. "Yes, much different. But how did you know where I was born?"

"I know a great deal about you, Alexandra. For example, you live in a condo and have a boyfriend named Tom. I also know Tom is out of the country, currently a guest of the Mexican government. I know you had a nasty run-in with a man named Bart Rogan and one of my other friends, but we'll get to that later. I also know you are a very talented public relations expert and journalist. Words are weapons in your hands. You can be lethal if provoked. I want to be your friend and not your enemy."

"Friend? You must be kidding me. What you really want is Piper. You want to take her away from me and use her to further your criminal enterprises. She is just a young girl. She's not your property. You can't just send her to work for you in Russia or wherever you have your hacking farm. She is my family, and I'll fight you to the death if I have to."

"Why so dramatic? Who filled your head with such nonsense? It's true she is very talented on the computer, but she needs her education and her family. You say you are her family; well, so am I. I took Constance and her mother into my house and cared for them. Her mother became very important to me, and she misses her daughter. So you see, Alexandra, we each have a connection to Constance. We both need to do what's best for her. I possess the resources to develop her God-given talents into something spectacular. You don't have the resources to come close to that.

"I have a proposition for you. Why don't you and Constance both work for me? You can help me develop my spa chain into a nationwide enterprise, and I'll make certain she gets the best education possible."

I couldn't believe my ears. He actually was trying to make me believe he was a legitimate businessman. He wanted me to do PR for his whorehouses disguised as spas. My blood boiled. I sneered at him across the table. I could reach down, draw my .38 revolver, and shoot him in the head just like Michael Corleone in *The Godfather*. Maybe it wasn't a great idea, but it was tempting.

"I don't want anything to do with you and your criminal enterprises. You disgust me. You prey on vulnerable young girls with your good looks and smooth manner. You turn them into drug-addicted zombie whores, ruining their lives. No, I won't work for you, but I will stop you. I don't know how and I don't know when, but I promise you, if you come near me or my family, I will send you back to hell."

My rant was interrupted by my phone ringing. I looked at the caller ID but didn't recognize the number. I let it go to voice mail. When I looked back up at Victor he had a broad smile on his face, perfectly straight white teeth gleaming in the candlelight.

"You are exactly like my friend said you were. You met him in Colombia. They call him El Alacran. He and I are working together now. We are going into the import business in New Orleans. He is very excited to reunite with you. He said you and he have some unfinished business. I don't think he's a big fan of yours, but if we can find a way to work together, I'm sure he would let bygones be bygones."

These two assholes together could only mean trouble for anyone who crossed them. Still, scared as I was, I couldn't hold back. "You can both go fuck yourselves," I yelled as I stormed out of the restaurant.

I was fuming mad as I left Baton Rouge in my rearview mirror. I knew I had serious trouble ahead. I could have taken the easy path and made some type of deal, but I remembered my mother's warning that the devil always collects. I wanted nothing to do with the devil's protégé sitting at the table with me. I picked up my phone to call Sophia and saw I had a message. It was from a California area code. Maybe it was Piper's mother.

"Hi, Alexandra, it's Piper. Don't be mad at me. I ran away. I felt like I was putting you and Tom in danger. I wanted to find my mother, so I came to California. I am in Los Angeles. Call me back on this number. It is a burner cell phone. Don't give this number to anyone."

Oh my God, she was in California. How the hell did she get to California? She must have had the same idea I had—that Victor would punish her mother. I pulled off at the next exit to call her back. My hand trembled as I pressed the callback button.

A little voice said, "Hello."

I couldn't contain my emotions. I burst out in tears. "Piper—" I cried some more, big bellowing sobs. "H-how are you? Are you okay? What happened? I was so worried!"

"Yes, I'm okay," she said, crying, too. "I am so sorry that I left the way I did, but I thought Victor would hurt you or Tom if I stayed around."

I paused to take a breath. I was almost angry, but not angry. *Should I be angry?* I thought. No. She was a little girl.

"It's okay, sweetheart. I know you meant well. I'm booking a flight right away to come out there. How did you get to LA?"

"My computer skills are a little better than I told you. I hacked your and Tom's phones to get all of the contacts from them. I Googled all of them and found Amanda's blog. I chatted with her for many days and nights. We became close friends. I told her my mother was missing and I needed to go to California to find her. She helped me run away that night at the cemetery and paid for my bus ticket. Don't be mad at her. She thought she was helping."

"I'm not mad. I'm just upset because I thought I lost you. I'm so relieved you are okay. I was so desperate to find you I went to Baton Rouge to meet with Victor."

"You met with Victor?" Piper asked.

"I was meeting with him when you called and left the message."

"Oh no. You are going to have to get rid of your phone. If Victor got close to you, he cloned your phone. That means he can look at your texts, get all of your contacts, and even turn on the mic to listen to conversations. He's already gotten the number of this burner phone for sure and is tracking my location. I have to go. Go online and book your flight and hotel. I'll find you. I love you."

That was it. She hung up. Holy shit, he'd cloned my phone. *I bet he did it that morning at Café Du Monde*, I thought. That's how he'd been able to track me. No wonder he'd been able to move in on the Dixie Mafia's territory. He'd learned how to spy on them digitally.

He might have been a master at eavesdropping, but he didn't know where Piper was. I'd be in LA tomorrow to bring her home.

CHAPTER TWENTY
MAKING ARRANGEMENTS

~੭

I SPED ALONG I-10 toward New Orleans, feeling more than a little paranoid. I'd just told a Russian Mafia boss and his Colombian drug cartel buddy to go fuck themselves. Was I crazy? Maybe so, but there was no way I was going to make any deals with Victor or any other criminals. I'd seen the consequences compromising values had on people's lives, leading to complete destruction.

I thought about my conversation with Victor, and for some reason it stirred maternal feelings in me. I hadn't considered having children anytime soon, but now I felt like I was a mother. My instincts were to protect Piper at all costs; I had to go to LA to bring her home, and that meant I had to leave the center unattended. My path was clear. Tom and Piper were my family, and they were my first priority. The center would still be there when I returned. At least that's what I hoped.

Tom. What about Tom? I picked up my phone to call Sophia. Wait. Piper said Victor cloned my phone. He knew where I was and whom I was calling. I pulled my car over again along the shoulder. I extracted the SMS card from my cell phone and threw it in the swamp. From this point forward I had no communication with anyone, and I felt vulnerable, knowing I still had to cross the Lake Pontchartrain waterway. This bridge was the place the Scorpion gang attempted to run me into the swampy waters. I took my gun out of its holster and placed it on the seat next to me. If El Alacran's thugs were going to attack me, they were going to pay a steep price.

Fortunately I made it to my condo without any trouble. Sophia was seated at the kitchen table when I entered the condo, drinking a freshly brewed cup of coffee. Just what I needed.

"Let me tell you what I've found out about Tom," Sophia said. "He's sitting in a jail in Southern Mexico. He's been arrested for rioting and resisting arrest. Those are serious crimes in Mexico. I don't know what he did to get arrested, but I know he's in big trouble."

"Shit, Sophia. Tom wouldn't do anything like that. He went to protest, not riot. He certainly wouldn't have resisted arrest. Getting arrested is the goal of the protests. It brings attention to the cause. No, there's more to his arrest than they are telling you. What can we do?"

Sophia thought for a moment before she spoke. "I'll have to go to Mexico. I have friends in the government who will help me. I may be able to get him released to my custody. There is a great deal of corruption in Mexico. Tom probably crossed the wrong people, and it won't be easy to get him out, but at least I can try."

Once again tears filled my eyes as I hugged Sophia. She'd returned to the city to help me without hesitation and without knowing what we were up against. I told her about my visit to the New Orleans central lockup and my trip to Baton Rouge. She was shocked to hear Victor's proposal to me. Sophia knew about phone cloning and told me to use only burner phones until Victor was out of my life. She booked her flight to Mexico and promised to do her best to get Tom back safely to the US.

I checked my blog and email. I had an email from my lawyer, Joshua Clark. He'd written in the subject line "Important," so I opened it immediately.

Dear Alexandra,

I have some urgent business I must discuss with you. I called your cell but it went straight to voice mail. Please contact me as soon as you receive this email.

Respectfully,

Joshua

I emailed him back advising him I'd lost my phone but would check my email regularly and needed to see him this afternoon, if possible. He must have been on his computer when I sent my email because he responded instantly, agreeing to see me right away. As I navigated traffic, I revisited my conversation with Victor. He knew Tom was in Mexico, saying he was a guest of the Mexican government. I didn't make anything out of it at the time, but now I knew he probably had something to do with the charges against Tom. Was it a part of his master plan? I just hoped Sophia could use her connections to spring Tom and bring him safely back to the United States.

I walked into the law office, and the receptionist ushered me into the coffee room, instructing me to make myself at home. It disturbed me to think how comfortable I'd become in a law office. Before moving to New Orleans, I didn't even know a lawyer, but now I was forced to deal with one regularly. Had life become so complicated that lawyers would be involved in all aspects of my life? I hoped not.

Both lawyers, Mr. Swartz and Mr. Clark, entered the conference room, and Mr. Swartz took the floor. "Hi, Alexandra, have a seat. We have a couple of matters to discuss. First, as you know, when you settled with ACC for poisoning your farm's well, they agreed to pay for the cleanup. They agreed to allow you to choose the contractor and gave you thirty days to make your choice. I received a letter from ACC's lawyer pointing out that it has been in excess of ninety days and you haven't advised them of your choice. They are threatening to pull out of the agreement if you don't choose a contractor within the next thirty days. Secondly, regarding the custody of Constance Sanders, the judge has ordered a conference of all parties in two weeks."

"Who has to attend the conference?" I asked.

"The judge usually wants all of the parties and their lawyers to attend. Will that be a problem?"

"I should be available, but I'm not sure Tom will be."

"I see," Joshua said. "The judge will probably allow me to waive his presence. It will probably be good enough that you attend as Mr.

Sanders's significant other. Now, what about choosing a contractor for the remediation of the well on your farm in Indiana?"

"I'll find a contractor within the thirty days," I said. "I have something else to talk to you about. As you know, I am on the board of Sarah's House for Battered Women and intimately involved in its operations. The director, Susan McAllister, was arrested for murdering one of the residents. I know she is innocent. Do you handle criminal cases?"

"No, I don't," Swartz said, "but Mr. Clark does."

This was fantastic news because I liked Joshua's confident manner and felt he was the right person to help Susan. I laid the entire situation out to him, even giving him Susan's family's background. I transferred a $5,000 retainer into his account as he instructed. He promised to go see Susan immediately and start working on her defense. I felt a little better about leaving town. I just knew Victor was the one causing all of these problems. The only way to stop the problems was to stop Victor.

I went to my condo and found Zach and his sister, Maddy, chatting with Sophia. I hoped they had some good news, because I could sure use it.

Not today. I guess it just wasn't meant to be. Zach had been ordered by Jaeger to complete another mission. It seemed El Alacran was in New Orleans, and Jaeger and the Dixie Mafia needed Zach take some cash to him as a down payment for a heroin shipment. I warned him that Victor had just told me El Alacran was on his team, and it looked like Zach was being used as a pawn in a deadly game of chess. Only this wasn't a game. We were caught in a life and death struggle for the dark side of New Orleans, the parts that had always been there but went unnoticed by most of us in our day-to-day lives. These were hidden places where people with dark hearts flourished. Zach said Jaeger already knew El Alacran was doing business with Victor, and the cash was an effort to break him away. I begged Zach not to go and to break his ties with all of them.

"Zach," I pleaded, "El Alacran is a murderer. I watched him give the order to cut off an innocent, young woman's head just because her father refused to do business with him. Five minutes later they brought her head in to show me. Nightmares still haunt my sleep from that sight. El Alacran wanted to kill me, too, and he would have if he hadn't been stopped by Sophia's brother. He won't hesitate to kill you and cut your head off—or worse, torture you first. Please listen to me."

Zach couldn't meet my eyes, knowing I was right, his hands trembling slightly as he hesitated to answer me. He was trapped; his choices were to go to jail for a long time and risk getting his sister killed or face El Alacran. Zach was suffering the consequences of his decision to get involved with these dark forces. I guess he felt like it was too late to turn back now.

"If I pull this off, Maddy and I will be free," Zach said. "If they kill me, at least Maddy will be free. She is my only family. Nothing will stop me from trying to save her. I have to take the chance."

"I know these guys well," Sophia said, her eyes seeming to glaze as she spoke. "They recruit young boys to be their foot soldiers from grade school, and most are killed by rival gangs. They threaten and kill entire families who don't cooperate with them. I have seen every member of an entire family murdered and their heads placed on poles outside of their towns as a warning to those who might defy the cartel. You can't reason with them. You must stay away from them or you will suffer a fate like the villagers I described. You should listen to Alexandra."

All of our pleas fell on deaf ears, and he decided to go anyway. Maddy sat next to him crying the entire time, pulling at my heart-strings knowing I was powerless to help them. She and Zach were all each other had, and she might lose him. Though she was innocent, drugs led Zach down the wrong path, and now they were threatening to destroy both of them. But that's what happened when you dealt with the devil; there was always collateral damage.

It was time for Zach to go to his meeting, and I asked Maddy if she wanted to stay with me at the center. She leaped at the chance, not knowing what else to do. If something happened to Zach, she would be all alone in this world, and that was a feeling I knew well. I had never realized how important having a family was to me. Even though Tom, Piper, and I were a little non-traditional, we were still a family.

Life at the women's center seemed normal. One of the youngest,

Karen, had stepped up to make sure certain meals were on time and chores were getting done. She was only seventeen but was an amazing person. I guess getting pregnant and having to be on her own made her grow up fast. I wondered what would have become of her, an unwed mother discarded by her parents, if the center wasn't available to her. Or even worse, what would have happened to her child. I shuddered to think of the consequences. Yet every day in this country, young girls were put in that position. They were easy prey for the Victors of the world. Without help, she would have no choice but to succumb to the life he offered.

These thoughts only reinforced my commitment to the center. I hoped I'd be able to bring Piper home and dedicate more time to helping these vulnerable but strong and deserving young women.

Maddy was mesmerized by the house, commenting that she had never been in such a fine place. As she walked in, she looked up in awe at the fifteen-foot ceilings finished with beaded board. I took her to the family room and introduced her to the women and children watching the Disney movie *Frozen* on TV. All of the children's eyes were glued to the large screen, fascinated even though they'd probably seen it five times. I guess everyone liked fairytales where the good guys won. They would surely need that belief later on when circumstances were challenging and evil reappeared, tempting them down the dark path.

I brought Maddy into Susan's office to assign her a room. Susan kept a chart of all of the residents, showing when they arrived, what room they were in, and when they expected to leave. She had more detailed records on her computer, but the chart was a quick visual reference, and I gave Maddy a room close to mine.

Maddy turned the television on in Susan's office to catch the news, being a bit of a news junkie. Other than that, she loved any shows dealing with healthy lifestyles. *Funny*, I thought, *how different her path in life was from Zach's*. The talking head was reporting on the increased number of young women missing from the streets of the city. They made it clear, without being politically incorrect, they weren't talking about soccer moms. They were talking about the city's working girls, and I was pretty sure I knew who was responsible. It had to be either

Victor or Clint and the rest of his Dixie Mafia buddies. More collateral damage. These young girls were in the middle of a war they had no power to stop. I only hoped Detective Baker could stop them before many more of those defenseless women were murdered.

It was getting late, and I was tired from my journey to meet with that demon Victor and all of the rest of the day's events. I showered and put on some comfy pajamas. Maddy did the same and joined me in my room. She told me all about her plans to someday be an advocate for organic food and fitness. She looked the part already, her skin completely clear and radiant. She was muscular yet still curvy and had unbound energy to go along with her physical beauty. We were just starting to get sleepy when Karen burst into the room.

"Ms. Alexandra, someone just dumped a body in the driveway!" she screamed. Maddy gasped and my heart stuttered. We were both thinking the same thing.

We ran outside. It was Zach.

CHAPTER TWENTY-ONE
LA OR BUST

~

MADDY SCREAMED AS she looked at her brother lying helpless on the pavement. His face was covered in blood, and blood flowed from multiple points on his body. He looked as though he'd been hit by a fast-moving train. He lay motionless on the pitted asphalt and, from a distance, was the very image of a gangland killing pulled from the pages of a prohibition-era newspaper. I ran to him and bent over as a thought came to me: *Blood is flowing; that means his heart is still beating.* And he was breathing.

"Quick, call 9-1-1!" I yelled. "He's alive. He needs to get to a hospital. Fast."

"Zach, Zach, what have they done to you?" Maddy moaned. She cradled him in her arms so his head wouldn't be on the filthy street. She thumbed the blood out of his eyes and stroked his blood-soaked hair. "You are going to be okay. The ambulance is on its way. You are going to be okay. You have to be."

I sat beside her and prayed his life be spared. Zach was trying to set his life straight. When would he be through paying for his mistakes? Where was that ambulance? It had better get here fast.

My prayers were partially answered as the ambulance pulled up next to Zach. I tore Maddy away so the paramedics could do their job. They shouted commands to each other, moving like a finely coordinated team. IV started, Zach was shifted to a gurney. It only took five minutes to get him secured in the ambulance and on his way to the hospital.

"Come on. Let's go to the hospital," I said.

Maddy and I loaded into my car and sped to Tulane Medical Center. For the second time in a week, an ambulance responded to a call at the center. The residents had to be freaked out. Poor Zach didn't look like he was going to make it. He'd obviously taken a severe beating. According to the paramedics, his pulse was faint, and though I hoped for the best, I prepared for the worst. Maddy was a mess, bawling and babbling at the same time. She couldn't get control of herself, and I couldn't blame her. Zach was a bad enough sight for me to have to witness; I could only imagine how rough it was for his sister to see him beaten, bloody, and hovering at death's door, her fear of losing him driving her to the edge of insanity.

When we arrived at the hospital, Zach was in surgery. We had no word on his condition, but I took it as an encouraging sign that they admitted him to surgery. They must have thought they could do something to save him and I felt like he was in good hands. The trauma unit at Tulane had seen its share of torn bodies. New Orleans had the highest murder rate of all American cities its size. The doctors at Tulane were experts at piecing together broken bodies. They dealt with beatings, knifings, and shootings every day, and this was just another case to them. But to Maddy, it meant everything since Zach was her last remaining family member. She rocked back and forth in the waiting room with her hands clasped in the praying position. She and I said nothing. She'd removed herself to a safe place in her mind; a place free from the hysteria she was fighting, wanting to escape everything and everybody.

A doctor emerged from the double doors leading to an operating room. "May I speak to the family of Zach Dawson, please?"

Maddy trembled as she rose to her feet. In a frail, distant voice, she said, "I am Zach's sister, Maddy Dawson."

The doctor nodded at me before he spoke to Maddy. "Ms. Dawson, your brother suffered a savage beating. He had a ruptured spleen and massive internal bleeding. He also had some serious contusions on his head. There doesn't appear to be any brain damage, but we won't be sure for a couple of days. Luckily, we got to him in time. A few minutes later and I don't know if we could have saved him. He is going to remain in intensive care for the next couple of days. There are always risks in a case like this, but if all goes well, he can start his long road to recovery. And it will be a long road, but from what I saw in there, your brother is a fighter. He's also a lucky man. Another five minutes…"

Maddy nodded numbly, the hope in her eyes fragile and heartbreaking.

The surgeon continued. "The police wanted to speak to him and I told them they'd have to wait a couple of days before he would be strong enough to talk."

"May I see him?" Maddy asked.

"Not tonight. If you come back tomorrow we will let you have ten or fifteen minutes with him. He needs his rest. He will feel pretty bad tomorrow. We will need to keep him sedated because he will be in a great deal of pain."

Maddy and I both breathed a deep sigh of relief. He was badly injured, but he was going to recover. There was no doubt in my mind who had done this to him. It was El Alacran, and I knew he didn't want to kill Zach. He wanted to scare me. That's why he dumped Zach at the center. He wanted me to know he was in town and above the law.

"Maddy, let's go back to the center and get some sleep," I said. "You can see Zach in the morning. I will be heading to Los Angeles. I would like you to stay at the center while I'm gone and help the girls. Do you mind?"

"No, I was hoping I would be able to stay there for a while. When Zach is finally able to get around on his own, I want to leave New Orleans and start fresh somewhere. I think he will be willing to go now. He's paid his debt to Jaeger and his Dixie Mafia friends."

The center was silent when we returned, a quiet calm throughout the house. Mothers had put their young ones to bed, and no one stirred when Maddy and I walked in. I hadn't realized it was two o'clock in the morning. I needed my rest if I was going to be on my game in Los Angeles. I was happy to know Maddy was staying at the center to watch over the residents in my absence. She seemed older than her years. I couldn't help but think it odd that Maddy, in her mid-twenties, and Karen, only seventeen, were taking on the responsibility of caring for all of these people. But that's what good people did. They rose to the challenges placed in front of them, and I wondered if I could do the same.

I had to.

A new day dawned, and I went to catch my ten a.m. flight. I packed fairly light, wanting to just get Piper and return to New Orleans. I would be in Victor's backyard in LA. I decided to leave my gun in New Orleans. I didn't want the hassle with TSA at the airport in either city and hoped I wouldn't regret my decision.

I had mixed feelings when the plane touched down at LAX: I was excited to see Piper, but I was not able to relax thinking of Victor's long reach. I hoped he wasn't tracking me. I left my phone at the center and hadn't purchased a burner yet. These were uncharted waters for me. I felt like I was sailing without GPS or even a compass. I walked from the plane down to baggage claim, but still no Piper. I took the courtesy van to my hotel and checked in to my room. I thought staying close to the airport was the best idea. Still nothing from Piper. When the phone in my room rang, I pounced on it.

"Ms. Lee, we have a package for you at the front desk."

A package? Who could have left me a package? It must have been Piper. I rushed down. The front desk clerk handed me a small box. I opened it to find a cell phone. I went back to my room and waited. Why wasn't she contacting me? What on earth was taking so long? Finally the phone rang. It was Piper. She said an Uber driver would pick me up in five minutes in front of the hotel. I was beginning to feel like I was the lead actor in a spy movie. All of this cloak-and-dagger stuff unnerved me. The driver brought me to Venice Beach.

I walked along the beachfront, looking at all of the painters, street performers, and small vendors to see if Piper's face was among them. I saw no one I recognized. The scene did remind me of the French Quarter. Lots of tie-dyed shirts, beards, and long hair. I walked along the car-free street lined with trinket shops. A person could buy a T-shirt with anything imaginable written on the front or back. The air was different, too; no humidity and a very pleasant seventy-two degrees.

I passed a shop with plastic and ceramic skulls for sale. A young man with wiry red hair and a T-shirt with "Day of the Dead" printed on the front called to me. "Alexandra, follow me. I'll take you to Piper."

Should I follow him? He could be one of Victor's guys. No way—he was exactly the kind of person I'd expect Piper to send to bring me to her. I followed him away from the beach to a shabby apartment above a small store. He said his name was Breezy. I figured it was a California thing.

There was Piper sitting on a couch in the cramped apartment, a sleeping bag covering the floor beneath her feet. She looked exhausted, her face pale and her hair unwashed. She smiled at me nervously. I held out my arms, and she and ran over and jumped right into them. I held her close, never wanting to let her leave my sight again. Is this what it felt like to be a mother? Holy shit. Now I had a lot more respect for what so many women went through. Part of me wanted to kiss her, and another part of me wanted to knock her into next week for scaring the shit out of me. I settled on hugging her tightly enough that she squeaked.

Then I extended my arms, pushing her back to look her up and down for damage. Other than the fatigue, she looked intact, her multi-colored hair shiny and stringy. "Don't ever do that to me again," I said.

"I'm sorry! I had to. I was imposing on you and Tom. You were both so nice to me. No one has ever treated me like that. You seemed to understand me and took an interest in really getting to know me. It freaked me out for a while. Just when I was getting used to thinking I could have a real family, Victor showed up. I knew he would hurt you to get his hands on me. I couldn't let that happen. So I ran away."

"That's crazy, Piper. We are family. Whatever troubles come our way, we'll face them together."

Piper's face reddened. She looked down at the floor for a second, and then back up into my eyes as tears ran down her tiny face. "Do you really mean that? You are my family? You won't leave me?"

I raised my hand and wiped her eyes. "I'm afraid we're all stuck with each other until the end. I won't lose you, Piper."

"I don't want to lose you," she whispered.

"Good, that's settled. Now tell me how you pulled all of this off, you little shit."

She smiled at me, relieved I wasn't mad and clearly proud of herself. "I hacked into your phone. I got all of your contacts. That's how I found Amanda. I told her where to park it so we could make a quick getaway."

"Clever," I said.

"Once I made it to LA, I connected with my friends in our underground network. We are a group of white-hat hackers who share secret hacking tactics. Some of them used to be black-hat hackers stealing money, crashing sites, and running scams. We don't allow any of that in our group."

"I didn't know clubs like that existed," I said.

"There are many of them. Alexandra, I want to find my mom. I know she's all messed up, but she's still my mom. Maybe we can take her back to New Orleans with us? What do you think?"

I smiled at her and said, "Sure we can. If she will come with us, we can take her to New Orleans and get her back on the right track. I'm sure you have a plan to find her and talk to her. Don't you?"

Piper told me all about her plan. Victor had a site on the dark net, a place that couldn't be accessed by ordinary browsers like Firefox, Google Chrome, or Microsoft Explorer. Surfing the dark web required a browser like Tor. It could surreptitiously access dark web sites. Victor's site was a hookup site. It displayed photos of young women who worked for him, and they could be booked for services at the spa. Some he allowed to do out-calls to hotels around the Los Angeles Convention

Center. Piper had it set up for a hacker friend to get a room in the hotel and book a hookup with one of the girls for a husband and wife date. Not just any of the girls; one whom she knew she could trust. Sasha, who went by her stage name Samantha on the site, was one of Victor's recruits from Ukraine. Sasha missed her family and wanted to get home to her war-torn country. Piper had already put her plan in motion. Sasha was to meet her date tonight.

I told Piper what had gone on in New Orleans since she left. She said Victor was behind everything that had happened. He had hacked Jaeger's phone years ago and has been following his every move. That's how he stayed ahead of Jaeger. Victor bragged about how he was a descendant of the Russian Czar who kicked the Huns out of Russia. Victor hated Jaeger and vowed to destroy him.

Piper summoned an Uber driver to take us to the hotel to meet Sasha. Her friend had already checked in and left passkeys for us at the front desk. We went to the room and waited for Sasha. We didn't have long to wait, because Sasha was prompt. I answered the door and she walked in.

"Hi, Sasha," Piper said, emerging from the bathroom. "I hope you don't mind that we tricked you into coming. This is Alexandra, my friend from New Orleans."

"Piper. Oh my God. It's really you," Sasha screamed. "You're all grown up. I haven't seen you in more than a year."

The two girls embraced. They looked like sisters reuniting after one being away at school. It was touching but soon turned to business.

"I can't stay long," Sasha said. "My driver is waiting in the lobby for me to finish. What are you doing here?"

Piper put both hands on Sasha's face. "Tell me, where is my mother?"

Sasha turned pale. She hesitated for a few seconds and then looked at me. She couldn't look directly at Piper to speak her next words. "Your mother is dead. Victor had her killed and her body taken out to sea."

Piper began to cry but was still controlling herself. "Tell me what happened."

"She told Victor you'd run away. He believed it and really didn't care, until one of the other girls told him about what you could do with a computer and he wanted you back. Your mother wouldn't tell him where you'd gone, so he did what Victor does. He killed her."

"But my father received a call from her," Piper said.

"That was Katerina," Sasha said. "She was trying to warn you. She paid with her life. Victor had her killed, too, for double-crossing him."

Now tears flowed freely down Piper's face. She wailed and wailed. I knew at that moment that I was going to get that bastard if it was the last thing I did.

After what seemed like hours, Piper finally composed herself. She said, "My mother and Katerina are both dead. There's nothing left for me here, Alexandra. Let's go home to New Orleans."

CHAPTER TWENTY-TWO
TROUBLES PILE UP

I OFFERED TO pay Sasha's way back to her home country. She refused. She knew if she left the spa, Victor's Russian Mafia wing would track her down and kill her and her family. She was trapped, a prisoner for as long as she could make them money. I asked her how we could help, and she said she didn't know yet but she was working on a plan. Something that would make Victor think she wasn't worth the trouble anymore. I didn't want to leave it like that, but I couldn't save everyone. She and Piper hugged and promised to stay in touch under the radar.

Then she messed up her hair and makeup and left the room after one hour, the allotted time for which she'd been rented, no longer a woman but a piece of equipment like a carpet shampooing machine. She had to be returned sustaining only normal wear and tear. Oh my God. What type of world were we living in today? She was a modern-day slave. Sure, it wasn't state-sanctioned like the slave trade was 150 years ago, but it was tolerated as a victimless crime. No wonder so many girls went missing from the streets. Many became sex workers forced by fear, drug habits, or both to work the streets.

Piper and I returned to New Orleans the next day. We snuck into the city, booking our trip under fake names and using fake IDs graciously supplied by Piper's underground friends. I felt like a criminal but also realized it was the best way to get home safely. Piper was quiet most of the trip. She needed the time to make some sense of the evil Victor had brought into her short life. I'd learned a little about evil myself. You couldn't just passively let it exist; you had to fight it with every fiber of your body or suffer the consequences. I'd told Victor and El Alacran to go fuck themselves, and I meant it. I was sure they would both be after me as soon as I surfaced.

We drove to the condo first. Sophia had already been to Mexico and back. I introduced Piper to her. They had similar life stories, having both lost their family members to crime syndicates. Sophia's father was murdered by a Colombian drug cartel, and Piper's parents were wiped out by the Russian mob.

"Tom is in a prison in Chilpancingo, Mexico," Sophia said. "The court has set his bond at $100,000 US. Like I told you on the phone, his charges are rioting and resisting lawful arrest. The prosecutor on the case is threatening to up the charges to eco-terrorism. My friends at Interpol believe the prosecutor and other local officials have been bribed to bring these charges. Interpol hooked me up with some of the local honest politicians. They are working behind the scenes to get Tom released to my custody. If the authorities agree to release him to me, he'll have to return to Mexico to face trial. I wasn't able to visit him, but he got word that we are trying to get him out. We should know something soon."

Piper's mood grew more somber with every word from Sophia's mouth. "Alexandra, that sounds really bad. Tom is in a lot of trouble. I'll bet Victor's mafia or drug cartel buddies are bribing the Mexican prosecutor. We may never see him again. They may kill him in prison."

"No, little one. They won't kill him," Sophia said. "They know Interpol is watching. Killing Tom would bring too much heat down on their heads. My American Interpol friends have put the US Embassy on notice that Tom has been detained. The embassy has made a formal inquiry into the charges. They wouldn't dare kill him now."

I wasn't sure if Sophia was just trying to calm Piper, or if Tom really was safe. My experience in Colombia led me to believe he was still in danger. I wanted to scream, feeling so frightened about what might happen to Tom, but I didn't for Piper's sake. I kept it together, at least for the moment. We needed to get Tom back to the United States as soon as we could. Piper's custody status conference was scheduled in a week. It would look bad if Mr. Clark had to report to the court that Tom was in a Mexican prison.

Piper and I left Sophia to head to Sarah's House. I hadn't been in touch with Maddy and wanted to get an update on Zach's condition. Maddy was talking to one of the residents when we arrived, and as soon as she laid eyes on me, she jumped up and ran to greet me.

"Alexandra, Zach is doing better. They've already taken him out of intensive care. He's in a room with a couch. I can stay with him overnight now. I am so glad you are back," Maddy said, bursting with enthusiasm. "Hi, Piper. Are you okay? We were all so worried about you."

"I'm fine," Piper replied. "I'm sorry I worried everyone, and I'm glad Zach's doing better. Alexandra told me what happened to him. Did he tell you who beat him?"

"He's not going there. We all know who did it. But what can he say? I was making a drug deal and got beat up? No one would care, especially the police. He just wants to put the whole matter behind him and get out of here," Maddy said. "Alexandra, a lady from the state came by while you were in LA. I put her card on Ms. McAllister's desk."

Lady from the state? That couldn't be good. What now? I went into Susan's office and found the card right where Maddy had left it. The lady from the state was Theresa Butler with the Louisiana Department of Family Services. She'd written a note on her card for me to call her as soon as I could.

It was too late to call tonight; it would have to wait until tomorrow. I was too tired to talk to anyone, anyway. I used Susan's computer to check to see if Piper had gotten my site back up on the web. I was a little surprised that it popped right up. The list of missing girls was growing larger by the week. I wondered how many groups like Victor's were out there and how many of the missing girls were victims of their evil schemes. I had to shut off the computer and cleanse my mind of these disturbing thoughts to sleep. It was difficult, but I simply had to. Piper and I both bedded down in Susan's queen-sized bed. I wanted her close. After a few minutes of reassuring each other, sleep came quickly to both of us.

Morning arrived with little fanfare. The center was so quiet and peaceful. No one would have ever known there were sinister forces brewing storms in the city. This center should have been a place of serenity. These poor women and children had already suffered devastating upheavals in their lives, yet evil found this refuge anyway. I guess you really couldn't hide from the forms evil takes. You could only fight it.

With these thoughts in mind, I called the Department of Family Services and asked to speak to Ms. Theresa Butler. She was pleasant enough, asking if she could meet with me this afternoon. I had to admit, it wasn't what I expected. She seemed genuinely interested in helping me get things back on track at the center. She said her visit was just a formality, something she had to do to complete her paperwork. *Whew, what a relief,* I thought.

I called Jess Johnson, and as usual she was in her office. She agreed to see me if I could get my ass in gear and make it there in the next hour. That was Jess: always on a deadline and expecting everyone else to be, as well.

"Come on, Piper," I said. "You are coming with me to meet one of the greatest ladies in this city."

That perked Piper up. When I told her Jess was Haitian, she got even more excited. "Do you think she knows anything about voodoo?" Piper asked.

"Jess knows everything about everything," I said. "Let's go see her."

I had already decided that wherever I went, Piper was going, too. I couldn't risk her getting separated from me again. Besides, I knew she and Jess would hit it off, Piper possessing the right kind of spunk for Jess. We arrived at Jess's office in no time. I'd been there so many times everybody recognized me. They all looked a little surprised to see me with a teenager. Stares and whispers marked our trek to Jess's office.

"Trying to make deadline and this damn computer won't work," Jess said as she stood behind her chair. A young man with spiked hair and horn-rimmed glassed was seated at her desk pecking away at her computer keyboard. "Who's this?" she said, looking at Piper.

"Jess Johnson, I want you to meet Constance Sanders. We call her Piper."

Piper smiled and nodded at Jess, calling on her street smarts to recognize a woman not to be trifled with. Jess sent a return courtesy nod Piper's way, never changing her game face, and got right down to business. "What can I do for you? You can talk in front of Henry here. He's in our IT department. I don't think he understands English." Henry wrinkled his nose and poked out his lower lip at her comment.

"I need your help," I said.

I ran through the entire story concisely like a journalist pitching a story to an editor. Jess had no patience for long-winded dissertations. Years in the newspaper business relating just the facts had honed her skills to machine-like efficiency.

"The bottom line, Jess, is I need *The Times* to research Victor Ivanovich's operation in other cities. I think he is moving into New Orleans the same way he's done in other metropolitan areas with convention sites. There are more working girls either missing or dead than usual. I think he's killing them off," I said.

She told me she'd already assigned a reporter to work on the story for the possible serial killer point of view. She said she'd get him to contact me to follow up on the lead I had and see if maybe Victor was behind all of the killings.

"Alexandra, I have something to talk to you about as well. *The Times* is working on a story about Susan McAllister and Sarah's House for Battered Women and Children. We've looked into the background of Ms. McAllister and know all about her mother's conviction for poisoning her father. We also found out her mother's family came to the United States from Russia. Aconite is made from a plant that grows in mountainous regions of Central Asia, Russia, Europe, and Great Britain. We discovered she visits her mother in prison every week.

According to our sources, she has been researching her mother's family and has recently made contact with her Russian relatives."

"That doesn't mean she did anything wrong," I said.

"No, but it does mean she had access to the people who could furnish the poison. Detective Baker is the lead investigator on the case, so you know she'll get a fair shake."

I knew *The Times* had to write a story about the death at the center, I only hoped it wouldn't stir public opinion against it. Piper sat next to me, pretending to listen to every word; her eyes were fixed on Henry groaning at the computer.

"There's something wrong with the server configuration," Henry blurted, clearly frustrated. "I'll have to take it with me to my office and see if I can reprogram it."

"Are you crazy?" Jess asked. "I have a deadline to meet. I don't have time for your computer crap talk."

Piper raised her hand like a student in a schoolroom, looking into Jess's eyes. "What is it, girl?" Jess barked.

"Can I look at the computer?" Piper asked.

Henry rose to his feet, casting his eyes up and down Piper. "I don't think that is a good idea," he said.

"Well," Jess said, "you don't seem to know how to fix it." She turned her eyes to Piper. "Go ahead and give it a try."

Jess's chair swallowed Piper whole. Her feet could barely touch the floor as she scooted the chair forward. When her fingers hit the keyboard, the clicking of the keys sounded like ten trains running down the same track. Within two minutes of feverishly typing, she said, "Try it now."

Henry gazed at the screen. "I'll be a son of a bitch. She's fixed it."

Piper slinked back beside me. Jess lifted the corners of her mouth, letting a smile take over her face. She winked at me then went back to our conversation about the center. I knew her smile meant she was impressed—seriously impressed—by Piper. I explained Victor's crazed desire to send Piper to Russia to hack computers for him. We agreed to dig deeper into the story to ferret out the truth of Tiffany's murder.

"Now get the hell out of here," Jess said. "I have a deadline to meet. Piper, you can come back to see me anytime. And don't you worry. This is our town, and you are one of us now. We don't like outsiders messing with our folks. Mr. Ivanovich may have to learn that the hard way."

We'd spent a little longer with Jess than I'd planned. We battled the traffic back to the center to meet Ms. Butler from the Department of Family Services. She'd arrived ahead of us and was chatting with some of the residents when we walked in. After the introductions, we walked to Susan's office. Piper sat in the desk chair to get on Susan's computer, and Ms. Butler and I perched on the couch, facing each other.

"So this is the young lady you went to California to retrieve," Ms. Butler said, eying Piper. "The ladies told me she's your boyfriend's niece. Is that correct?"

"Yes," I said. I went on to explain Tom and I were given temporary custody by the court since Piper was abandoned by her mother and her father was killed. "We are seeking permanent custody and hope to have the entire matter concluded in a month."

She raised one eyebrow as she listened to the saga of Piper's life. "Interesting," she said. "Now let's talk about the unfortunate events that led to the poisoning of Tiffany and the arrest of Susan McAllister. I have spoken to Detective Baker, who informs me Ms. McAllister is in jail and not likely to be released anytime soon. Are you running the center in her absence?"

"Yes, I am committed to helping these women and ensuring the center's work goes on. Susan McAllister is innocent. She wouldn't hurt anyone. She is dedicated to the mission of this sanctuary for abused women and children. I'll stay here as long as necessary."

"I see," she said. "My department will have to launch a full investigation into the center. There are children here, and the department must be certain they are safe and well provided for. The director of the department asked me to personally investigate allegations that the children are at risk. I will bring in a team to help me interview each and every resident. I have asked the state fire marshal to examine the building and to write a report on its compliance with the fire codes. I'll render a report to my supervisor when I finish. We will advise you of the action we intend to take at that time. Do you have any questions?"

"What do you mean by action you intend to take?"

"We have several options, ranging from no action at all to removing all of the children from this center and closing the entire facility down."

"Oh my God," I said as I gasped for air. "Closing the facility down? Where would these poor people go if you closed the center down?"

"If their mothers cannot provide for them—and I assume they can't or they wouldn't be here—we would make the children wards of the state and place them in foster care. The ladies would be responsible for themselves. There are some assistance programs, but that is not my department. The women would receive the proper referrals. Ms. Lee, surely you understand the gravity of this. A resident of this facility was murdered on these premises, and the director who oversees them was charged with her murder. We can't allow children to be at risk. They are better off in foster care."

Ms. Butler's expression changed. She focused her eyes narrowly on me as she picked up her purse to leave. "You may want to consider getting a lawyer."

She turned and walked out of the office without saying goodbye or even looking back.

CHAPTER TWENTY-THREE
THE STATE

~

GET A LAWYER. Why would I need a lawyer? Theresa Butler was on a mission to close the center. I didn't know if someone was pulling her strings or if she was acting on her own, but either way, she had the power to shut us down. I couldn't let that happen. What would Sarah think? The center was the legacy she left on earth. No way was I going to let her down. And what about Susan? She'd poured her heart and soul into this place. If the center were closed, where would she go?

I didn't like the direction things were headed, and I was so tired I couldn't think straight. I needed sleep in the worst way. Maybe tomorrow I'd have clearer thoughts on how to get out of this mess. I asked Piper to sleep in Susan's room with me, wanting to keep her close so no one could hurt her. I fell into an uneasy sleep, waking every two hours to assure myself Piper was still next to me. Thoughts swirled through my mind like a tornado cutting through our cornfield back on the farm in Indiana. Was Tom okay? Would the charges against Susan stick? What would Victor do to us? How could I battle all of the forces trying to destroy the people I love? My thought storm raged through the night without letting up. Finally the sun signaled the beginning of a new day.

What was going on with Susan's case? I picked up my phone and called Detective Baker. When he answered, he seemed a little more distant than normal. "Detective Baker, have you been able to develop any new information on Tiffany's connection to Victor Ivanovich?"

"Ms. Lee, you will have to direct your questions to Inspector Jaeger. He is in charge of the investigation of Tiffany's murder, and I am not at liberty to discuss this matter with you. It is police business. You may want to call Jess Johnson if you want to know the information the police department has released to the press. I have to take another call now." Baker hung up the phone.

What the hell was going on? Baker spoke in a lower pitch than usual. He had never been so formal with me. Something was definitely wrong. I phoned Jess without putting my phone down.

"Alexandra, I was just about to call you," Jess said. "Demetre came to my house early this morning to drink coffee with me. He felt like he needed to speak to me face-to-face about the investigation into Tiffany's murder. He's been removed from the investigation."

"Removed. Why? He was the lead investigator."

"He's been disciplined by the department for getting you into the jail to see Susan McAllister. They feel like he has compromised the investigation by allowing a suspect in an ongoing investigation to speak to a co-defendant. Inspector Alric Jaeger has been placed in charge of developing the case. He has convinced the chief and the district attorney's office to investigate your and Ms. McAllister's involvement in a prostitution ring operating out of the center. You'd better get a lawyer."

My pulse quickened. Beads of sweat formed on my forehead, my hands felt clammy, and I nearly dropped the telephone. "Me? I am a suspect in a prostitution ring? How could they possibly think I'd do anything like that?"

"Baker knows it's bullshit, but his hands are tied. He told me a couple of the women at the center are telling the police you and Susan approached them to turn tricks for you. They claimed you told them if they wanted to stay at the center, they'd have to work off their room and board."

"Who? Which ones? Someone is putting them up to saying those things. Surely Detective Baker knows they are lying."

"Of course he does, but it doesn't matter what Demetre believes. He can't go near the case. Jaeger is running the show now. Alexandra, you are going to have to fight this yourself. I'll help as much as I can, but it's up to you to set things straight. Be careful who you talk to at the center. Somebody there is telling the police you are running a prostitution ring. Whatever their agenda is, they've convinced the police to go after you. This whole matter has the smell of Louisiana politics at its worst. You are caught in the political meat grinder, and they'll bury you if you don't fight back," Jess said.

Jess spoke from experience. She'd spent years reporting below-the-belt body blows thrown in the Louisiana political arena. It wasn't a place for the faint of heart. In 1930, Louisiana's sitting governor, Huey Long, ran for the United States Senate. Every newspaper opposed him. To silence a particularly bothersome pair of critics, Long recruited some henchmen to break into their hotel room in the middle of the night and kidnap both men and tie them to a tree on election day. Long won the election and was never charged with kidnapping. That was just the way the game was played in Louisiana. Everyone knew it, and everyone expected it.

No sooner did I hang up with Jess than I received a text from Charlotte.

Alexandra. I need you to come to Superior Sugar's office now.

I'm tied up at the moment. Can it wait?

No! I need you here now.

Holy shit, Charlotte. This was the second time she was panicking—not her normal style. Piper was up and ready, so we scooted to Superior Sugar headquarters. When I pulled into the parking lot, I noticed all of the flags were at half-mast. Charlotte met me at the door, and just like the last time I saw her, she had reddened puffy eyes from crying. She broke down into tiny fragments when I hugged her. She sobbed and wailed, making sounds that reminded me of the primal scream made by a woman during natural childbirth. I knew immediately what had happened. Mr. Morris had died. She didn't need to say it.

I kept my arm around her and walked to her office. "It's okay, Charlotte. He's out of pain now. I know you'll miss him, but he's no longer suffering."

Piper sat next to me and leaned in to rest her shoulder against my arm. I put my arm around her as we watched Charlotte dry her tears with a tissue. "Mr. Morris was such a good man. His heart was pure gold," she said.

Before she could complete her thoughts, Mandy Morris burst into the room dressed all in black as usual. "What is the meaning of this?" she asked Charlotte, shaking a cluster of legal-size papers stapled together.

"I don't know what you're talking about," Charlotte answered, temporarily shocked out of her tearful state by Mandy's insolent tone.

"This is a copy of my father's will. He has left everything to me except the ownership of that stevia company. He's split the ownership of it eighty percent to you, Charlotte, and twenty percent to you, Alexandra." Her eyes shot invisible laser beams at Charlotte as she spoke. "Have you been fucking my father? Is that why he left you the company? I can understand him giving a portion to Alexandra. She's talented and essential to the company's success. But not you."

Charlotte shot to her feet and headed around the desk toward Mandy. Her eyes were ablaze with rage, and she clenched both fists. Mandy took a step back. I lunged between them to stop the carnage. Charlotte drew deep breaths in and out trying to calm herself. Her face blazed red.

"Get away from me, you psycho bitch, before I scratch your eyes out of your head," Charlotte screamed. "I quit. No notice. No time to train someone to take my place. I quit. You and your pervert uncle can sell your poisonous sugar on your own."

Mandy turned and tromped out of the door. Charlotte started emptying her desk drawers. I retrieved boxes from the recycle bin, and just like that she was packed and out the door. As we walked to her car carrying the boxes, she looked at me with a steady flow of tears rolling down her face. I knew she would miss Mr. Morris, but she'd miss Superior Sugar, too. Charlotte's marketing work helped build Superior

Sugar. Her heart had to be broken. I asked if she wanted me to go to her house with her and hang out and talk.

"No, Alexandra. I just need to be alone for a while. You and Piper can call me later. I am sorry to say that Mandy will probably cancel your contract, as well. We will have to get to work on the stevia company soon. I will need the income," she said.

Boy, was she right about needing the income. My funds were getting low, and I wouldn't have any steady income if I lost the Superior Sugar account. I'm sure the account was lost. Mandy may want me to work for her, but I'd just be trapped in the middle between her and Charlotte. I didn't want to work with Garrett Morris, anyway. Mandy was hard enough to take with her dark side dominating her personality, but Garrett was another thing altogether. He was a sick pervert, and they were the perfect pair to push life-shortening sugar on the uneducated public. With all of my other problems, now I had no dependable income.

The thought of being broke occupied my mind as Piper and I went back to the center. When we arrived we were greeted by the sight of a metal herd of state motor pool cars in the driveway. Inside, Theresa Butler led a team of Department of Family Service workers through the building. She hadn't bothered to call me to let me know she was coming. Her surprise attack must have been part of her master plan. When she spotted me, she walked my way.

"Ms. Lee. These workers are going to need privacy to interview the residents and inspect the premises. Is there any place you can go while we do our job?"

Any place I can go? This bitch is starting to piss me off, I thought to myself. This center was a sanctuary for abused women and children, not a springboard for some political agenda. I was about to tell her how I felt when Inspector Jaeger walked into the center with four uniformed officers and two plainclothes detectives flanking him. He strutted to me and gave me a sideways glance before he surveyed the state workers pairing up with the residents to question them.

Jaeger turned his attention to Ms. Butler and said, "I want a typed copy of every statement you take from the residents. My investigators will debrief each of your people when they are finished. I want a dossier on every person who's been here in the last six months. If they have a job, I want to know about it. If they leave at night, I want to know where they go. Susan McAllister's office and bedroom are now crime scenes. I want them sealed off. Is that clear?"

"Yes, sir," the officers said. I watched as Ms. Butler sidled up to Inspector Jaeger to get within whisper range.

She faux-whispered, making certain I could hear, "You can count on my complete cooperation. Something is terribly wrong here. Trust me, we will get to the bottom of it."

Jaeger acknowledged her comment with a slight nod of his bald head as he turned his attention to me. "Ms. Lee, it would be in your best interest to leave us. You might just dig yourself a deeper hole if you attempt to stay here."

Young Karen Durio, who'd watched the entire orchestrated drama play out, said, "Don't worry, Alexandra, I'll watch over things here until you are able to come back."

I forced a smile and cast it in her direction. God I hope she was being sincere. I was still a bit stunned by what was happening. I took Piper by the hand and headed to my condo. Traffic was heavy, which usually added to my stress level, but for some reason today it was welcome. None of the people in the cars were out to get me. They just wanted to get home to their families, and I just wanted to keep mine together.

When I walked into my condo, Sophia was packing her bags to leave. "Alexandra, I have some bad news. The prosecutor in Mexico has filed terrorism charges against Tom. They have a hearing tomorrow to increase his bail. I need to be there to see what I can do to help. Things are going to get messy, I'm afraid."

I was afraid to think how things could get any messier than they were now. Poor Tom. I wanted to scream and break down in tears, but I feared I'd make matters worse for Piper. I couldn't get on the plane with Sophia, either, though my heart longed to. I had to deal with Jaeger, Butler, and Victor. I told Sophia about Jaeger's comments. She looked at her feet and shook her head side to side. "He's after you, Alexandra. For some reason he wants you out of his way."

Piper cowered in the corner of the kitchen and began to cry. "It's me he wants. Victor wants me, and Jaeger wants to use me to get to Victor. I am causing all of this trouble. It's why I ran away in the first place. I should have stayed in California and never contacted you. I hate myself for doing this to you and Tom."

My heart fractured into small pieces listening to this tiny child consumed with guilt. I began to cry along with Piper. Even battle-hardened Sophia sobbed. I reached out my arms and brought her to my chest, holding her for a tearful minute.

"None of these problems are your fault, dear. Sometimes life isn't fair. When tragedy strikes you need your family next to you to help you overcome the trials of life. We are a family. I will always be there for you. You didn't cause Victor's criminal acts. The evil inside him has taken hold and controls him. The same is true of Jaeger. He is so obsessed with putting Victor in jail as revenge for what happened to his parents many years ago that he's blind to anything but evil. We are victims of their greed and rage. We must stick together as a family, and we will see this through. Evil only triumphs when good people do nothing. We are going to fight them together."

"I hear what you are saying, but I still feel guilty," she said.

Sophia finished packing and said, "My flight leaves in three hours. How about we go eat and then you can take me to the airport?"

Since neither Piper nor I had eaten all day, I suggested we go to Whole Foods. Good food was what we needed to change our mood. I wanted some chicken in curry sauce so bad I would have sold an arm to get some. Piper wanted a spinach salad. Strange choice for a teenager, but she loved it. Must have been the hippie genes passed down from the Sanders side. Sophia had eyes only for the paella. Good thing our New Orleans Whole Foods believed in diversity. The food was excellent. I added Tabasco to my curry to spice it up more than normal.

We dropped Sophia off at the airport. I resisted the urge to quiz her about what Tom might be facing, not wanting to upset Piper anymore.

I could always text her after she got to Mexico. Piper and I went back to the condo and passed out in the bed. We both knew I was going to have to deal with Ms. Butler and Inspector Jaeger tomorrow.

CHAPTER TWENTY-FOUR
THE LEGAL SYSTEM

~

"WAKE UP, ALEXANDRA. I've brought you coffee," Piper said as she crawled into bed next to me. "Maybe if we start the day off differently, things will get better?"

Yesterday was so bad, things had to get better. Or at least I hoped they would. My thoughts turned to Charlotte. I wondered if she was okay. She just lost her job and a dear friend. We both had to put some serious effort into the stevia company if we were going to be successful. Neither of us knew how to run a business. We had to learn fast if we hoped to succeed. How could I focus on business, though, with my family and myself in such jeopardy?

I checked my blog and saw that many more young women were going missing in New Orleans. Their disappearances had to involve Victor and the Dixie Mafia's ongoing war for control of the dark side of the city. Who was looking out for these poor unfortunate women? No one.

"Do you think Tom will be okay?" Piper asked. "I am worried about him."

"Yes, I don't think anyone will hurt him. Sophia will find a way to help him," I replied.

Even though I told Piper Tom would be okay, I didn't really believe it. I'd learned money spoke loudly in politics. Hell, it screamed in Louisiana, twisting values and laws. I could only imagine how bad things were in Latin American countries if my experience in Colombia with political corruption was typical. Tom was in real danger of going to prison or worse. Every cell in my body wanted to go to Mexico to be with him. I had to fight the urge as hard as I could. He would want me to look out for Piper. I pinned all of my hopes on Sophia.

Mr. Swartz had emailed me yesterday, wanting to see me. I'd forgotten to give him my burner cell phone number. Piper and I had some fresh blackberries from Whole Foods for breakfast. When we finished, I phoned Mr. Swartz. He asked me to come to his office as soon as I could and to bring Piper. He wouldn't tell me why, explaining he needed to see me in person. I had a sinking feeling he had bad news for me.

We took the short drive to Mr. Swartz's office. It was a typical summer day in New Orleans. The sun was slowly roasting the plants, churning out eighty-three-degree waves before ten o'clock in the morning. Yes, as everyone felt compelled to say, it was going to be a hot one. The bleached blond weather babe predicted a high temperature of ninety-eight degrees. The air was still and heavy. Air conditioners worked overtime to cool offices, homes, and cars. I worked hard to keep myself cool from all of the heat generated by Victor, Jaeger, and Ms. Butler.

We were greeted by the friendly receptionist and quickly escorted into the conference room. Mr. Swartz joined us with a single set of papers in his hands. He sat across the table from me and drew a deep breath before speaking. He wasn't his machine-like self. He seemed a bit unnerved. Before he could speak the first word, we were joined by Mr. Clark

"Alexandra, I'm afraid I have some very bad news for you. I have asked Mr. Clark to join us. Before you and I speak, I'd like you to listen to what he has to say," Mr. Swartz said. "You may want Constance to leave the room while we talk."

Piper slowly hooked her arm in mine and snuggled up against me. She looked up into my eyes, shaking her head from side to side. She wanted to stay in the room with me.

"I know what you have to tell me is bad news or Mr. Clark wouldn't be here. Her mother and father kept her in the dark for too long about matters that directly impacted her life. My parents did the same to me. I will not repeat their mistake. Whatever you have to say, you can say to both of us."

Mr. Clarkwas much more composed. His expression was compassionate. "Ms. Lee, you hired me to defend Susan McAllister on the murder charges brought against her. Ms. McAllister is my client, not you, even though you paid my fee. My duty is to protect her rights and defend her against the charges leveled against her. You and I do not have attorney-client privilege. I have had an ongoing dialog with the district attorney's office since I took the case.

"I have been advised by the assistant DA that they are about to charge Ms. McAllister and you with letting the premises for prostitution. The police, under the direction of Inspector Jaeger, have questioned several women at the center who claim you and Ms. McAllister forced them to turn tricks while they lived at the center."

I almost swallowed my tongue. "What the hell are you talking about?" I yelled. "Which women said that? It's a complete lie."

"Please," Mr. Clark said, "let me finish. The police have not disclosed the names of the women yet since no charges have been filed. The police also claim they've examined Ms. McAllister's computer and found emails from you and her setting up dates with several men. The authorities are searching for the men as we speak. The forensics team dusted the keyboard for fingerprints and found yours on the keys. It is possible the police may charge you as an accessory to murder."

I sat, stunned. "How could anyone think I could do any of these things? They can't be serious. Will you represent me, Mr. Clark, if they arrest me?"

"I can only represent you if both you and Ms. McAllister waive the conflict of interest I have. You see, there may come a time when they offer one or the other of you a deal to testify against the other. I would have to resign as attorney for both of you. You and Ms. McAllister would have to get two new lawyers. She has already agreed to that condition. Will you?"

"Yes, I absolutely will. Mr. Clark, neither of us has done anything wrong."

"Please, Ms. Lee. Do not say anything more right now. With Constance and Mr. Swartz in the room, there is no attorney-client privilege and they can be compelled to repeat what you say. We'll talk at a later time," Mr. Clark said.

Piper was wiping the tears from her eyes as she listened. I was scared to death but tried to hold it together. Mr. Swartz's complexion turned pale as Mr. Clark left the room, leaving him alone with Piper and me.

He timidly directed his eyes to me and said, "Alexandra, I'm afraid there is more bad news. The Department of Family Services for the State of Louisiana has filed an intervention in your lawsuit to gain permanent custody of Constance. They have gotten an order signed removing her from your and Mr. Sander's custody and placing her in foster care. You must turn her over to the state as soon as we finish talking."

Piper bawled out loud, taking large breaths of air as her chest heaved with each crying spell. I put my arm around her and hugged her as close as I could. "How can they do this? She doesn't even have her clothes with her."

"We can bring her things to her tomorrow. I am so sorry for you, Ms. Lee. I know you are taking good care of Constance. We have to prove it to the court. The state has made some very serious allegations against you and Mr. Sanders. The judge must have felt placing Constance in foster care was the best course of action at this time. Let me show you the petition the state's attorney emailed me."

Mr. Swartz slid the petition across the table to me. Piper stood behind me to read along. The document contained a great deal of legalese which I didn't understand, but the main allegations against me were as plain as day. I read each one out loud as if I were a hangman reading the charges against a condemned man before I pulled the lever to drop the trap door.

"*Alexandra Lee and Tom Sanders have placed the minor child, Constance Sanders, in danger by the following more particular but not exclusive acts:*

I. *Cohabiting in a dwelling with only one bedroom forcing the minor to sleep on a couch while they sleep together without the benefit of marriage.*

II. *Placing the minor child in danger by allowing her to stay in said dwelling, which was the scene of a violent confrontation with a known murderer whose murderous actions were directed at Alexandra Lee.*

III. *Associating with a convicted felon currently recuperating from injuries suffered in an alleged drug deal gone bad. Allowing the said felon into the dwelling with the minor child present.*

IV. *Taking the minor child to a facility from which they said Alexandra Lee and co-conspirator allegedly ran a prostitution ring.*

V. *Taking the minor child to the facility though a resident was murdered and the director, Alexandra Lee's alleged co-conspirator, was arrested and charged with murder.*

VI. *Alexandra Lee and Tom Sanders failed to adequately supervise the minor, allowing her to run away to Los Angeles, California, placing herself in grave danger.*

VII. *Tom Sanders is currently incarcerated in a Mexican prison charged with, inter alia, eco-terrorism.*"

I'd read enough. Mr. Swartz sat in his chair with his face in his hands rubbing his eyes. He moved his hands to his temples and said, "I'm not going to lie to you, Alexandra, the situation is very grave. We have to get the evidence necessary to refute these allegations the state has made. The court is not going to place Constance in your custody if there is any chance she would be in danger."

"I understand. Can I have a few minutes to speak with Piper alone?"

"Sure," Mr. Swartz said. "I'll go into my office and call Family Services to pick up Constance."

As Mr. Swartz left the room, Piper buried her face into my chest. Through tear-soaked, muffled tones, she said, "I don't want to leave you."

"I know. This is something we must do. Don't worry. I will never let them take you from me. I will fight until my dying breath to beat these trumped-up charges and get you back. We have to think with a clear head now. You are tough. I need you to keep it together. We can communicate through my blog. You can use the code name Penny to communicate. You can hack into my site and set up a private communication between us. You have my burner phone number. Don't give it to anyone except Tom, Jess Johnson, or Sophia. I will need your help fighting these SOBs. If they arrest me, contact Sophia Garcia and get her to help clear these charges. Can you do that for me?"

The tears in Piper's eyes were replaced by determination. She said, "I will. No way they are going to keep you in jail if I can help it. I've lost my mother and father. I can't lose you, too."

Mr. Swartz returned to the room to tell us the Department of Family Services was on their way to pick up Piper. She was being remarkably strong. She'd seen so much turmoil in her short life. She was treating the current situation as just another chapter in the book of life. I wasn't faring so well. My tears started flowing when Mr. Swartz said the state would be there in a few minutes. I realized the difficult position I was in. The police had a fairly solid circumstantial case mounting against me, and the state's intervention petition in Piper's custody suit made me and Tom look like unfit caretakers. I had the real prospect of going to jail, and so did Tom.

Ms. Butler arrived at Mr. Swartz's office with a social worker and a deputy sheriff. I kissed Piper and they took her away. My mind was reeling. My whole world was turned upside down. I just wanted to go home and cry. I left Swartz's office and headed to my condo.

I arrived at my place to find Zach and Maddy camped on my front steps. Zach had a gauze bandage wrapped around his head. He had two black eyes, and one was swollen shut. Maddy helped him to his feet and escorted him into the kitchen.

"We apologize for barging in on you without calling first," Zach said. "Your phone went straight to voice mail every time we called. I needed to talk to you, so here we are."

"It's okay," I said halfheartedly. "I didn't have any plans. I don't mean to be rude, but I've had a really bad day and I just want to go to bed."

Maddy sensed my tension and asked if she could get me anything. She offered to go to the store for me or order some take-out. I explained the highlights of the day—or more accurately, the lowlights.

Zach shook his head side to side. "I'm not surprised. You are caught between some powerful, warring factions. They have no limits to what they will do to get what they want. Jaeger may be the most dangerous of them all. Even the Dixie Mafia has its limits. After all, they have to live here after the war is over. If Victor wins, so does he. Victor has to play according to the dark side of the city's rules. But Jaeger is obsessed with putting Victor in jail, and he doesn't care who gets hurt in the process. When it's all over, he will just go back to Germany, leaving all the carnage behind. He is a very dangerous man."

"What do you need to talk to me about, Zach?" I asked.

"When I met with the Scorpion, he told me all about your visit to Colombia. He said you made him lose face with his men. Some kind of macho thing, I guess. He is committed to supplying drugs to New Orleans. As you know, he graduated from Tulane University. His son is a freshman at Tulane, majoring in chemistry of all things. So he wants to spend time here. He has chosen sides in the war. He is with Victor. Alexandra, he hates you. His men beat me until I couldn't walk. They would have killed me had he not stopped them. He said he was letting me live so I would be able to give you a message. He's going to get you."

"He's going to get me?" I asked. "What the hell does that mean?"

Zach paused for a few seconds to muster his courage to deliver the next line. "He said he wants to cut your head off and put it in a box and send it to your boyfriend, just like Camila. I'm not quite sure what he meant, but that's the message he wanted me to give you."

Zach and Maddy told me they were leaving town. We exchanged phone numbers, promising to keep them private. They left me by myself, and I was once again all alone. Really alone. Piper was in foster care and Tom was in jail. No one was going to help me fight this battle. This must have been what the Spartans felt like at the Battle of Thermopylae. The odds were stacked against me. My only choice was to fight to the death.

I got on my knees to pray. I asked my two guardian angels to help me find a way through this mess. I threw the prayer to the heavens then went to bed wondering if I'd be arrested or killed tomorrow.

CHAPTER TWENTY-FIVE
ALONE

THERE WAS SOMETHING about the morning that always inspired me. Maybe it was the freshness of the plants covered with dew or the gradual spreading of the sun's light. Whatever it was, I really enjoyed the refreshed state of mind I woke up with. I sipped my coffee at my kitchen table wondering what this day would bring. I had choices: I could go to work for Victor and my troubles would vanish as soon as I agreed to his terms; I could snag Piper and leave town; or, I could stay and fight. The only thing I couldn't do was nothing. *So, Alexandra, which is it going to be? Fight or flight? You have to decide soon or the demons will decide for you.*

No sooner did I ask myself this question than my phone rang. "Alexandra, this is Inspector Jaeger. I'd like you to come to the police station and clear up some matters for me. Do you mind? Maybe this afternoon, if that is convenient."

I hesitated for a moment. Should I call Mr. Clark before I answered? That would be the cautious action to take. Screw it. I was on my own and I knew it. I made sure my voice was cool and composed. "I would be happy to. Let's say around three."

"That will be fine," Jaeger said.

I hung up and let loose a few vicious words into the air. *Oh, how I wish I could act directly on my feelings!* I thought. But I had responsibilities. Piper. I wondered how Piper was dealing with her foster family. I checked my blog. She'd hacked my site like I'd asked and left me a private message.

"Hey, I'm with my foster family. They are cool. They've given me my own room and a macked out computer. I have full lightning speed access to the Internet. I'm good. Don't worry about me. I can hang here for as long as you need me to. I'll stay in touch. If you need me to do anything for you on the web, I won't have any trouble getting it done. Love and miss you, Piper."

Was the answer to my self-directed question ever really in doubt? Fight and fight hard was what I was going to do. I was going to fight for my family. They couldn't have Piper, they couldn't keep Tom, and they couldn't put me in jail. Even though Susan wasn't my family, they couldn't have her, either. And I was going to start by going to the dark side of the city to look one of its demons in the eyes. I strapped my .38 to my ankle, put on some pants with loose-fitting legs, and struck out for the French Quarter.

I walked into Clinton Cunningham's strip club early in the morning. Just like the last time I was here, people were drinking and a dancer feigned obscene acts with a pole on the stage. This was the dark side of New Orleans. The side where people with no destination parked their lives, counting the days until there were none left to count. They drank every waking hour of every day, numbing the pain of lives littered with uncorrected mistakes. Clint was the mayor of this city, hidden in plain sight. No one cared what these people did as long as it didn't hurt the tourist industry. It had its own ecosystem operating in the shadows.

I marched into Clint's office. He sat behind his desk with two goons occupying two of the three chairs in his office. He continued counting a stack of dollar bills as I sat in the chair directly in front of him. I knew he wasn't worried about me taking his money. I occupied a different world than him. I lived in a world of strict rules, honesty, and fair play. His world didn't concern itself with those pesky concepts. Might, power, and position held the seams of his shadow world together.

I sat in silence for a few minutes while he finished counting. He looked up at me and said, "I thought I'd see you soon. Things not going so well for you?"

"You know what's happened to me. You know Jaeger is trying to frame me. Are you a part of his plan?" I asked.

"Ha, ha, ha," he laughed. "You know, for a smart girl, you sure are stupid. You've gotten yourself caught up in a game you don't know how to play. You were fucked before you even knew it."

"Why don't you tell me what the rules are then if you know so much," I said with a disdainful expression on my face.

"I'm not trying to frame you. I'm trying to do the same thing you are. I am fighting for survival. My men don't have an education but have street smarts. Women who have self-image problems, drug addictions, and mental problems, who can only make a living selling their bodies? I give them a world to live in. Not a pretty world like yours. Just a place for them to survive. You know what else, Miss High and Mighty? They are happy to have it."

"I need you to call Jaeger off of my ass," I said.

Clint looked around at the two goons and told them to leave the room. When we were alone, he said, "We come from different worlds, but we have something in common. We live in New Orleans. Jaeger and Ivanovich aren't from here. They are fucking with our world. So, at least for now, we are on the same side. I will tell you this. If you continue to be Miss Goody Two Shoes, you'll get your ass handed to you. Wise up. Bend the rules until they almost break if you want to survive. Use what you have and hit them below the belt. I won't hurt you, but I won't help you, either. I'll give you this advice. Be careful who you trust. Things aren't always what they seem. You're a smart girl. You'll figure it out. Now get out of here unless you want to see things that will give you nightmares."

I walked out of his office into the New Orleans sun, still puzzled what he meant by "things aren't always what they seem." The heat dragged me from my thoughts, pushing me to find shade or air conditioning. This was summer sun. It wasn't ten o'clock yet and sweat beads formed on my forehead as soon as the thick air hit me. Clint wasn't going to be an ally in my fight, but he wasn't coming after me, either. I took some comfort in knowing he wasn't putting a target on my ass, but Jaeger was another story. He was going to be hard to shake. I needed some good advice to figure out the best way to deal with him.

Jess Johnson had to be my next stop. She would make sense out of the players in this game. She'd dealt with the dark side of the city for more than thirty years. Just like always, I walked through the halls of *The Times* as though I was just another employee. No one made eye contact with me, though there were a few distant smiles. They knew my situation. For God's sakes, this was a newspaper. Nothing went on without them knowing.

"Come in and sit down," Jess said as I stood at her door. "You look like you could use a cup of coffee." She summoned an intern to bring us each a cup. *Weird,* I thought. *We still drink coffee in the middle of the hot days of summer. And we still love it.*

"Jess, Alric Jaeger is trying to charge me with letting an establishment for prostitution and accessory to murder in Tiffany's death. It's all bullshit. Jaeger wants to use Piper to smoke out Victor, and he knows I'm in the way."

"I know. They've taken Demetre off of the investigation. We had dinner at my house last night. He disclosed the evidence they have against you. The charges are bullshit. There's just not much he can do. Jaeger's got the chief's ear. He's letting Jaeger run with the investigation. The politics are thick on this investigation. The mayor wants to run for governor. Historically, New Orleans's politicians don't do well in Baton Rouge or North Louisiana. He thinks if he shows the public he's cracking down on trafficking in women, he'll get some support in those areas of the state. He might be right, too. You are unfortunate collateral damage."

"Have your reporters turned up any information that may help me?" I asked.

"They've been conducting extensive background research on Victor

Ivanovich and Alric Jaeger. I don't know the details yet, but it seems Jaeger has a blood vendetta against Ivanovich."

"I know. He blames the Russians for what happened to his family during World War II."

"The Russians were afraid that the Germans living in Russia would turn against the Russian government, so they deported millions of Germans, and many of them died during the exodus. The Russians claimed they were all Nazi sympathizers." That was more than I had known, but it didn't matter. I couldn't worry about crimes against long-dead people. Not when Tom, Piper, and I were in grave danger.

Jess went on to tell me Jaeger had a legitimate reason to investigate Victor's criminal activities. Victor's group hacked into several German banks, stealing millions of Euros. The banks put pressure on the German authorities to pursue Victor. Jaeger was more than happy to take up the cause. The rumors were that he'd get a fat reward from the banks if he brought Ivanovich to justice. It would be enough for him to retire anywhere in the world. I could see the attraction. If he got Victor, he'd end his career on a high note. He'd be a hero in Germany and would be set for life financially. Rewards like that would tempt lesser men.

I asked Jess to check into his family ties. I felt like there was more to Jaeger's motivation than what we knew. His pursuit of Victor was definitely personal. But it was also a long time ago for him. Something told me the exploitation of women got under his skin in a way that the hacking and drug trade didn't.

I so enjoyed talking to Jess. She was a rock for me, and nothing seemed to faze her. She assured me if we had to go down, we'd go down fighting. I wasn't interested in going down at all. My family was at stake. Time flew by and I remembered I had to drag myself to the police station to meet with Jaeger. I said farewell to Jess, hoping I'd see her again without bars separating us.

The afternoon sun beat down on the streets without mercy. Summer was in full bloom. People walking the streets moved slower this time of year. Most tried to stay indoors. For the first time I observed the street people who couldn't get out of the heat. They had nowhere to go.

How do they handle it day after grueling day? I wondered. These were the bottom one-percenters. They searched for places to hide from the midday sun. Unlike the goons I'd been associating with, they wanted shade to avoid the scorching sun, not to hide their criminal acts.

I was surprised when I entered the police precinct to find smiling faces greeting me. Several officers whispered, "We're with you," as I walked by. Wasn't it funny how the person on the front lines knew what was really going on when the brass didn't have a clue? Maybe the ones in control knew but had personal agendas they cloaked in veils of righteousness. It felt good to know these uniformed officers still believed in me.

Jaeger directed me to the interview room. I knew what that meant. He didn't want me to clear up anything; he wanted to interrogate me. I knew how this process worked. He would try to convince me he was my friend, looking out for my best interests. Then, when my guard went down, he'd hammer me with evidence or an outright lie to get me to confess to something. I braced myself for the roller coaster he was about to put me on.

"Tell me how long you've known Susan McAllister and the circumstances of your involvement with her and the murdered girl, Tiffany," Jaeger said.

I told him the entire story of how Sarah introduced me to Susan and her work at the Center for Abused and Battered Women and Children in LaPlace, Louisiana. I related all of the details of Sarah's murder, my inheritance, and my donation of Sarah's house to the center. I was sure he knew it all, but I played along with his cat-and-mouse game. I made the story take twice as long as it should have, just to fuck with him.

Jaeger listened without interrupting. He sat stone-faced, not reacting to any part of the story. He was a seasoned investigator. He showed only the emotion he wanted me to see. I edited my story, making sure I didn't reveal any information that might be harmful if Victor heard it. I knew he'd cloned Jaeger's phone and could have someone listening to our entire conversation.

Next he asked me to tell him how I came to be awarded custody of Piper. Once again I provided the details I thought he needed to know.

I held back the existence of the recording on Ethan's phone. I decided I would rather play that card at a later time.

After I had given him all the information he asked for, his tone changed, and he became hostile and gruff. "Ms. Lee, are you involved in the prostitution business?"

I wanted to kick him in his old, worn-out balls so hard they ended up in his foul mouth. I controlled myself, fighting my natural farmgirl instincts. "Never," I answered.

Jaeger displayed a forced smile, revealing his tobacco-stained, wide-spaced teeth. He plopped some photos in front of me in what he must have thought was one of those gotcha moments. "How is it then you were photographed visiting known human traffickers?"

I picked up one of the photos with my right hand as I sat back in my chair. I studied it carefully to figure out where the photographer had hidden. I wanted to make sure I knew where the photographer was in case I visited Clint's strip club or Victor at Gino's Restaurant again. After a few moments, Jaeger grew impatient.

"Well, Ms. Lee, do you have an answer to my question?"

"You know as well as I do, Inspector Jaeger, that there is a demonic battle raging for control of the dark side of New Orleans. My family and I are caught in the middle. We are not participants in the war like you, Inspector Jaeger. We are innocent bystanders. I will not allow myself or any of the people I love to become victims or collateral damage, as you military types say. Why was I meeting with Clinton Cunningham and Victor Ivanovich? I went to confront the demons where they lived. I wanted to look them in the eyes and see what types of monsters I had to deal with, much the same as I am doing now with you. As long as these demons threaten my family, I will chase them from the shadows where they dwell into the light to fight them on my terms, to the death if necessary. Does that clear things up for you, Inspector Jaeger?"

He was stunned by my candor. I had caught this seasoned interrogator off guard. He had no immediate response. Before he could regain his composure, I received a text from Piper. She sent me a copy of an article from a London tabloid. I scanned it quickly. The gossip rag featured two underage prostitutes who'd accused Jaeger of extorting sexual favors from them. The girls were both Romanian and probably working for Victor. Interpol pulled him back to Paris pending an investigation. No charges were filed, and Jaeger wasn't disciplined. I started to understand Jaeger's obsession.

When he finally found his stride again, he said, "Ms. Lee, I understand collateral damage better than you think. You are playing a game you can't win. You'd better back off and let me take care of Victor Ivanovich."

"As long as my family is in danger, I'm not backing off of anything. This isn't London," I said as I rose and walked out of the room without glancing back at his astonished face.

CHAPTER TWENTY-SIX
WHERE DEMONS DWELL

~

I COULDN'T DECIDE if Jaeger was a closet pervert or another victim of Victor's devious mind. He looked to me like he could be either one. He definitely wasn't a clean cop. He'd been involved with the Dixie Mafia and drug cartels. I couldn't help but think that once he'd climbed in bed with them he picked up some of their habits. He sent Zach to see El Alacran, knowing the dangers. He didn't blink an eye when Zach was beaten within an inch of his life. Even Clint kept Jaeger at arm's length. *No*, I thought, *there's no doubt he's a dirty cop*. He knew I wasn't involved in Tiffany's death, but he was willing to arrest me just to use Piper as bait. I wondered exactly how he was going to use Piper. There were too many mysteries circling around me to come to a conclusion.

I went to the condo to chat with Piper via the web. She was really good at this web stuff. She linked her computer and mine so we could video chat. I sat in front my computer at the kitchen table with a cup of coffee. She was in her bedroom at her foster family's home. She toured me through the room with the camera on her phone. It had obviously been a boy's room at some time. There were posters of football players, MMA fighters, and Louisiana's own Britney Spears decorating the walls. Absolutely no pink anywhere, but there were plenty of blues and blacks.

Piper smiled from ear to ear as she looked at my face spread all over her computer screen. "Alexandra, I miss you so much. These people are nice, but I want to be with you and Tom. Have you heard from him?"

"Not yet. Sophia's in Mexico, so I'm sure we'll hear something soon. Don't worry, we'll all be back together soon." I only hoped I wasn't lying to her.

"So, let me tell you what I've found out since I sent you the text. There were two girls in London who accused Jaeger of trying to extort sex from them in exchange for having their prostitution charges dropped. They were only sixteen years old. I hacked into the computer of the creepy tabloid that reported the story and found all kinds of cool stuff. The tabloid had recordings of the telephone messages from Jaeger setting up meetings with the girls. His messages said if they cooperated with him and did him favors he'd drop their charges. His tone was so lecherous I was totally grossed out."

"That's pretty good, but it's not exactly a smoking gun. He may have been talking about their legitimate cooperation in exchange for dropping charges. Police and prosecutors do that all the time," I said.

"True. The girls' names and cell phone numbers were in the tabloid's records, too. I got in touch with both of the girls. They were really pretty cool. I told them what Jaeger was putting us through, and they really dished on him. They didn't have anything to do with Victor; that was just a cover Jaeger used to hide his true intentions. They spoke to the tabloids because they were paid big bucks to tell about all of the British politicians they were sleeping with. They were promised anonymity. I'm sure the promise didn't include hackers like me," she said, giggling at herself. "They aren't in the game anymore and don't want to be exposed. Interpol didn't believe their allegations about Jaeger because the tabloids had paid them for the story. So it all went away for Jaeger."

I thought for a minute while I sipped my coffee. "I'll bet Jaeger thinks Victor put the tabloids on the story. Or maybe he just thinks they were Victor's girls. Just added fuel for his vendetta against Victor."

"There's more," Piper said. "Seems Jaeger has a granddaughter who is a high-priced hooker. I tracked her down using some special software my friends and I hacked into and improved while I was living in California. His granddaughter goes by the name Ms. Kitty and has a website on the dark web."

"Dark web again," I said.

"The dark web or deep web is actually the majority of the Internet. They are sites hard for Google to index because they're either changing all the time or they require interaction. These sites are designed to be inaccessible to ordinary browsers. They offer nothing for the search engines to hook onto—the opposite of your average commercial site, which spends loads of money on search engine optimization: registration, keywords, and so on. With the dark web sites, you have to know the exact address and sometimes passwords. It's all word of mouth."

"And it's all criminal activity?"

"Mostly. Maybe some hidden political stuff, like in China or something, I don't know, but what I've found are ads for erotic services from sex workers as well as sites that sell drugs, weapons, and just about anything else you wouldn't want people to know you're buying or selling. Ms. Kitty bills herself as an exotic escort. Her rates are 1,500 euros a night. Her clients pay all of her expenses. She usually works on the French and Italian Riviera. Her site is linked to all of Victor's sites on the dark web," Piper said.

"Holy shit. Linked to Victor's sites? That must really piss Jaeger off. No wonder he hates Victor so much. I still don't know why he's putting you and me in the middle of all of this."

"I don't either, but I can't wait until it's over and we can be together again," Piper said. This time her voice cracked. She was about to start crying. "Gotta go."

The connection went blank. I knew she didn't want me to see her cry. Frankly, I wouldn't have been able to take it. My emotions were in a knot. I missed her, and Tom, too. What was he going through in Mexico? He must be scared to death. I wondered if he knew what was happening to us here in New Orleans. I really hoped not. It would only make things worse for him.

Oh shit, I'd completely forgotten that I had to go to Mr. Morris's wake. Charlotte had texted me the time and funeral home location. She really wanted me to come. I thought how awkward it was going to be with Mandy and her creepy Uncle Garrett there. But Charlotte needed my support, so I jumped in the shower and put on a black dress I hadn't worn since Sarah's funeral. Memories flooded my mind. The emotional tsunami caught me completely off guard. I began to cry, and all of my fresh mascara ran down my cheeks. *Crap*, I thought, *now I have to wash my face and reapply my makeup.* That's when I heard a knock at my door.

I thought it was the cute girl selling Girl Scout cookies again, so I got a twenty-dollar bill from my purse. When I opened the door, there stood Victor Ivanovich and El Alacran. I jumped back at the sight of them. Victor's green eyes nearly sparked the air between us. Damn, he was good looking. The Scorpion even looked respectable in his beige suit with a blue shirt and yellow tie. Both men grabbed their coat jackets with their hands, opening them as they said, "We come in peace." That was a statement I highly doubted. Since I had a dress on I didn't have my gun strapped to my leg. I decided to let them in anyway. If they wanted to hurt me they would have others with them. And they wouldn't be nicely dressed, standing at my front door so everyone could see them.

"Excuse me for a second. I have to unplug my curling iron." I went to the bedroom and took the SMS card out of my phone. Piper would have been so proud. Victor couldn't clone my phone now. When I returned I said, "I have somewhere to be, so get to the point. What do you two want?"

El Alacran spoke first. "See how these American women are, Victor? They don't offer you any hospitality. They don't have proper manners. My son is a chemistry student at Tulane. I've told him not to get involved with an American woman. Colombian women know how to treat a man."

I narrowed my eyes and clenched my jaw. As if any self-respecting American woman would want his slimy, black-hearted son. I didn't say that, though, I just gave him my best go-to-hell look. He smiled back at me, the no-good bastard. It was obvious there was no love lost between the two of us. I never felt hatred for anyone like I did for him. He was responsible for killing Sarah. I watched him kill Camila in Colombia. He would have killed me, too, if he could have.

I turned my eyes to Victor. "Look, Alexandra," he said, "maybe we got off on the wrong foot. I would like to start over. We have so many common interests now. We both want that German asshole Jaeger off our backs. Word is he's going to charge you with the murder of one of the poor unfortunate girls under your care at that home you run. Your friend Susan is already in jail, and you're sure to be next. We also both want what is best for young Constance. Her mother misses her. I miss her. Now that her father's dead and her uncle's in jail in Mexico, she needs to be back in the loving care of her family. We appreciate all that you've done for her, but it's time she came home."

My blood began to riot in my veins. My face turned red and my heart rate increased. I wanted to keep controlling myself, but it was nearly impossible. His patronizing tone and the memory of Piper's grief was just too much to bear. My blue eyes flashed at his green, serpent eyes. My hands turned cold and clammy. I balled my fists.

"Who do you think you are fooling? Piper's mother is dead. You murdered her. She sent Piper to her father's house in Chicago to get her away from you. You only want her for what she can do for your criminal enterprises. I told you before, Tom and I are her family now. She hates you. She knows what you are and what you did to her mother. I'll see you in hell before I let you have her."

"I was hoping your current legal troubles would make you see matters a little more clearly," Victor said as he focused his emerald green eyes on me. He seemed not the slightest bit affected by my accusations. "I can see you are not quite ready to be reasoned with. Soon, I think you'll come around. And, by the way, I spoke to my friends in the Mexican Justice Department. They think your boyfriend is part of an international terror group. They intend to make an example of him. If you ever think we can talk more civilly, call me. I think I can convince them he's just a harmless environmentalist."

El Alacran breathed in and out like a man who'd just run a

marathon. His hate-filled eyes met mine, and he said, "My friend here is very tactful. I do things differently. If you don't do what we want, puta, I am going to cut your head off and put it in a box and send it to your boyfriend in the Mexican jail. Once he has a chance to cry and scream, I'm going to cut his head off and send it to his hippie parents in California. You hear me, bitch?"

Victor grabbed his arm and led him to the door. Victor flipped a business card on my table and said, "My number's on the card if you want to talk."

They left the condo, and I took a few minutes to calm down. These were definitely two different types of demons. They both dealt in depravity and death. One was a little smoother than the other, but they were both death dealers. I was in a world of shit and so was my whole family. I collected myself and put my SMS card back in my phone. I'll bet Victor shit in his $500 pants when he couldn't clone my phone. Score one for Piper and me.

Even though I'd foiled his attempt to clone my phone, they'd delivered the message. Play ball with them or they would destroy Tom and me. Victor showed me he had control of Tom's fate in Mexico. He also let me know he'd release his rabid dog, El Alacran, on me if he didn't get what he wanted. I couldn't make any deals with them. They would kill me no matter what I agreed to. It didn't really matter because I wasn't agreeing to anything anyway. The fight was going to be to the death.

I put my gun in my purse and headed to the funeral home. I hoped the wake would be less dramatic than the first part of my day. Too much to ask for, I feared.

I found Charlotte as soon as I arrived at the funeral home. The seating was a little disturbing. There was a friends-of-the-bride-and-friends-of-the-groom thing going on. Mandy and Garrett Morris were on the left side of the aisle, and Charlotte and most of Superior Sugar's employees were on the right side. I felt the tension in the room as soon as I entered. What struck me as strange was that the family was dry-eyed, laughing and joking, while the employees were somber, silent, and crying. Role reversal on display, to say the least.

I walked to the front of the room, being careful not to view the body. I didn't like carrying the image of a person in their casket around with me. I preferred to remember them in life. I gave my condolences to Mandy and Garrett before I joined Charlotte on the other side of the room. My poor friend was hopelessly grief-stricken, her eyes nearly swollen shut from crying. She greeted me with a half-smile as I sat beside her.

"Alexandra, I don't think I can face the world without him," she whispered. "He was always there for me. He was a great man." She broke down again, whimpering as she cried.

It was a pitiful sight to see, but I couldn't help but think that all of his problems were solved now. He was at peace. His family, well, that was another matter altogether. He'd left his daughter, Mandy, and his brother, Garrett, behind to sort out their lives. Garrett was a gambler and a sexual deviant. Mandy was a more lamentable creature. Her life shifted with the most dominant male influence in her life at the time. I hoped she would find someone other than Garrett to influence her. I remembered how many people warned me to stay away from him when they found out I was working for Superior Sugar. I knew he went to dog fights but had no idea the depth of his depravity. I just knew I didn't want anything to do with him.

When Charlotte's crying spell settled, I took her by the arm and led her out of the viewing room to the funeral home's kitchen so we could talk. She needed to get out of that room for awhile. This whole place was pretty sterile; not the cozy café I would have chosen, but at least there were no dead bodies in the kitchen and we were alone. We poured ourselves a cup of coffee then went and sat in the lobby together.

"Charlotte, I am so sorry for your loss. I know he meant a great deal to you."

She looked out the window at the swaying trees and said, "More than you'll ever know, Alexandra. He was such a good person. He didn't deserve the problems his family gave him. He always tried to do the right thing."

"I didn't know him well. But I could tell he was a wonderful person," I said.

She really didn't hear my words. She was in her own world of memories. "When he discovered the contribution sugar made to the world's obesity epidemic, he decided he couldn't stay in the business any longer. That's when he opened the stevia company. He didn't want to be in a business that hurt people."

Mandy approached us as we spoke. I prepared myself for a rant but was surprised by her conciliatory attitude. She sat next to Charlotte and took her hand. It took a moment for Charlotte to comprehend who'd taken her hand. Before she could react, Mandy said, "I'm sorry for the scene I caused at Superior Sugar the other day, Charlotte. I was overwhelmed with grief at the loss of my father. I want you to know how much our family appreciates you. You've shown unconditional dedication to my father throughout the years you've worked for Superior Sugar."

Charlotte seemed comforted by Mandy's gesture. I doubted the sincerity, but it didn't matter to me as long as it made Charlotte feel better. It did make me wonder what Mandy was up to. Maybe I was being a little too paranoid. Then she turned to me.

"Alexandra, I hope you will continue your relationship with our company. We need you more than ever now. This isn't the time to talk about business, but I would appreciate it if you would come to our office in the next few days to talk about how we could work together."

She stood and walked away, her long black dress trailing behind her. Charlotte said I should meet with her. I really didn't want to think about it now. Fortunately, I received a text from Jess Johnson before I could respond to Charlotte.

Demetre and I would like to meet with you tomorrow.

What now?

CHAPTER TWENTY-SEVEN
HUMAN TRAFFICKING

WHEN I RETURNED to my condo, my bed sucked me into it. I threw my clothes off and debated with myself about the need to take my makeup off. I lost the debate and was thankful the task was mindless. I fell into bed like a live oak tree toppled by a hurricane. Healing, dreamless sleep left me motionless on my bed. I awoke the next morning without having ruffled the covers. I'd slept on top of them and didn't move enough during the night to disturb them more than slightly.

I brushed my teeth, finding I'd regained the energy sapped from me yesterday. I looked at the clock. Holy shit, it was ten o'clock in the morning. I'd never slept that long in my life. I pushed the button on the magic machine and called Jess.

"When would you like to meet?" I asked.

"How about in an hour at the Community Coffee shop by the newspaper?"

"I'll be there."

When I hung up the phone, I opened my computer to read my blog site. Louisiana had become a hot spot for missing young women. Girls from Shreveport to Morgan City were reported missing. The numbers weren't large by Los Angeles or New York standards, just excessive for Louisiana. All were between sixteen and twenty-two, and most were considered runaways by the police. I knew better. It wasn't a coincidence that Victor was moving his operation into New Orleans at the same time as the spike in missing girls.

Piper had left me a sweet message. She wrote, "I hope you sleep well tonight. I miss you and love you. Can't wait to be back with you. :)"

I sent her an "I love you" message back. I didn't have time to write more because I had to head out to meet Jess and Detective Baker. I made sure I had my pistol strapped to my leg before I left. From now on, I resolved not to go anywhere without it. It took me a few minutes to drive to the coffee shop, and I made sure I wasn't being followed.

Jess and Detective Baker were already seated when I arrived. I loved the smell of freshly brewed coffee that dominated the shop. They had chosen seats in the back corner with their backs to the wall. I had to sit facing them, leaving my back exposed. I wasn't comfortable sitting like that, but I knew these two wouldn't let anyone sneak up on me.

Jess always dressed comfortably. She looked professional and feminine at the same time. She chose dark colors even in the summer, probably because she was always seated at her desk in the air conditioning. Detective Baker, on the other hand, always wore a suit that screamed, "I'm a cop."

Jess took the floor. "Alexandra, I've been researching Victor Ivanovich's past. He was descended from one of the Russian Czars. His family always enjoyed great wealth. That is, until World War II broke out. Both his maternal and paternal grandfathers fought against the Germans. They were both killed in action, and the family lost all of its wealth. His family background plagued him in communist Russia. He grew up a scrappy street kid in Moscow. He was smart and ambitious. He formed his own gang, which took advantage of the breakdown of the Soviet Union. He brutalized his way to the top of the Russian Mafia hierarchy."

Baker joined in. "He's found a way to make political connections in Baton Rouge. He is the one who has gotten the Department of

Family Services to go after the center and you. We are fairly sure that the girl poisoned at the center was working for him. My hands are tied. Jaeger has used political pull to get me thrown off of the investigation. He's even gotten a couple of CIA contractors helping him. He has convinced Homeland Security that Victor is a threat to national security because of his hacking operation in Russia. Jaeger wants to use your girl, Constance, as bait to bring charges against Victor."

"I don't get it. How is Piper bait if she's in a foster home?" I asked.

"His plan is a little twisted but also clever when you think about it," Baker said. "Victor intervened in your lawsuit on behalf of the little girl's mother to get custody of her. If he won, he'd have the girl. If you and Tom won, Victor could kidnap the girl and claim she ran away or it was just a civil matter. Not likely law enforcement would get involved. But if the State of Louisiana had custody and the child was in foster care, and *then* he kidnapped the girl, the state would have to pursue criminal charges and track her down. Victor would certainly be prosecuted along with anyone who helped him. So Jaeger placed her with a family who's letting her have all the freedom she wants to tempt Victor to take her."

Jess chimed in, "I think this Butler woman with the Department of Family Services is involved somehow. She's way too committed to taking Piper away from you not to be. Something is rotten with her. Jaeger knows Piper is a computer prodigy. He's convinced Homeland Security if Victor gets her, she'll be a danger to national defense."

"She's just a child. She's not a danger to anyone," I said. "She deserves a normal life just like everyone else. They are treating her like a pawn in some international game. I won't stand for it."

Jess said she was still putting her story together on Victor and wasn't even close to going to print. He had concealed his illegal activities very well. Baker said there was some software given to the police department by Homeland Security that searched the dark web and mapped the connections to sites and people. It helped reveal the identities of the people behind the sites. The Defense Advanced Research Projects Agency, DARPA, had developed an Internet search tool to help bust human traffickers. The problem was only one person in the New Orleans Police Department was trained to use it. There was no way Baker could get Jess access to it.

"Is it on the police department central server?" I asked.

"Yes," Baker said with a broad smile. He knew what I had in mind. I'd get Piper to hack into it. She'd already mentioned software she and her friend in LA developed. She'd used her software to track down Jaeger's granddaughter's website. If anyone could get to the software, Piper could.

I told Jess and Baker what Piper had found out about Jaeger's past. Detective Baker said if I could prove any wrongdoing on Jaeger's part, it would go a long way toward getting him removed from the investigation of Tiffany's death. Baker went on to say that all of the NOPD cops were in my corner and would help any way they could. It felt good to hear, but I still had to clear my own name. They had all been sidelined.

How was I going to get the evidence Detective Baker needed to eliminate Jaeger from the investigation? More importantly, how was I going to prove neither Susan nor I killed Tiffany? I had no way to track down what I needed to clear my name.

I went back to my condo, and Zach was sitting on the steps waiting for me. We went inside and closed and locked the door. "I thought you left town," I said.

"I sent Maddy to one of her friend's," Zach said. "I was called by Clinton Cunningham. He wants you and me to go to a party together tonight."

I searched his eyes to make sense of what he'd just said. "A party? Are you crazy?"

"It's a party thrown by some wealthy old guard folks in New Orleans," Zach said. "Clint felt like we ought to go. He's gotten us an invite. He said to dress sexy and bring a mask. It's one of those kinky kind of parties."

I still didn't get it. "Why does he want us to go to a kinky party?"

"He said things aren't always what they appear to be. We should go and keep our eyes open. Clint added Victor is bringing in high-priced female talent for the affair, free of charge. It's part of his wooing of the New Orleans city fathers."

Clint must have his reasons for sending me to an event for Victor. He wanted Victor out of town as much as I did. Zach gave me one of the party invitations and told me he'd be at my condo at eight o'clock tonight. I didn't think it was the type of party I'd go to by choice, but what the hell did I have to lose? The thought of nailing Victor made me anxious to go. I wanted to see who would show up to a soiree like that.

Zach left to catch the streetcar to whoever's house he was crashing at for the night. The gay culture in New Orleans had created a close-knit family; they really took care of each other. It wasn't unusual for gay residents to offer their couches and floors to out-of-towners coming to party in the Big Easy. In addition to Mardi Gras, Southern Decadence was a city-wide event that drew gay people from around the world. They filled up the hotels and couches of the entire city. It was quite a spectacle to behold. They were one large family, and they treated each other like family. They had spats but coalesced if someone outside their community threatened them. It was a shame everyone couldn't treat each other like that all the time.

I'd barely had time to clean my place when I had another knock at my front door. It was Ms. Butler. She was here to do a court-ordered home inspection of my living arrangements. I thought it odd that she just showed up without an appointment. Then I remembered she didn't have my cell number, and I'd told Piper not to give it to anyone. So I decided to let her in. She took the tour of my small condo in less than five minutes. Not much to see.

"Would you like a cup of coffee?" I asked.

"Yes, Ms. Lee, as a matter of fact I would. How long have you lived in this place?"

"Not long, about three years," I answered.

Ms. Butler took a sip of coffee. "Mmm, that's good," she said. "It's a nice condo, but don't you think it's too small for you and Constance? She doesn't have a bed to sleep in. A girl her age needs some privacy and a place to sleep. I don't mean a couch, either. What about her clothes?

Where are you going to put her clothes? She doesn't have a dresser of her own. Where will she do her homework? Here at the kitchen table?"

All of the rapid-fire questions were not really designed to get an answer. They were supposed to make me see how untenable my condo was for custody of Piper. I dodged the opportunity to answer them. I told her we were looking for a more suitable place as well as a school where she'd feel comfortable. Of course she didn't listen to my answers. That's not why she was really here. She was looking for reasons to take custody away from Tom and me.

"I understand Constance's uncle is in jail in Mexico. Is that correct?" she asked. "Can you give me any time frame when you expect him to be released, or is he going to have to serve time in Mexico? I know the charges are very serious. The Mexican government considers him a terrorist."

Wow. How did she know that the Mexican government was considering filing eco-terrorism charges against Tom? It could have come from Jaeger, but I didn't think he was interested in Tom. The more likely source was Victor. Jess warned me he'd gotten the Department of Family Services on my ass. When I saw her sidle up to Jaeger at the center, pledging to work with him, I'd bet she was just a spy for Victor. If so, there was no use in trying to make nice with her.

"Tom has been arrested as an environmental protester. He was peacefully protesting the planting of genetically modified corn in the southern part of Mexico. The government currently forbids GMOs in the south because they are a danger to native corn that has been the chief source of food for Mexicans for centuries. He's a hero in my book. Now, are we done here?" I asked.

She left with a confident look on her face. She'd obviously gotten what she'd come for. She could tell the court my condo was too small for the proper care of a young lady. I had to find a way to expose her for the fake she was. Maybe Piper could use her magic fingers to dig up some dirt on Ms. Butler.

I emailed Piper her mission to check into DARPA's web surfing program and also to find out what she could about Butler. Piper bounced right back to me. She'd already hacked DARPA's program.

That was the software she and her California friend had improved. She could find out anything about anybody on the dark web. She went right to work digging into Victor's connections to Tiffany and everyone else on the web. If it were there, she'd find it.

She said finding the dirt on Butler might require some of her black hat tactics, so she contacted some of her friends in LA to do the dirty work for her. They would need a day or two but would find every secret she had. Piper said they would even be able to tell me if she wore thong underwear or granny panties. I suspected that mental image would take some serious scrubbing to erase.

I had to hustle. Time had flown by. I needed to find a dress and mask for the big event tonight. Zach told me it was a dressy affair. Of course it was some type of party involving high-priced call girls; sex had to be on the menu. I picked a dress that accentuated my boobs. I hadn't displayed them to the city since Tom and I started dating. I squeezed them into a push-up bra, allowing their abundance to overflow. The tight bra I chose guaranteed there would be no wardrobe malfunction. I put my hair on top of my head and donned some of Sarah's dangling earrings. I broke out my Jimmy Choo shoes and some sparkling bracelets. I overdid my makeup. I was farmgirl-turned-Cinderella again, ready for the ball. Only there wouldn't be any Prince Charming at this event. Just a bunch of horny rich people walking the edge of morality.

I looked at myself in the mirror. I was sexy in that slutty kind of way. A few years ago I would have been proud of the way I looked. But not now; I was embarrassed. I was no longer interested in having random men lust after me. I wanted a family life.

CHAPTER TWENTY-EIGHT
DARK WORLD

ZACH SHOWED UP in a blue outfit accented by a feathered peacock mask. I was afraid to ask why he owned such a thing, though it looked good on him. I followed the instructions on the invitation to a spacious house on the lakefront, the grounds finely landscaped with crepe myrtles and roses. I had no idea whose house it was, but I knew they were rich. The street was lined with expensive cars. The New Orleans Mercedes dealership didn't have that many S-Class cars. This place screamed money.

Zach and I showed our invitations at the door and then made our way inside to the center of the house. The furnishings were all contemporary. The floor was made of wide pine planks, dark stained, but everything else was light. The open floor plan allowed us to circulate from room to room without any obstruction.

Elegantly dressed people with faces covered by masks chatted in the great room. Scantily-clad women flirted openly, performing pre-sex acts for all to see. I blushed under my mask. Zach confided he'd been to many parties like this. These were rich, bored elites spicing their lives with rented sex partners. He warned me the swapping would begin soon. I braced myself, not knowing if my Midwestern upbringing would allow me to endure the spectacle. I didn't want to be here. These people were not living authentic lives. They were distracting themselves with sex, booze, and drugs. All were used to stimulate dopamine production in their brains, the feel-good neurotransmitter that elicited the pleasure response, making us temporarily feel good. But it didn't last. The after-crash put the addict in a worse place than they were before the high. As Mr. Morris had explained to me, sugar produced similar dopamine reactions, and that was why people found it hard to cut back—because they were addicted.

Even though I wanted no part of their world, I had to mingle. What had Clint meant, things weren't always what they seemed? Zach and I drifted from cluster to cluster of people jabbering on about themselves. It was easy to spot Victor's girls because they were the young and pretty ones. Most attendees were middle-aged men, with a sprinkling of older women. They sipped their wine and in some cases whiskey, keeping their eyes on the quarry supplied by their host.

All of the conversations I participated in eventually drifted their way to sex. Couples paired off and disappeared into rooms as the night progressed. I engaged with as many people as I could, using my Lois Lane instincts to glean information from each of them. No one used his or her correct name. Around eleven o'clock the alcohol broke down all inhibitions. The scene descended into a full-blown orgy with people-tangles everywhere I looked; couples, groups, male on male, female on female, and every other combination imaginable. My church upbringing urged me to get the hell out of there. I didn't want to blow my cover, so I feigned a migraine. I've never said no in so many ways in my life. The best answer was to say Zach and I were newlyweds. That got some people's imaginations going, but they didn't push it, other than to remark that we certainly were getting an education. Yeah, just not the one they thought.

I couldn't stand what I was seeing any longer. I made Zach take me out of there.

My stomach turned somersaults as I tried to make my eyes unsee what they insisted on seeing. So that was what rich people in New Orleans did for amusement. Surely not all of them? I scanned the repulsive images in my mind to identify what Clint wanted me to see. Maybe it was Victor's girls? I still had no idea, and Zach couldn't figure it out, either, though he wasn't repulsed by anything he'd seen. He'd walked those paths before, and now he was paying the price.

"In my younger days I would have been right in the middle of the action," Zach said. "All drugged up, prostituting myself for more drugs. I don't miss that lifestyle at all. Maddy and I want a stable life doing healthy things. We're going to work and pool our money so someday we'll save enough to be organic farmers."

I was elated to hear the change in Zach. He'd finally gotten himself on track. I dropped Zach at his friend's house and headed to my condo. I took another shower before going to bed just because I felt dirty after witnessing the dark world in the suburbs of New Orleans. I had no idea parties like that went on in the city.

The next day I had an appointment to see Mr. Swartz. When we sat down in his office to talk, he was stiff and formal. I knew he couldn't have good news for me. He always stiffened up when he had to tell me something I didn't want to hear. I guess it was a defense mechanism he'd developed practicing law. He must have had to deliver bad news quite often.

"I have been contacted again by ACC's lawyers," he said. "They are insisting you make your choice of contractors. They say if they don't hear from me within two weeks, the deal is off. I know Tom wanted to supervise the work, but given his current situation, I don't see how that is possible."

"I am sorry for the delay. I know we are not keeping up our end of the bargain, Mr. Swartz. I'll definitely have a name for you within two weeks. Tom should be back from Mexico soon."

Oh my God. Did I just lie to my lawyer or was I just doing some wishful thinking? I was going to have to make the judgment call myself if Sophia didn't spring Tom soon. I missed him every night and every day. It was so hard waking up without him next to me.

"There's a second matter we need to discuss," Swartz said. "We had a telephone conference with the judge in your custody case yesterday after the Department of Family Services visited your house. Of course your current legal problems were discussed. I assured the court you were being wrongfully accused. The judge said time would tell, but even if you were cleared, your living arrangements would have to change for her to consider awarding you custody of Constance. She could not place a child in a living arrangement without a bed of her own. Have you given any thought to what you can do about finding a new place?"

"Yes, we have looked at several places. I know we will have to move, but with everything that is going on moving hasn't been my priority," I said.

"It needs to become a priority if you hope to win custody of Constance. We need to have a plan ready in two weeks detailing how you intend to take care of her," he said. "I am sorry to load you up with these requirements, but I have no choice. The court has asked the child's mother to do the same. Her lawyer informed me she intends to take Constance back to California to live. The Department of Family Services' attorney advised the court that the foster parents were prepared to care for the child until custody was awarded. From what I can tell, right now, you are the court's third choice for custody."

"Oh shit. Mr. Swartz, you think I might lose her, don't you? I can't let that happen. May I visit Piper, I mean Constance?" I asked.

He picked up the phone and called the attorney for the Department of Family Services, the foster mother, and the judge while I waited. They agreed to the visit on the condition that I went to the foster family's house immediately. Not a problem. I really needed to see Piper. I missed her. I didn't know what I'd do if the judge sent her to California.

I left Mr. Swartz's office racking my brain for a solution to my living arrangements on my way to the foster family's home. I didn't want to make any plans for Tom and me with him still in Mexico. How the hell was I going to get a new place in the next two weeks? Holy shit, my new place might be a jail cell if Jaeger had anything to say about it. And even if that didn't happen, I'd need Tom's signature on a lease to get a big enough place because my income would fall short of what was needed.

The foster family's house was in a swanky subdivision. The family obviously had money. A very pleasant woman in her mid-forties greeted me at the front door. She showed me into her family room. When we passed the kitchen, I did a double take. There, seated at the kitchen table, was one of the couples I'd seen last night at the party. I was sure it was them. What was going on here?

I looked at the lady escorting me and said, "Oh, I'm sorry. I didn't know you had company."

"No problem. That's my brother and his wife from Los Angeles. He's in town for business. He works for some European company. I'm not sure what he does. Something to do with the Internet, I think."

Holy shit, now I knew why Clint sent us to the orgy party. He wanted me to see these people. That means the European company he worked for was really Victor's mafia group. Probably Ms. Butler was working with Victor, too, placing Piper in this foster home at Victor's request. He'd outsmarted Jaeger. He must be planning to kidnap Piper and make it look like she ran away, or maybe he had something else planned. Whatever he had up his sleeve involved these Californians. He thought his fingerprints weren't on this subterfuge. Well, he was about to find out he was wrong. I was going to fix his ass.

Piper ran into the room and jumped on me. She threw her arms around my neck and hung on. I put my arms around her back and spun around. Her legs flew through the air as we twirled, and the joy in my heart was hard to contain. I could never be separated from this little girl.

We sat on the sofa next to each other, and I whispered to her, "Piper, I need you to find out some information for me. Listen carefully. I think your foster mother's brother is working for Victor. I need you to find out everything you can about them. I need proof that they are connected to the Russian Mafia. It's the only way I'm going to convince the court to let you stay with me."

"I can do that," she said. "Now let me tell you what I found out digging in Ms. Butler's life. She recently deposited $25,000 into her checking account. The check was written by a bank in the Cayman Islands. The company who wrote the check is named the European Collaborative Organization. I tracked its incorporation papers to

Liechtenstein. The Collaborative is owned by Victor Ivanovich. Copies of the incorporation papers will be in your email tomorrow. You will also receive a copy of the check made out to Ms. Baker. I can't tell you who got this for me or how they did it, so you can't give it to the police or any other authorities. Maybe you can find another way to use the information."

I grabbed Piper and kissed her cherub cheeks. "Piper, you are amazing. I can use this all right. Finally, some ammunition to fight back with," I said. "Today is getting better with every passing moment."

Piper's foster mother came into the room. She apologized for the interruption but said it was time for Piper to get cleaned up for supper. I hated to leave, but I had my work cut out for me if I was going to put all the information together into some sort of strategy to beat these bastards. Piper and I kissed and hugged, and I left her with her foster parents and Victor's pals from California.

I couldn't help but think about what Tom had said to me long ago when I was battling Bart Rogan: "These devils are like cockroaches; they thrive in the darkness and shadows. Shine a light on them and they scatter." That's what I needed to do; use my talents as a writer to expose them. How could I do that without compromising Piper or her friend? The only way they could have gotten this information was through illegal means. I couldn't put them in jeopardy. I pondered the questions while I drove. Nothing came to mind, so I asked my mother and Sarah for guidance. As I drove I got a gut feeling I needed to go to the shelter. Maybe it was my mom and Sarah guiding me, or maybe it was intuition. Whichever it was, I was going to follow it, learning long ago to listen to my intuition, knowing it spoke to me for a reason.

I drove to Sarah's House. I found Karen Durio in the family room breast-feeding her infant. I told her I was her proud of the care she was giving her baby. I asked how she'd chosen to breast-feed. She was only seventeen years old. She explained she'd been on the Internet ever since she learned she was pregnant, preparing herself to be a mom. She'd learned breast-feeding boosted the immune system. When she finished, she asked if she could speak to me privately.

We sat in Susan's office with our chairs close enough to hear each other's whispers. "Two other girls came to the center on the same day Tiffany arrived. I thought it was a little odd that so many women needed help on the same day. I grew suspicious when I saw they all knew each other. Something was wrong with them. They didn't seem to fit in here. Yesterday, they were in the bathroom together. I needed to wash my baby's face, so I waited by the door for them to finish. I heard them say they felt bad for what they did, but Tiffany had to go. Victor insisted. It was either her or them. I don't know exactly what they meant, but I thought you should know."

"Do you know the girls' names?" I asked.

Karen pulled out her cell phone. "Not their real names, but I have their pictures if that will help."

She handed me her phone and I texted the photos to myself. I'd send these to Piper, hoping she'd recognize them. I thanked Karen and warned her to stay clear of those two and keep this between us. She assured me she wouldn't say a word to anyone.

I left the center and headed back to my condo. So that was how Victor pulled this whole frame-up job. He had sent three girls into the center. Tiffany's job must have been to lure the Dixie Mafia's girls to a hotel, thinking they were going to turn a trick. She sent the Uber driver to pick them up. When the girls refused to cooperate, she or one of Victor's goons killed them and disposed of the bodies. When Jaeger found out Tiffany was working for Victor, he texted Tiffany's photo to Clinton Cunningham. He didn't know Victor had cloned his phone and had intercepted the photo and message. That must have been when Victor gave the order to the other two girls at the center to poison Tiffany and frame Susan. Victor had done his homework on Susan and knew her family's history, planning to frame her all along. He was brilliantly diabolical. He just didn't count on Karen's loyalty to Susan and me. He also didn't know how incredible a hacker Piper was.

My next step was to tie these two girls to Victor, if possible. I sent the photos to Piper with instructions to find their true identities and get back to me as soon as possible. I couldn't wait to hear back from her. When Piper's email arrived on my blog, I wasn't disappointed.

CHAPTER TWENTY-NINE
TURNED INSIDE OUT

THERE WERE TWO emails from Piper, one sent earlier in the day. It contained videos of the two girls whom Jaeger had taken advantage of in London, and Piper had concealed their identities with clever video editing, covering their faces digitally with an editing program. I didn't know how she did it, but the little minx talked the girls into allowing her to use their names and videos if necessary. That wasn't all she'd done to Jaeger. She'd hacked his phone and sent the videos to him, making it appear they were all over the Internet. I'll bet he crapped his pants when he saw them.

I nearly broke my fingers opening Piper's second email. She'd attached a diagram of all of Victor's websites on the dark web. There were photos of girls who appeared on multiple sites. She had even recorded the dates, times, and locations the photos were taken. In some cases, when the photo had been taken by a cell phone, she gave me the registered owner of the phone and added that she could give me the complete address book as well as the most recent calls.

She also delivered what I was most interested in: a picture of Tiffany, whose real name was Althea Antipov, from Ukraine; the other two girls—both Americans from Los Angeles; and complete dossiers on all of them. There were photos of each of the girls on many of Victor's websites. Piper had hacked the phones of the two girls and had printouts of the telephone numbers they'd texted. The phones led back to Victor. Though one of the correspondences definitively linked them, or Victor, to the death of Tiffany, a.k.a. Althea, I had enough to clear Susan of the murder. I wanted to do backflips.

I took all of the information and wrote an article detailing Victor's background and connection to the porn and hooker sites. I described the various services the girls offered as well as how long they'd worked for him. I included gobs of photos of each of the girls from the sites on which they were featured.

Then I wrote the story of Victor's connections in Baton Rouge, displaying the check and deposit to Ms. Butler's account. I attached the corporate papers from Lichtenstein showing Victor as owner.

When I finished writing the article, I picked up the card Victor had given me when he and El Alacran visited my condo and called him. Somehow, he knew it was me when he answered the phone.

"Well, hello, Alexandra. What a pleasant surprise. How may I help you?"

"No, Mr. Ivanovich, it's how I can help you that's important," I said. "Do you have a private email address? I need to send you an article I'm turning in to *The Times* today. I'd like you to review it for accuracy. If you have any suggestions, I'd love to hear them. Once you've read it, call me back at this number."

Victor gave me his email address, and I sent him the article, subject line: The End of Anonymity. In the body of the email I wrote, "Call me if you'd like to talk." Of course I didn't hear from him, but his silence spoke volumes.

My happy dance was interrupted by a call from Detective Baker. "Alexandra, Inspector Jaeger has gotten a material witness warrant for Constance Sanders and has taken her into his custody. They are not at the police station. He's taken her somewhere else off the grid. I don't know the details of how and why, but I thought you should know."

Holy shit. He is using her for bait, I thought. Piper had to be in danger. Surely he wasn't able to track the videos back to her. Was he capable of hurting her, or worse? These and more horrible thoughts went through my mind. I had to find her. But how? I called her phone. No answer. I did the only thing I could think to do. I raced down the streets of New Orleans to the French Quarter. I burst into Clinton Cunningham's office.

"Jaeger's taken Piper. Where the hell is she?" I screamed.

Clint sat behind his desk as if nothing were wrong, smiling at me, amused by my hysteria. "Go home and wait for your friend Zach to come to see you. You'll get your answers then," he said.

"I'm not going anywhere until I know where Piper is."

"You don't have a choice. You aren't in control of this situation. It's going to have an ugly end if you don't listen, you hard-headed little bitch."

I wanted to lunge across the desk and knock his tobacco-stained teeth down his double-chinned throat, but that voice inside me spoke again: "Calm down and go home." As much as I hated it, I had to listen. I had no other choice.

The drive to my condo was excruciating. I was at the mercy of the Dixie Mafia, Russian Mafia, and a German pervert cop with nothing to lose. Jaeger must have gone off the deep end when he saw the videos, knowing his career was over. He must have reckoned this was his last chance to get Victor, and he was going to use Piper to do it. My hands trembled as I gripped my steering wheel. Tears flowed down both sides of my face. I sent a silent prayer to heaven, hoping my mom and Sarah would look after Piper. Oh my God, I was petrified.

When I arrived at the condo, Zach was once again sitting on the steps, still bandaged, looking emaciated from the weight he'd lost during his stay in the hospital. I felt sorry for him. I knew he'd made the choices that put him the terrible position he was in, but I thought he'd suffered enough for his mistakes. *When do you get a second chance?* I wondered. Sarah sought redemption and she paid with her life. Was that going to be Zach's fate, too?

"Hi, Alexandra. Let's get inside before we are spotted," Zach said.

We hurried inside the condo and sat at the kitchen table. "What's going on with Piper?" I asked.

"I'm not really sure. I got a call from Clinton Cunningham a short while ago. He told me my debt to him would be paid in full after I did one last thing for him. He instructed me to come to your condo and wait with you for a few hours. Then he wanted me to ride with you back to the French Quarter to his strip club on Bourbon Street. He instructed me to stay out of sight until then."

"I don't understand. I just left his club. He could have told me all of that himself. Why all of the cloak-and-dagger?"

"I don't know. I know it has something to do with the telephone call you made to Victor Ivanovich. But that's all I know."

I struggled with the idea of sitting in my kitchen doing nothing while Piper was in the hands of Jaeger, but what could I do? I didn't know where he'd taken her. I called Detective Baker again, and he had nothing new on Jaeger's whereabouts. My stomach turned flips as I waited. I rubbed my fingers across my forehead over and over like Aladdin rubbing his lamp, as if a thought would pop into my head to bring this episode to a happy ending. The clock seemed to move backward. Funny how time crawled when you were waiting for a disaster to strike. I tried occupying myself with my blog but couldn't face reading the posts about missing young girls. Piper and Tom had become my life. They were still both in jeopardy, and I was confined to my condo, waiting for something. What I was waiting for, I did not know. Was I supposed to trust Clint? No way. But I did trust my inner voice, and it was telling me to be patient.

Finally my phone rang, and I sprang on it like a leopard on a gazelle. Caller ID said it was Sophia. *Oh God*, I thought, *something's happened to Tom.* "Alexandra, I have some news for you...Tom is being released."

"What? What did you say?"

"Alexandra, it's true. The Mexican Secretariat of Foreign Affairs office called the American Embassy to confirm Tom would be released from jail today. The prosecutor brought Tom into court this morning and told the judge that Mexico was dismissing all charges. He will be free to leave later this afternoon as soon as the paperwork is complete. I am trying to book us a flight to the States tomorrow morning."

I cried joyous tears because Tom was coming home. I was worried I'd never see him again, but now a miracle was bringing him home. Home to me. But our entire family had to be reunited before I could rest. I needed to find Piper. Where the hell had Jaeger taken her?

"Thank you, thank you, thank you, Sophia!" I said, nearly screaming into the phone. Zach watched me in astonishment, my elation and enthusiasm lighting his face up like a Japanese lantern. He was happy for me. Soon his expression dimmed as the reality of our current situation brought us both back down to earth.

Zach and I talked about Tom coming home. I think he was trying to take my mind off of Piper for a few minutes. He liked Tom and thought he was good for me. He said he'd seen a huge change in me since Tom and I had gotten together. He was right. I'd never considered having a family life. I'm sure the dream was buried somewhere in the very back of my mind, but I feared the vulnerability that came with family ties. After all, my mother and father both passed when I was still young. My father lived longer than my mother, but his mind left him when I was still in high school. I associated family with a broken heart and loss. If you loved them, they were taken away from you. I wanted to avoid that pain, and I'd tried. But now I had a family I couldn't live without. Tom and Piper were my family, and I couldn't bear the thought of losing them like I'd lost my parents.

The silence was broken by Zach's cell phone ringing. When he hung up he said, "That was Clint. He wants us to go to his bar now. He said don't waste any time and to get there as fast as we could."

What the hell? Should I just blindly trust him and head to the bar? Was this some sort of trap? Were Zach and I going to get beaten or killed? I really wasn't sure what to expect. But, if I stood even a small chance of getting Piper back safely, I had to go. I had to accept the consequences of my decision to save her from the demons who were terrorizing us. I had my .38 strapped to my leg. I was determined to use it if I had to.

Zack and I sped along the busy streets on the way to the Quarter.

He grabbed onto the dash of my car and cinched his seatbelt as tightly as he could. I kept my eyes focused on the traffic ahead as I weaved in and out, cutting cars off, ignoring the blaring horns and the extended middle fingers. I glanced at Zach. His eyes were closed, and I would have thought it cute were it not for the circumstances. Neither of us spoke a word. Neither knew what fate awaited us.

We parked and ran down Bourbon Street to Clint's bar. We zipped by the dancers and security and burst into his office. Clint was seated at his desk, and Jaeger was standing in front of him, holding Piper tightly just above the elbow. She looked fine, but my blood boiled at those thick, meaty fingers digging into her thin arm. Before I could even blink, Clint threw up his right hand at me like a cop halting oncoming traffic.

"Don't say a word," Clint barked. "I'll do all of the talking." As soon as he spoke, two of his goons walked into the room and stood in the corner with their guns drawn.

"Is it all set up?" Jaeger asked.

"Yes," Clint answered as he rose to his feet and opened a closet door. "You two get in here and stay quiet. No matter what you hear, do not say a word until I tell you to come out."

Jaeger threw me a confident look and dragged Piper into the closet as Clint shut the door behind him. Clint looked at me and gave me a knowing wink. I was nearly at panic stage by then, but something told me to remain composed. I sat in a chair as instructed but reached down and put my hand by my .38 revolver.

Clint yelled to his men, "Okay, bring them in."

One of the goons walked out and repeated the command to some of Clint's men in the bar. After a few long minutes, Victor Ivanovich and El Alacran walked into the room. Clint put his right hand up just as before. Victor flashed a nervously confident smile at me. The Scorpion scowled. I was sure he would eat me, bones and all, if Victor gave the word. I had no idea where this scene was headed. Zach began to tremble at the sight of El Alacran. Not surprising after the beating he'd taken.

Victor spoke first. "Do we have a deal, Mr. Cunningham?"

"Yes, Mr. Ivanovich, we do."

"Then let me see the goods."

"It's time, Mr. Jaeger," Clint said.

As soon as he spoke, Jaeger opened the door. He stood next to Piper with the same tobacco-stained smile I'd seen before. Clint's two goons edged their way to flank Jaeger on either side. Clint nodded to Jaeger, and he let go of Piper's arm. One of Clint's men walked Piper to me. I noticed how pale she was, her thin face cracking a smile as she threw her arms around me.

A shocked Jaeger looked at me and then Clint. "What the fuck is going on here?" he yelled.

The huge goons on either side of Jaeger grabbed him and pinned him against the wall. Clint looked at me and Zach with eyes as cold as a Montana winter. "Take her and get the hell out of here. Now!"

El Alacran squinted his eyes and wrinkled his nose, a face of complete confusion. "Yeah, what the fuck is going on?"

Victor put his hand on the Scorpion's forearm to silence him. Victor's movements were quick and confident. He let El Alacran know all of these actions were part of his agreement with Clint. Only two men in the room knew the answer to the questions Jaeger and the Scorpion had asked. Victor and Clint had struck some deal that included Piper and me being reunited. It slowly dawned on Jaeger that his fate was not so certain. Piper was not the prize the two bosses were exchanging. Jaeger was.

Whatever their deal was didn't concern me, because I had Piper and that was the only thing that mattered. Zach jumped to his feet, and the three of us ran from the room without looking back. We didn't stop our gallop until we were in my car, Piper breathless, half crying, half laughing. I knew what it was like to be in that condition, and I knew she'd be just fine with a little time, a few hugs, and maybe some food.

We sped home as fast as we could. I didn't dare stop for fear that killing the three of us might be a part of Victor's and Clinton's deal. It all happened too fast to make sense of it.

At the condo, Zach was the first to speak. "I don't know what deal they made, but I think we are safe now. I watched these guys work for years. If they intended to hurt us, we wouldn't have been allowed to leave that room. No, they didn't want us there to witness their next moves."

I gave Piper a few of the hugs she needed and then a few more. I wouldn't let her escape even briefly from my grip. I stroked her hair as we talked to Zach. "It was like the devil's demons had come to collect his black soul and take it away. They swooped in, grabbed their bounty, and retreated back to the shadows. Maybe we just witnessed an evil man being taken to hell," I said.

Zach and Piper both nodded. My phone rang as I spoke, so I dug it out of my purse. The caller ID said, "Tom Sanders." Holy shit, Tom was calling me from his phone.

CHAPTER THIRTY
A New Home

~

"Oh my God, Tom, is that you?"

"Yes, pretty girl, it's me. They let me out this morning and just gave me back my phone. Sophia is with me and we are getting the hell out of here tomorrow morning. I miss you so much. I can't wait to see you. How's Piper?"

Tears, tears, and more tears streamed down my face. "She's fine. Hurry home. We all need to be together."

I wanted to talk to Tom for hours, but he was still in the police station and he had to make certain he could get a flight out. He'd seen all he wanted of Mexico for a while. We agreed to tell each other everything that had happened when he returned. Real food and some sleep in a real bed were on his mind. I just needed to spend time with Piper sorting everything out. I really couldn't make sense of how quickly the situation was changing or why. I was happy to have Piper, but I didn't trust Victor. And what was happening with Jaeger? He seemed totally caught off guard by Victor's and Clint's moves.

"Piper, why did Jaeger bring you to Clint's bar?" I asked.

"He came to my foster family's home and flashed some

official-looking papers that said 'Warrant' on them. My foster parents verified with their attorney that the warrant was legal. Her brother tried to stop Jaeger from taking me, but Jaeger pulled out his pistol and threatened to shoot the guy. When we got to the bar, Clint told Jaeger that Victor was coming to pick me up. I was as surprised as you to see what happened."

I knew something had transpired to change the entire course of events that Victor had put in motion. For some reason, he had changed direction and put his gears in reverse. I wasn't sure my troubles with Victor were over, and I didn't know what to expect next.

Knock, knock, knock loudly rang out from my front door. I unbuckled the strap holding my .38 in the holster, sent Piper to the bedroom, and told Zach to open the door. He flung the door open and jumped back, expecting the worst. Clint and two of his monster men stood outside.

"May we come in?" Clint asked.

What was I going to say? No? I couldn't shoot all three of them, though the thought did cross my mind. "Yes, come in," I said.

My meager kitchen was getting crowded. I had never had this many people in my condo at one time. Clint asked me to keep Piper in the bedroom because what he had to say wasn't for her ears to hear. I politely told him to go to hell and asked her to join us. She wasn't leaving my sight with these guys around.

He laughed. "You can be a badass little bitch when you want to be, can't you?"

I didn't answer. I just kept my gaze steady, locking our eyes together. Even though I was peeing my pants with fear, I couldn't show it. My stomach and heart knew I was afraid because they were both broadcasting it loudly. But scared or not, I was going to protect my family.

Clint sat at the kitchen table and rocked back in the chair, his fat belly too much for his feet to bear. "I'm here because there are things you need to know. You'll figure out what just happened or at least some of it. Nothing I say can be repeated or there will be consequences."

The room fell deathly silent. We all knew what consequences

meant. I wasn't sure why he was here to explain what had happened, but I was glad he was. I didn't want to live with the fear of thinking either he or Victor would be coming for Piper or me.

Clint continued, "Victor and I have been in a bloody battle for control of the dark side of New Orleans. There have been casualties on both sides. I've lost some good men and working girls. I took down some of his best people, too. You wouldn't understand, but my people are my family just like this little girl is yours. We may live by a different set of rules, but we have each other, and that's all we have. Our war stalemated, neither of us gaining an advantage. That all changed when you sent him the article you'd written. He knew you could get your friends at *The Times* to print the article or put it on your damn blog. Either way, he would be exposed to law enforcement all over the world. So he approached me with a deal. He said if I gave him the girl, he'd get out of New Orleans."

"That bastard!" I yelled.

Clint put his finger to his lips, shushing me. "I told him that deal wouldn't fly, and I proposed to trade him the German cop instead of the girl. He needed to get Jaeger off his ass, anyway. Plus, those two guys really hate each other. He agreed, so I convinced Jaeger that I had the goods on Victor, using your article, and told him we could use the girl to lure Victor to my bar. Then I'd help Jaeger nab him. You know what happened next."

"What happened to Jaeger?" I asked.

"That's not your business. He was a corrupt, child-molesting, extortionist cop. Whatever happens to him, he deserves. You see, missy, in my world, the devil is always right around the corner to collect his due. What's important is that Victor is out of New Orleans and off your ass. That means the DA will be dropping the charges against your friend, Susan McAllister. The bribed state worker, Ms. Butler, will drop her claims against your center and custody of the girl. And, of course, Victor has already seen to his bribed Mexican prosecutor dropping the charges against your boyfriend. There is still one problem. We sent word to the judge in your custody case that the state would be backing off, but she still insists that you find a bigger place to live before she can sign off on you getting custody of the girl."

I finally felt like I could take my hand off of my gun. Clint wasn't here to hurt me. It looked like Victor had given up on Piper, and New Orleans, for that matter. "Was the judge on the take?" I asked.

"For God's sakes, no," Clint chuckled. "Let me tell you something about how things work in this city. We operate in the shadows. We don't go into your world. There is an understanding between us and law enforcement. As long as we obey a certain set of rules, such as staying out of sight, we are allowed to exist. The cops and judges understand what we do is going to go on no matter what they do. It's better for them to deal with the devils they know than the devils they don't know. So we are all part of a large dysfunctional family of sorts. You need to stay in your world. You don't belong in ours."

After he said what he came to say, Clint stood and waddled out of the door with his two thugs trailing behind. So Victor didn't want to be exposed. *I guess if I expose him now, I'll be inviting trouble for myself and my family. It's better to leave well enough alone*, I concluded. Anyway, I was happy to hear that Piper and I were safe. It was icing on the cake to know that charges against Susan would be dropped and things at the center would return to normal.

As Clint stepped out of the door, he turned to say, "Victor is gone for the time being. I don't know if he'll try to come back to New Orleans, but you should watch out for that Alacran asshole. He didn't seem too happy with the deal."

I knew the Scorpion had it in for me. I offended his macho ego in Colombia. He tried to intimidate me, and it didn't work. He couldn't take it, so I knew he would try to get at me some way, but I couldn't worry about him now. There was nothing I could do to stop the crazy bastard except stay vigilant. When Clint left us, I wanted to spend time with Piper.

Zach sensed that we wanted to be alone, so he excused himself to go give Maddy the good news. He was finally free from the Dixie Mafia. He and Maddy could pursue their organic farming dream, and I was happy for both of them.

Piper had nerves of steel. None of this seemed to bother her. "Let's go to Whole Foods. We can get some great food and have a celebration dinner. Victor is going to leave me alone! Maybe I shouldn't be celebrating when I know he killed my mother, but I lost her long ago to heroin. Victor just finished her body off. She was hopelessly addicted and miserable. Her arms and legs were so riddled with needle marks that her veins were collapsing. I know she is in a better place now. And me…I have a family I can depend on to take care of me. You do love me, don't you, Alexandra?" Piper said.

"I love you with all my heart and more than you will ever know," I said.

I could tell Piper was not used to showing emotion. She had built her own great wall, just like the ancient Chinese, to keep people out. I understood why, knowing she was raised in such a volatile environment. Her mother took a wrong turn in life and Piper watched her gradually decay. Other people came and went from her life, and she couldn't afford to get close to anyone. If she invested any emotion in anyone, she might lose them, too. Nothing had been solid or permanent in her world.

I vowed to change that for her. I, too, had found a missing piece of myself. I had no idea I wanted to care for a child. My career ambitions seemed to drive me. Maybe Piper had brought to light a need deep inside me I didn't know existed. Whatever had happened, I liked it. My priority was my family.

Piper and I readied ourselves for a popcorn-and-movie night after our Whole Foods dinner. We told stories, giggled, and watched two movies as we consumed our popcorn. I went to sleep anxious for the reunion with Tom in the morning.

I slept a little later than usual, and Piper fetched me a cup of coffee to help me rise and shine. We dressed and headed to the airport. We arrived more than an hour before Tom's flight, so we spent time in the airport shops. I bought Piper a New Orleans Saints cap. She looked so cute with it on her small head adorned by rainbow-colored hair. I chuckled to myself about how the Saints and Piper didn't seem to go together.

Finally Tom's plane touched down, the excitement building in me from my toes to the top of my head. As he and Sophia walked from the gate, I ran to him. He threw his strong arms around me and drew me close. I felt his ribs as we hugged. He'd lost some weight while in the Mexican jail but was still a strong, handsome man. When my inspection of Tom was over, we walked hand in hand to Piper. She hopped in the middle of us smiling as we made our way to baggage claim. Sophia watched our reunion with loving approval. Family was important to her, too, and she knew she was a member of our extended family.

Tom told me all about what he'd learned in Mexico. The industrial corn farmers had created a genetically modified version of corn. It grew very quickly and was programmed to react well to pesticides. These corporate conglomerates were pushing their Frankencorn on the Mexican government, forcing local farmers out of business, destroying a way of life that had existed for hundreds of years. Worse, the pollution that went with large farming operations would destroy the natural balance of the habitat of the wildlife in the region; the environmental consequences promised to be horrendous.

"I can see fighting these Goliath companies is nearly impossible," Tom said. "They have the resources to lobby or outright buy politicians. I was placed in jail for no reason. They kept me there simply because they could. Sophia told me what happened in New Orleans while I was locked up, and I felt so guilty for abandoning you and Piper. My family was threatened and I was miles away, helpless. I can't leave you and Piper again. We have to find another way to fight these devils. Alexandra, one of the big companies trying to push their Frankencorn was Aggrow. They are one of the worst offending industrial farm companies in the world. They are also the company that is leasing your land in Indiana. We may not be able to stop them in Mexico, but we sure as hell can stop them on your land in Indiana."

We agreed to get them off the land in Indiana. I brought Tom up to date on everything that had happened since Sophia went to Mexico. "We have to find a place to live that the court approves," Tom said. "And we have to find a contractor to clean up the well on the farm in

Indiana." He had that take-charge attitude that I loved. He'd rearranged his priorities and focused on Piper and me. I found it so sexy.

On our ride home from the airport, I received a text from Charlotte: Call me.

She and Mandy Morris wanted to come by the condo to talk to Tom and me. *They must have mended their differences*, I thought. I really didn't want to deal with anything new, but Charlotte made it sound crucial we meet, so I agreed to see them. They arrived at the condo shortly after we'd stashed Tom's luggage in my bedroom. Sophia excused herself and headed back to her hotel.

In true form, Mandy Morris took the floor. "Alexandra, Charlotte told me what you've been through in the last few weeks." She turned to Piper. "You are such a treat for us all. I really like you, Piper. I know the judge wants you to get a larger place to live. So I've spoken to my dear friend Bob Broussard, and he's agreed to sell Alexandra and Tom his father's condo on Bourbon Street."

"Oh boy, oh boy. That's the best news I've ever heard!" Piper screamed. "When can we move, Alexandra? Can we start tomorrow?"

Tom sat back with a pensive look on his face, and I was more than a little shocked. I wasn't sure I could live in a place where Bob Broussard had killed so many women. It would be too weird, but Piper was so excited. She wanted to live in the Quarter, and so did Tom. They both seemed to draw energy from that part of the city.

"Why does Bob want to sell the condo?" Tom asked.

Mandy took a moment to respond. "He knows he will never go back there. His doctors say the memories associated with the condo would jeopardize his recovery. He has always liked Alexandra. We both appreciate the work she has done to help build our fathers' companies. Selling it to you two would keep it in the family, so to speak, and make the judge happy. She wouldn't hesitate to give you and Alexandra permanent custody of Piper if you had a three-bedroom place to live in. Bob's agreed to lower the price to make it work and even finance the purchase. So, what do you say?"

Tom looked at me for approval. I had my reservations, but what could I say? Living in the Quarter was a dream come true for Tom and

Piper, and me, too, if I were being completely honest. I just wasn't sure about Bob Broussard, Mandy Morris, and this particular condo. But in the end, if this was what my family wanted, I wouldn't say no.

"It is a gracious offer for sure. I have one requirement, though. All of the bathtubs have to be replaced. Bob placed all of his victims in those tubs. No way I could get in them," I said.

Tom's smile stretched from ear to ear, and so did Piper's. "Okay, that won't be a problem. I'll take care of getting them replaced." He turned to Mandy and Charlotte and said, "We'll take it. First, we'll have to make sure it's okay with the judge. If it is, we'll start the process right away."

CHAPTER THIRTY-ONE
DEATH IN THE DARK

~

TOM AND I spent our first night back together wrapped in each other's arms, the moonlight sneaking through the bedroom blinds. It felt so right. I really didn't fully comprehend how much I had missed him until we were reunited. Piper tossed and turned, thinking about moving to the Quarter. The following morning we piled into my car and went to see Mr. Swartz and Joshua Clark.

Swartz was a bit more relaxed in this meeting. "I'll call the judge right now. I'm sure she will not have any problems with the new living arrangements." He and Mr. Clark left us in the conference room and retreated to his office to have one of those secret conversations lawyers have. When they returned, both lawyers were smiling for the first time since we began the custody proceeding.

"What did she say?" I asked.

"She gave her preliminary approval to the move. We'll still have to have an evidentiary hearing to formalize the custody arrangement, but there shouldn't be any problem as long as nothing happens to upset the apple cart. I'll be able to do the legal work for your purchase of the condo from Mr. Broussard as soon as you arrange the financing," Mr. Swartz said, his formal demeanor returning.

"Woohoo!" Piper yelled. "We are going to live in the French Quarter!"

Mr. Swartz gave us a moment to celebrate, then brought up another more troublesome subject. "Now, what are we going to do about getting you a contractor to remediate the pollution on your farm in Indiana? The other side is pushing for answers."

"Sorry for dropping the ball on that," Tom said. "We'll talk it over and get back to you a little later."

We left Swartz and went straight to Tom's bank. We filled out all of their paperwork and waited in the lobby for them to examine our finances. Soon they gave us the good news. We qualified for the loan if the appraisal supported the purchase price, and I had no doubt it would. We were purchasing the condo at a 25 percent discount. The bankers knew the value of the condo, too, since Tom's bank was the same bank Mr. Broussard had used.

We went back to my condo, and Tom left us to talk to his bosses about returning to work. Piper and I headed to the center. We were greeted by a thinner version of Susan McAllister. She smiled as we approached.

"Susan, you look great," I said.

"Yes, I've been on the indictment diet. I wouldn't recommend it, but it sure works," she said as she laughed. "It feels so good to be home. I missed all of the girls and their children. Alexandra, we have a new resident who would like to speak with you."

A new resident who knew me? Was this a new move by Victor? "What's her name?"

"Her name is Adrian Guidry. Would you like to meet her?" Susan asked.

"Okay, can we meet in your office?"

Susan nodded and left to get Adrian. I was on my guard, thinking the worst. Adrian walked into the office with a timid smile on her face. I'd seen her before but couldn't figure out where. As soon as she started talking, I remembered. She was the stripper at Clint's bar who'd winked at me the first time I went there. I remembered her auburn hair and her bright blue eyes.

"Hi, Alexandra, I am so happy to finally talk to you. You have changed my life," Adrian said.

Susan stood to leave, but Adrian asked her to stay. "Susan, you have created such a wonderful place for women and children with no other place to go. Many of us would be on the street without Sarah's House."

Adrian was a pretty girl but couldn't be more than nineteen years old. "Adrian—that's a lovely name," I said, watching her twirl her hair around her finger. "Where are you from and how did you end up dancing in a bar on Bourbon Street?"

"I was born and raised in Morgan City. My father was an oil field worker and a National Guardsman. He used to come in my room every morning before he went to work to tell me good morning. He would wipe the sleep from my eyes as he hummed his favorite song. When I asked him what he was wiping from my eyes, he'd say stardust. His National Guard unit was shipped to the Middle East, and he was killed in action when I was only ten years old. I had a hard time after that. My mother died when I was seventeen. I was doing drugs and getting into trouble most of the time. The police in Morgan City arrested me over and over. I decided to leave when I was eighteen and came to New Orleans. Clinton gave me a job dancing. I chose the stage name Stardust, and people started calling me Dusty. The name has stuck, and I like it because it reminds me of my dad."

"That is a sad story, Dusty," Susan said. "Do you have any family?"

"None that aren't in jail. There's just me," she answered. "I probably would have started turning tricks were it not for you, Alexandra."

"Me? Why?" I asked.

"When I first saw you walk into the club, I thought you were a dancer, too. I went near the door to listen to what you and Clint were saying, wanting to know about my competition. I heard you tell Clint you wouldn't make any deals with him. Nobody ever stands up to Clint, and I said to myself, 'If she can be that brave, maybe I can, too.' Then when I heard how you fought to get the little girl back, you inspired me to change my life. I don't have to be a dancer or make a living on my back. I am here to stay on my feet, find a real job, and finish my education. Maybe I'll even go to law school. Thank you, Alexandra."

I felt a swell of pride surge up my spine. I had never considered myself an inspiration to anyone. I was just a small-town girl from a corn farm in Indiana. I wondered how many lost souls there were like Dusty in the city; surely too many to count. It was funny how one story like hers and a thank you could make all of the trouble worth it.

Susan didn't miss a beat. "Why that's wonderful, Dusty. You would make a fine lawyer."

Piper and I left the center and met Tom at home. The day had been wonderful for him as well. He was relieved to find that he still had a job. The company he worked for was also environmentally concerned and supported his peaceful protests with ROLL. They did not know about his activities with the non-violent sister organization ROLF. It was a good day all around.

The next day Tom asked if I could invite Zach and Maddy over for coffee. Tom and I had something we wanted to discuss with them. They arrived in the early afternoon. Zach's injuries had mostly healed, and Maddy was her usual ball of energy describing how she and Zach had been researching organic farming on the web. She went on and on about their future plans, creating the opening Tom was looking for.

"Zach, Maddy," Tom said. "Alexandra told me all about the help you gave her when I was in Mexico. It was a very brave thing risking your life to help her. She also told me that you and Maddy would one day like to farm organic vegetables. As you know, Alexandra has farmland in Indiana. It is currently under lease by Aggrow, a land-destroying, chemical-spewing, conglomerate monster. Their lease is ending at the end of this month. We won't renew it. Would you like to start your organic farming operation on Alexandra's land? We'll put up the seed money and we'll all share the profits."

Zach fell completely quiet. He rubbed his ears as if he wasn't sure he'd heard what Tom said. Maddy smiled and looked at her brother, who looked a little dumbfounded, waiting for him to answer. Slowly the words sunk in as he decided Tom and I were serious. A smile conquered his face, and he shouted, "Hell yes!"

"That's fantastic," Tom said. "I've been networking through the company I work for and found a California company who does environmental remediation. Their founder also has an organic vegetable farm. I've spoken to him. He's agreed to meet us in Indiana to sign the contract to remove the poisons from the well. He'll also be an adviser to you and Maddy on organic farming. As it turns out, my mother and father have already visited his farm. He's the real deal."

Maddy jumped up, ran around the table, and hugged me. She grabbed Piper, and the two spun around doing a happy dance. She asked me what my hometown was like. I told her all of my stories about growing up in Silbee. It sounded perfect to her. She told me she'd start a fitness program for the residents free of charge. I thought of the three frumpy old ladies who'd been my mother's friends, dressed in leotards, and had a great chuckle. *That would really be a sight to see,* I thought.

Tom and Zach diagrammed the farm, sectioning the parts right for growing vegetables without irrigation. They'd calculated the temperature changes and figured not many vegetables would be appropriate for the harsh Indiana climate. They factored in building a greenhouse to cope with the fall temperatures. Profit wasn't our motive. We wanted to do our part contributing to a sustainable way of living for all Americans, having no idea where our efforts might lead. But, we did believe it was the right thing to do.

Maddy and I talked about my family home. I told her she could do whatever she wanted to it. No one had lived in the house for quite some time, and it would require a mammoth effort to clean and organize. She said she was more than ready to take that on. I had no doubt about that. She was a solid ball of energy. I was sure my mother was smiling down from heaven at the thought of having such a sweet person rattling the pots and pans in the family home again.

Piper had long since gotten bored with our conversation and was using Google Earth to view the French Quarter and the condo we were closing on in the morning. The bank had quickly approved our loan using an updated appraisal to verify that the value of the condo was much greater than what we were paying. It was settled that after the closing tomorrow, Tom, Maddy, and Zach would hop a plane to Indiana, and Piper and I would start painting the garage at the condo in the French Quarter. We all called it a day, knowing tomorrow would be long for all of us.

Tom, Piper, and I went to the closing at eight in the morning, and by nine we had the keys and were on our way to the French Quarter to walk through the rooms. The color scheme was a little dated for my taste, so Piper and I chose new colors to paint the entire condo and modernize it. We bought all the paint we needed and stored it at the condo. My plan was to have the garage, kitchen, bathrooms, and bedrooms painted when Tom returned from Indiana. There was a great deal to be done, but excitement was powering us.

Piper and I took Tom to the Louis Armstrong International Airport and dropped him off. We scooted back to the Quarter to start painting. Since my skills were a little rusty, I parked my car in a parking garage down the street, not wanting to get paint on my car. Piper and I walked to the condo enjoying the sights, sounds, and smells of the French Quarter. We painted and laughed, having a great time all day. We got poboys for dinner, figuring we had worked off the excess calories. Maybe not the best choice, but it didn't hurt to splurge every once in a while. Besides, we had to stay in the Quarter and get takeout to finish our painting job on the garage. Piper had gotten most of the paint on herself. She looked like modern art.

Darkness fell, and before we knew it, it was nine o'clock and time for us to quit for the night. We cleaned our brushes and a little off our faces. I had paint down the legs of my pants to my tennis shoes. Piper had it all over her clothes, face, and hair. We looked as though we'd rolled in it.

We held hands, chattering away about our talent as painters all the way to my car. The parking garage was almost completely empty, the lights near my car not working. When I looked closer, I saw the bulbs were smashed. There was glass on the concrete floor under each of the light fixtures. *Damn vandals*, I thought. Why would they want to bust these lights out?

I didn't have time to answer my own question. El Alacran sprung out of the stairwell by my car brandishing a long machete-like knife in his left hand. Before I could react he was on me. He balled his right fist and knocked me to the ground, the punch landing right on my jaw. I was dazed and a little out of it as I hit the concrete floor with a thud. Piper ran at him swinging wildly. He pushed her to the ground and she fell against the car. He had a crazed look in his eyes, like the one I'd seen in Colombia just after he killed Camila and threatened me.

"Now, you American puta, I'm going to teach you to fuck with me. Victor isn't here to save you. I'm going to cut this little smart-ass computer bitch's head off while you watch. Then, I'm going to cut yours off and roll it down the stairs like a bowling ball."

While he was yelling, he was pointing the machete at me. Then he turned his back to me and walked toward Piper. She was pinned against the car. I could see tears and a terror-filled expression on her face as the machete caught a ray from a distant light and glinted in her face. I slowly regained my senses as El Alacran took deliberate steps toward Piper. I pulled up my pants leg and pulled my .38 from the holster. I took aim and squeezed the trigger gently just like my father had shown me so many years ago. The bullet hit him in the upper right-hand corner of his back and spun him around. He looked at me in disbelief and took one step toward me. It was the last step he ever took. I shot him in his black heart. He catapulted backward, hitting the trunk of my car and rolling to the ground not five feet from Piper.

I sprang to my feet, opened the car door, and threw Piper inside. I walked back over to El Alacran. His chest was not moving. I saw a black form rise from his body and whisk away into the ground. I stood over him ready to fire again, but it wasn't necessary. He was dead. There was no doubt El Alacran was dead.

CHAPTER THIRTY-TWO
THE RETURN

I KNOW I saw evil leave his body, and it scared the living hell out of me. I'd heard stories about souls leaving the body since I was a child but never thought I'd actually witness it. I shuddered, thinking of where that soul was going. Then I looked up to see Piper staring at me from the back window of the car. She strained her neck to see if the Scorpion was dead. I glanced back at him and wondered for a brief moment if he would get back up, if he had some deal with the devil for extra lives. It didn't seem that far-fetched once I'd seen that black form emerge from his body.

I started shaking to the point where I could barely hold the .38. Should I put it down or back in my holster? I decided the safe thing to do was to snap it back in its ankle holster. Devil or not, he wasn't getting up like the monsters did in horror movies. He was gone for good. He was permanently and irrevocably dead.

When Piper saw I was trembling, she opened the door and called 911. I kept my eye on the Scorpion's body just in case I was mistaken. Funny how the movies had taught us not to trust that evil could be killed. Maybe it couldn't. Maybe it just made its way into some other body. From what I'd witnessed, it was always around. The evils of the world were like weeds in a garden; they would always find a way to grow back. Good people needed to stay vigilant.

While Piper spoke to the 911 operator, I called Detective Baker. He said he'd come right away. My mind ran the scene over and over again like an instant replay from an ESPN broadcast. I couldn't get the picture of El Alacran's face when I shot him out of my mind. Soon the flashing lights and sirens arrived. Baker came shortly afterward and took Piper and me to the precinct for questioning. Baker and I both knew it was just a formality. He was happy there was one less drug lord plaguing the streets of New Orleans, but we both also knew that it was like swatting mosquitoes. You could never get them all.

While we were in the interrogation room, a detective brought in a computer and put a disk in it for Detective Baker. The garage had a working surveillance system. My entire encounter with El Alacran was recorded. There could be no question about the righteousness of the shooting. Still I struggled with the fact that I'd just taken a man's life. His face, the look in his eyes when he knew he was dying, stained my thoughts. I had to find a way to reconcile it in my mind, never dreaming I'd kill anyone. I wondered what the judge in Piper's custody case would have to say about me having custody of Piper now.

When I finally had a chance to call Tom, he and Zach had finished arranging for the contractor to remediate the well in Indiana. Tom immediately dropped everything and jumped on the first flight back to New Orleans. Zach and Maddy agreed to stay in Indiana and oversee the job, but I needed Tom back in the city next to me. It was time to make some sense of our crazy life. We needed to move into our new condo and get Piper enrolled in school. The judge still had to rule on our custody arrangements. My mind was working overtime.

As I drove home, I looked at the sky. Silently I asked my mom for strength. No words were spoken to me from the heavens, nor did I hear my familiar inner voice, but what I did see was a peculiar cloud formation. Just for a moment it looked like a girl smiling at me. Then I realized it looked just like Camila. Was she smiling because her killer had been dispatched, or was it because she had found peace? Maybe I just needed to see something like that, or maybe it was really there. It didn't matter which one it was because it worked. I smiled right back at her, my inner critical voice silenced, calmed down, and giving me some rest.

Piper and I picked Tom up at the airport. We didn't talk much on the way to my old place. We still didn't have furniture in the Bourbon Street condo, and the painting wasn't complete. There was time to do all of that tomorrow, or the next day, or the next. I just needed to be held in Tom's arms. That was exactly what he did all through the night. He stroked my hair and told me everything would be alright. Every time I awoke, he was stroking my hair or kissing me gently. I don't believe he got any sleep that night.

Piper ran into our room in the morning with a cup of coffee in each hand. "Can we start moving into the Quarter condo today? Can we please?"

"We sure can," I said. "But first we have some painting to do. This time let's try to get some on the walls."

We all laughed. Family was just what I needed. I'd learned a great deal about myself over the last few months. I wasn't a loner after all. I was a family woman. Sure my family was a little unconventional, but we were a family, nonetheless. I drew strength from them, and I'd learned I'd go as far as I needed to protect them. I didn't regret shooting El Alacran. I was haunted by the memory, but I didn't regret it. Sometimes the evil in the world forced you to kill to protect your family. Not your property, your family.

Piper turned on the television to check the weather forecast. She loved seeing the bottle-blond weather babe try to look intelligent when she tried to speak like a meteorologist. Piper said she'd never seen so much hairspray on thin hair until she moved to New Orleans. I'm not sure if she was talking about the women or the men. New Orleans had to be the comb-over capital of the world.

The news was on instead of the weather. We all paused when we heard the reporter say, "The body of a law enforcement officer was discovered leaning against an above-ground grave in the historic Lafayette Cemetery. The officer, Alric Jaeger, died of an apparently self-inflicted single gunshot wound to the head. Mr. Jaeger, an Interpol agent, had recently been placed under investigation as a result of molestation accusations leveled against him. The grave was that of a young child murdered by a German immigrant in the early 1800s. The child was a resident of the Irish Channel. Lafayette Cemetery is the final resting place for many of the poor working-class immigrants who lived in the Irish Channel section of New Orleans. The police report indicated that no foul play was involved. Mr. Jaeger's body will be transported back to his native land in Germany."

We all sat in shock. I found it hard to believe that Jaeger shot himself. More likely he received street justice. He was a law enforcement officer who had crossed the line. That made him fair game in this city. I couldn't help but think he got what he deserved. He crossed into the world of the shadow demons to do what they did. I guess he got what they got. Once he went in, he couldn't find his way back out. As sad as it was, I knew actions had consequences, and Jaeger's karma finally caught up with him.

A week later we'd completed painting and furnishing the condo. I had to admit it was beautiful. Piper and Tom loved living in the Quarter. I wouldn't say we were a conventional family, but then again, nothing was conventional in New Orleans. And in the French Quarter, normal was just weird. I worked during the day with Charlotte, promoting our stevia company. Since we now had a large place with three bedrooms, Tom and I had the privacy to make love at night, and boy, did we ever. The energy of the French Quarter was quietly thrilling: tourists mingling with locals, artists of all types filling the streets by day, and jazz and blues ruling the night.

Mr. Swartz escorted Tom, Piper, and me into court for the custody hearing. He presented the evidence to the judge, showing her photos of the condo and Piper's bedroom. He detailed our finances so she could confirm we had the ability to take care of Piper. When he finished he asked the judge if she had any questions.

She looked directly at me. "Ms. Lee, the court has your entire record before it. You have indeed had some brushes with death. At first, I was concerned about the safety of Constance in your custody. Then I realized you and I have a great deal in common. You did not seek out the troubles that came into your life. They found you. You chose to help people and protect them from evil. I do much the same every day, and my job may be even more dangerous than yours. I get death threats on a regular basis, but that doesn't stop me from doing what's right, nor should it stop you. Evil will always find good people, and good people must always fight it. That's the way the world is made. You are hereby awarded the permanent care, custody, and control of Constance Sanders. A judgment will be signed accordingly. Court is adjourned."

We went to Brennan's Restaurant to celebrate and asked Mr. Swartz and Mr. Clark to join us, but their schedules wouldn't allow it. I really think Swartz was scared to go anywhere with us. He'd seen us weather some rough waters, and he didn't seem the type to appreciate adventure. I wasn't so sure about Joshua Clark who appeared more adventurous. One of the beautiful perks of living in the French Quarter was that the fine restaurants were within walking distance of our new home, like Brennan's on Royal Street. After we ate, we took a carriage ride around the Quarter.

I received a call from Sophia. "Hi, Sophia, are you back in Paris?"

"Yes, Alexandra. It is beautiful this time of year. Congratulations on getting custody of Piper," she said. "I'm calling to give you a heads-up. The Indian government has dropped all charges against Bart Rogan. He is free to leave India any time he chooses. I don't know any of the details, but you can bet money changed hands somewhere. I thought you'd want to know. Bye."

Holy shit, I thought, *I hope that asshole has learned his lesson and will leave us alone.* We've had enough trouble to last a lifetime. I wanted to have a normal life and enjoy my normal family. Wow, who was I kidding? There was nothing normal about us.

Tom chose to curtail his environmental protests for a while and concentrate on family life. We enrolled Piper in a private school with a strong computer science program, and I spent my days working on my business. Mandy Morris tried to persuade me to stay involved with Superior Sugar, but I just couldn't. Zach had educated me on the addictive nature of sugar and its contribution to the obesity crisis around the world. He convinced me it contributed to drug abuse. I preferred to help promote our organic vegetables and stevia.

"Okay, Alexandra," Mandy said. "At least stay in touch with me. Piper loves the haunted tours, and she can tag along anytime."

I wasn't too sure about letting Piper around Mandy. She and her group seemed unusually weird even by New Orleans standards. Something wasn't right about them. Mandy continued to visit Bob Broussard every week. I didn't want Piper sneaking off with her to see that serial killer. He'd killed seven women and his own mother. He was right where he needed to be, in a psychiatric prison, and Piper was better off hanging out with kids her own age.

Life was going well for a change. Then late one night I got a call. I answered my phone without even thinking to check the caller ID.

"Hello, this is Alexandra," I said.

"Hi, Alexandra, this is Bob Broussard. I was in the neighborhood today and I almost stopped in to see you. I would love to catch up sometime and talk about our common interests."

I sat up straight in bed. *Oh shit. Bob Broussard calling me?* He must have gotten out of the mental institution somehow. That couldn't be good.

About the Author

John Moore was born in Louisiana. His grandmother's ancestor's roots were planted before the Civil War. His grandfather emigrated from Italy to open a family grocery store in the early 1900s. His mother married a military man who adopted him and his two brothers. The family lived in several states like most military families do. John pursued careers that enabled him to travel the world, and he gained a deep appreciation of cultural differences. He settled in South Louisiana to enjoy the warmth of Southern living and pursue his writing career.

The Crescent City Murders
A Three Book Series

If you enjoyed *The Devil Always Collects* and *Chasing Shadow Demons* be sure to check out the third book in the series, *Return of the Devil's Spawns*.

Visit John Moore's website
www.johnmooreauthor.com
to learn more.